EDWARD MARSTON was born and brought up in South Wales. A full-time writer for over forty years, he has worked in radio, film, television and the theatre and is a former chairman of the Crime Writers' Association. Prolific and highly successful, he is equally at home writing children's books or literary criticism, plays or biographies.

www.edwardmarston.com

THE
RAILWAY DETECTIVE

EDWARD MARSTON

Allison & Busby Limited
11 Wardour Mews
London W1F 8AN
www.allisonandbusby.com

Hardcover published in Great Britain in 2004.
This paperback edition first published in 2005.

A CIP catalogue record for this book is available from
the British Library.

28

ISBN 978-0-7490-8352-6

Typeset in 10.75/16 pt Sabon by
Allison & Busby Ltd.

The paper used for this Allison & Busby publication
has been produced from trees that have been legally sourced
from well-managed and credibly certified forests.

Printed and bound by
CPI Group (UK) Ltd, Croydon, CR0 4YY

In loving memory of my father,
who spent his working life as an engine driver,
and who instructed me in the mystery
of steam locomotion.

The landed proprietor often refused admission to the trespasser and his theodolite. At Addington the surveyors were met and defied in such force, that after the brief fight they were secured, carried before a magistrate and fined . . . The engineers were in truth driven to adopt whatever methods might occur to them. While people were at church; while the villager took his rustic meal; with dark lanthorns during the dark hours; by force, by fraud, by any and every mode they could devise, they carried the object which they felt to be necessary but knew to be wrong.

JOHN FRANCIS
A History of the English Railroads (1851)

CHAPTER ONE

London, 1851

Euston Station was one of the architectural marvels of the day. Even the most regular passengers on the London and North Western Railway could still be impressed by the massive portico with its four Doric columns built of adamantine Bramley Fall sandstone, flanked by two pairs of pavilions, and standing on the north side of a large open space. The addition of two hotels, one either side of the portico, introduced a functional element that did not lessen the stunning impact of the facade. Those who passed through the imposing entrance found themselves in the Great Hall, a combined concourse and waiting room. It was a magnificent chamber in the Roman-Ionic style with a high, deeply coffered ceiling that made newcomers gape in astonishment.

Caleb Andrews did not even notice it, nor did he spare

a glance for the majestic curved double flight of steps at the northern end of the hall that led to a gallery and vestibule. Only one thing in the station interested him, and that was the locomotive he and his fireman were about to drive to Birmingham. Andrews was a short, wiry character in his early fifties with a fringe beard that was peppered with grey. There was a jauntiness about him that belied his age and that concealed his deep sense of dedication to his work. Caleb Andrews was a man who thrived on responsibility.

'It's a fine day, Frank,' he observed. 'We should have a clear run.'

'God willing,' said Pike.

'God doesn't come into it, man. *We* are the people in charge. If we do our jobs properly, everything will go well. The important thing is to get there on time. Do that and we'll earn ourselves another pat on the back.'

'That would be nice, Caleb.'

'It would indeed.'

'Extra money would be even nicer.'

Andrews gave a hollow laugh. 'From *this* company?'

Frank Pike nodded resignedly. Now in his thirties, the big, shambling man from the West Country knew that they would only get their stipulated wage. Fireman Pike had a round, flat, moon face that was marked by routine exposure to the elements and, as a rule, darkened by a somnolent expression. His large hands were badly scarred by his trade. He had the deepest respect for his companion and was delighted to work alongside him.

Technically, a conductor was in charge of a train, but not when Caleb Andrews was there. The driver always asserted his authority and his colleagues knew better than to arouse his combative streak.

The two men were on the footplate, checking that everything was in readiness. Pike had got up a good head of steam and his fire shovel was at hand to add more fuel from the tender when necessary. The engine was throbbing with suppressed power. Andrews studied his instruments with a mixture of pride and affection. A locomotive was much more than an inanimate piece of machinery to him. She was a trusted friend, a living creature with moods, likes and dislikes, a complex lump of metal with her own idiosyncrasies, a sublime being, blessed with awesome might, who had to be treated correctly in order to get the best out of her.

'Mr Allan knows how to design an engine,' he said, appreciatively.

'She's one of the best,' agreed Pike.

'Mind you, there's still room for improvement. They ought to let me spend a week or two at Crewe. I could point out a number of things that would make her run better yet use less oil.'

'You always were a man of opinions, Caleb.'

'They're not opinions – they're plain common sense. The people who can give the best advice about how to build a locomotive are the men who drive her.'

'I got no complaints.'

'That's because you're too easily satisfied, Frank.'

'I do what I'm paid to do, that's all.'

There was an air of fatalism about Pike. Though Andrews was very fond of him, he had long ago accepted that his fireman lacked any real urgency or ambition. Frank Pike was a reliable workhorse, a quiet, efficient, unassuming, conscientious man who never questioned what he was doing or looked beyond it to something better. Andrews, by contrast, had enough aspiration for the two of them. He was bubbling with energy. While most men of his years were anticipating retirement, all that he could think about was promotion.

Like his fireman, Andrews wore a uniform of light-coloured corduroy and a cap. Pulling a watch from his pocket to consult it, he clicked his tongue in irritation.

'What's keeping them?' he said.

'There's minutes to go yet, Caleb.'

'I like to leave on time.'

'We will,' said Pike, turning round to look back down the train. 'I think they're loading the last box now.'

Andrews put his watch away and gazed back down the platform. It was a short train, comprising an empty first class carriage, a bright red mail coach, a luggage van and a guard's van. The locomotive and tender bore the distinctive livery of the northern division of the company. The engine was painted green, with main frames a paler shade of the same hue. Smoke box and chimney were black. The dome was green, as was the base of the safety valve, though the casing of the latter was polished brass. Hand-rails were covered polished brass and splashers

12

were brass-headed. Wheels were black. The front cylinder caps were made of iron, polished to a sheen. Before she set out, she was positively gleaming.

'Come on, come on,' said Andrews, tapping his foot.

Pike gave a tolerant smile. 'You're too impatient.'

'I want to be on my way, Frank.'

'So do I,' admitted the other. 'I always feel a bit nervous when we've so much money aboard. It must worry you as well.'

'Not in the least.'

'But we must be carrying a small fortune.'

'I don't care if we've got the Crown Jewels tucked away in the luggage van,' boasted Andrews, sticking out his chest. 'Makes no difference at all to me. Besides, we have plenty of guards on board to watch over the mail and the money. No,' he went on, 'the only thing that unsettles me is time-keeping. I've a reputation to maintain.' He heard a shrill blast on a whistle. 'At last!' he said with relief. 'Stand by, Frank.'

'I'm ready.'

'Then let's take her to Birmingham.'

With a venomous hiss of steam and a loud clanking of wheels, the engine moved slowly forward as she pulled her carriages on the first stage of their fateful journey.

By the time they hit open country, they had built up a steady speed. Caleb Andrews was at the controls and Frank Pike shovelled more coal into the firebox at regular intervals. The train surged on, rattling noisily and leaving clouds of dark smoke in its wake. Its iron wheels clicked rhythmically on the track. Having driven over the route many times, the two men were familiar with every bridge, viaduct, tunnel, change of gradient and curve in the line. They were also known to many of the people who manned the various stations, and they collected endless waves and greetings as they steamed past. Andrews acknowledged them all with a cheerful grin. Pike lifted his shovel in response.

It was a glorious April afternoon and the men enjoyed the warm sunshine. After the harsh winter they had endured, it was a pleasant change. Their work took them out in all weathers and they had little protection against wind, rain, snow, sleet, or insidious fog. Driver and fireman had often arrived at their destination, soaked to the skin or chafed by an icy blast. Even the heat from the firebox could not keep out all of the cold. Today, however, it was different. It was a perfect day. Lush green fields surrounded them and trees were in first leaf. The train was running smoothly over the flanged rails.

Forty miles passed uneventfully. It was only when they had raced through Leighton Buzzard Junction that they had their first hint of trouble. One of the railway policemen, who acted as signalman, stood beside the line and waved his red flag to stop the train. Andrews reacted immediately. Without shutting off steam, he put the engine into reverse so that her speed was gradually reduced. Only when she had slowed right down was the tender hand-brake applied along with the brake in the guard's van. Since she had been moving fast, it had taken almost half a mile to bring her to a halt.

Driver Andrews opened the cylinder cocks with the regulator open, so that steam continued to flow without working on the pistons. The water level in the boiler was maintained. Andrews leant out to look at the bulky figure of another railway policeman, who was striding towards them in the official uniform of dark, high-necked frock coat, pale trousers and stovepipe hat. He too had been signalling with his red flag for the train to stop. Andrews was annoyed by the delay.

'You'd better have good cause to hold us up,' he warned.

'We do,' said the policeman.

'Well?'

'There's a problem with the Linslade Tunnel.'

'What sort of problem?'

'You're not going through it, Mr Andrews.'

Tossing his flag to the ground, the policeman suddenly pulled a pistol from his belt and pointed it at the driver. Following his example, a group of armed men emerged swiftly from behind the bushes on either side of the line and made for the mail coach and the guard's van. The latter was easy to enter, but the locked doors of the mail coach had to be smashed open with sledgehammers before they could rush in and overpower the mail guards in their scarlet uniforms. While that was happening, someone was uncoupling the mail coach from the first class carriage in front of it.

As he watched the burst of activity, Caleb Andrews was outraged.

'What's going on?' he demanded.

'The train is being robbed,' replied the policeman, still holding the weapon on him. 'All you have to do is to obey orders. Stand back.'

'Why?'

'Do as I tell you.'

'No.'

'Stand back!' ordered another voice, 'or I'll shoot you.'

Andrews looked up to see a well-dressed man at the top of a shallow embankment, aiming a rifle at him. There was an air of certainty about him that suggested he was more than ready to carry out his threat. Pike tugged anxiously at his friend's elbow.

'Do as they say, Caleb,' he advised.

Andrews was truculent. 'Nobody tells me what to do on my engine,' he said, as he was pulled back a little. 'I won't let this happen.'

'They have guns.'

'They'll need more than that to frighten me, Frank.'

'Will we?' asked the bogus policeman.

Having hauled himself up onto the footplate, he levelled the pistol at the driver's temple. Pike let out a cry of protest but Andrews was unmoved. He stared at the interloper with defiance.

'Take her on, Mr Andrews,' said the other, crisply.

'What do you mean?'

'Drive the train, man.'

'Not without the mail coach, the luggage van and the guard's van.'

'You won't be needing those.'

'I've got my responsibilities,' argued the driver.

'Your only responsibility is to stay alive,' said the policeman, letting him feel the barrel of the weapon against his skull. 'Now – are you going to obey orders?'

Andrews put his hands on his hips. 'Make me,' he challenged.

For a moment, the other man hesitated, not quite knowing what to do in the face of unexpected resistance. Then he moved quickly. Grabbing the pistol by the barrel, he used the butt to club the driver to the floor, opening up a gash on the side of his head that sent blood oozing down his cheek. When the fireman tried to intervene, the gun was pointed at him and he was forced to step back. Badly dazed, Andrews was groaning at their feet.

'Don't hit Caleb again,' pleaded Pike.

'Then do as I tell you. Start her up.'

'Let me see to that wound of his first.'

'No,' snapped the other, turning the pistol towards Andrews. 'Drive the engine or your friend is a dead man.'

Pike obeyed at once. More concerned about the driver's safety than his own, he released the brake as fast as he could. Andrews, meanwhile, had recovered enough to realise what had happened to him. With a surge of rage, he threw his arms around the ankle of the man who was trying to take over his beloved locomotive. His recklessness was short-lived. It not only earned him two more vicious blows to the head, he was dragged to the edge of the footplate and tossed to the ground.

Horrified at the treatment of his friend, Pike could do nothing to help him. With a loaded pistol at his back, he set the train in motion and prayed that Caleb Andrews had not been too badly injured in the fall. The locomotive, tender and first class carriage trundled forward, leaving the mail coach, luggage van and guard's van behind. Had he been able to glance over his shoulder, Frank Pike would have seen a disconsolate group of guards, surprised by the speed of the ambush, relieved of their weapons and forced to dismount from the train and remove their shoes.

When the engine had gone a hundred yards and started to pick up speed, the man who had pretended to be a railway policeman gave Pike a farewell slap on the back before jumping off the footplate. He made a soft landing on a grassy verge and rolled over. The fireman soon saw why he had been abandoned. Ahead of him in the middle distance was the opening of the Linslade Tunnel, but there was no way that he could reach it. A whole section of track had been levered off its sleepers and cast aside. Those behind the ambush were bent on destruction.

Seized by panic, Pike did what he could to avert disaster, but it was in vain. Though he put the engine into reverse and tried to apply the brake, all that he did was to produce a firework display of sparks as the wheels skidded crazily along the rails. Seconds before he ran out of track, Pike had the presence of mind to leap from the footplate. Hitting the ground hard, he rolled over then watched in alarm as the locomotive veered over sharply, like a giant animal shot for sport.

The noise was deafening. Ploughing after the engine, the tender and the first class carriage ended up as a tangled mass of iron, seen through a fog of billowing smoke and angry steam. Frank Pike had to hold back tears. When he jumped to the ground, he had twisted his ankle but he ignored the pain. Pulling himself up, he turned his back on the hideous sight and limped back along the line to the fallen driver, hoping that Caleb Andrews was still alive.

CHAPTER TWO

As soon as he entered the room, Robert Colbeck knew that a serious crime must have been committed. The air was thick with pungent smoke, and Superintendent Edward Tallis only reached for his cigar case when he was under severe pressure. Seated behind his desk, the older man was scanning a sheet of paper as if trying to memorise important details. Colbeck waited patiently for the invitation to sit down. Tall, slim and well-favoured, he was impeccably dressed in a dark brown frock coat, with rounded edges and a high neck, well-cut fawn trousers and an Ascot cravat. Catching the light that streamed in through the window, his black leather shoes were shining brightly. In the prosaic world of law enforcement, Inspector Robert Colbeck stood out as the unrivalled dandy of Scotland Yard.

Tallis tossed him a cursory glance then waved a podgy hand.

'Take a seat,' he barked. 'We have much to discuss.'

'So I understood from the urgency of your summons,' said Colbeck, lowering himself onto a chair. 'I came as soon as I could, sir.'

'And not before time. We have a robbery on our hands.'

'What kind of robbery, Superintendent?'

'The worst kind,' said Tallis, putting the sheet of paper aside. 'A mail train was ambushed on its way to Birmingham. It was carrying a large consignment of gold sovereigns for delivery to a bank in the city. The thieves got away with every penny.'

'Was anyone hurt in the process?' asked Colbeck with concern.

'Only the driver, it seems. He was foolish enough to offer resistance and suffered for his bravery. The fellow is in a sorry state.'

'Poor man!'

'Save your sympathy for me, Inspector,' said Tallis, ruefully. 'All hell broke loose when word of the crime reached London. I've been hounded by the commissioners, harried by the railway company, hunted by the Post Office and badgered by the Royal Mint.'

Colbeck smiled. 'I thought I caught a whiff of cigar smoke.'

'Anybody would think that *I* was the culprit.'

'Only a bold man would ever accuse you of breaking the law, sir.'

Tallis bristled. 'Are you being facetious, Inspector?'

'Of course not.'

'I'll brook no disrespect.'

'I appreciate that, sir.'

Tallis glared at him. The Superintendent was a stout, red-faced, robust man in his fifties with a military background that had deprived him of his sense of humour and given him, in return, a habit of command, a conviction that he always made the right decisions and a small scar on his right cheek. Tallis had a shock of grey hair and a neat moustache that he was inclined to caress in quieter moments. A lifelong bachelor, he had no family commitments to deflect him from his work in the Detective Department of the Metropolitan Police Force.

'This is no time for drollery,' he warned.

'I was merely making an observation, Superintendent.'

'Keep such observations to yourself in future.'

Colbeck bit back a reply. There was an unresolved tension between the two men that came to the surface whenever they were alone together, and the Inspector had learnt to rein in his urge to provoke Tallis. The Superintendent had a violent temper when roused. Colbeck had been at the mercy of it once too often. He probed for information.

'What exactly happened, sir?' he asked, politely.

'That is what I'm endeavouring to tell you.'

'I'm all ears.'

Clasping his hands together, the Superintendent recited the salient details of the case, stressing the importance of prompt action by Scotland Yard. Colbeck listened carefully to the account. Several questions raised themselves and he put the obvious one to Tallis.

'How did they know that the train was carrying so much money?'

'That's for you to find out, Inspector.'

'They must have had help from an insider.'

'Track him down.'

'We will, sir,' promised Colbeck. 'What interests me is that the locomotive was forced off the tracks and badly damaged.'

'It will be out of service for weeks, I'm told.'

'Why on earth did they do such a thing? I mean, the gang had got what they wanted from the train. There was no need to derail the engine like that. What was the intention?'

'Ask them when you catch up with them.'

'The other thing that worries me,' said Colbeck, reflectively, 'is the ease with which the security arrangements were breached. The money was loaded in boxes that were locked inside Chubb safes. I read an article about those safes when they were installed. They were reckoned to be impregnable.'

'Two keys are needed to open them.'

'As well as a combination number, Superintendent.'

'Only one key was carried on the train,' noted Tallis. 'The other was in the possession of the bank to whom the money was being sent.'

'Yet, according to you,' Colbeck pointed out, 'the safes were opened and emptied within a matter of minutes. That could only be done with a duplicate key and foreknowledge of the combination number. There's collusion at work here.'

Tallis heaved a sigh. 'This robbery was extremely well planned, Inspector. I deplore what was done, but I have to admire the skill of the operation. We've never had to deal with anything on this scale before. That's why we must solve this crime quickly and bring the malefactors to justice,' he went on, banging a fist on the desk in exasperation. 'If they are seen to get away with such a daring exploit, there'll be others who will surely try to copy them.'

'I doubt that, Inspector. Most criminals, fortunately, have no gift for organisation and that's the essence of this robbery. Several men were involved and their timing must have been excellent.'

'Yes,' conceded Tallis, grudgingly. 'They knew what they wanted and took it – including the mail bags. The Post Office is hopping mad about that.'

'It's the people whose correspondence has gone astray who should be really alarmed,' said Colbeck, thinking it through. 'Those mail bags were not taken out of spite. Some envelopes will contain money or valuable items that can be sold for gain, and – by the law of averages – there'll be letters of a highly sensitive nature that may give the villains opportunities for blackmail.'

'That never occurred to me.'

'I'll wager that it occurred to them.'

'The scheming devils!' said Tallis, extracting a cigar

case from his pocket. 'Robbery, blackmail, wanton destruction of railway property – these men must be rounded up, Inspector.'

Colbeck rose purposefully to his feet. 'The investigation will begin immediately, Superintendent,' he said, firmly. 'What resources do I have at my disposal?'

'Whatever you ask for – within reason.'

'I presume that the railway company will be offering a reward?'

Tallis nodded. 'Fifty guineas for anyone who can provide information that will lead to an arrest,' he said, selecting a cigar from the case. 'This is a poor advertisement for them. It's the first time their mail train has been robbed.'

'I take it that I'm to work with Victor Leeming on this case?'

'Sergeant Leeming is on his way here, even as we speak.'

'Good,' said Colbeck. 'When he arrives, we'll take a cab to Euston Station and catch the next available train to the scene of the crime. I want to see exactly where and how it all happened.'

'You'll need this, Inspector.' Tallis picked up the sheet of paper. 'It has all the relevant names on it – except those of the criminals, alas.'

Colbeck took it from him. 'Thank you, Superintendent.' His eye ran down the list. 'The driver is the crucial person – this Caleb Andrews. I hope to speak to him in due course.'

Tallis lit his cigar. 'You may need to have a clairvoyant with you.'

'Why?'

'Mr Andrews is still in a coma, and not expected to survive.'

The table in the stationmaster's office at Leighton Buzzard was not the most comfortable bed, but the patient was quite unaware of that. Lying on the bare wood, with a blanket draped over him, Caleb Andrews seemed to have shrunk. His head was heavily bandaged, his face pallid, his breathing laboured. One arm was in a sling, one leg in a splint. He looked as if he were hanging on to life by the merest thread.

Keeping vigil beside the makeshift bed, Frank Pike was torn between fear and guilt, terrified that his friend might die and filled with remorse at his inability to protect the driver from attack. There was another dimension to his anguish. With a pistol held over him, he had been forced to drive the locomotive off the track, something that was anathema to any railwayman. It was no consolation to him that Caleb Andrews had not been able to witness the awful moment when their engine plunged into the grass verge and shed its load of coal and water. Pike winced as he recalled it. His employers were bound to blame him.

He reached out a hand to touch the patient's shoulder.

'I'm sorry, Caleb,' he said. 'I had no choice.'

The older man's eyelids flickered for a second and a soft murmur escaped his lips. Pike needed no interpreter.

Caleb Andrews was reproaching him. The driver had been in the same situation as him and he had shown that there was, in fact, a choice. It was between refusal and compliance. While one man had the courage to refuse, the other had opted for compliance. It made Pike feel as if he had betrayed a dear friend and colleague. He drew back his hand involuntarily, no longer entitled to touch Andrews.

Covered in blood, the body had been carried all the way back to the station so that a doctor could be sought. The fractured leg and the broken collarbone were not the real cause for concern. It was the head injuries that made the doctor pessimistic. All that he could do was to clean and bind the wounds. Given their severity, he could offer no hope of recovery. Whatever happened, Pike realised, he would come in for censure. If the driver lived, he would be sure to admonish his fireman for cowardice. If he died, there would be many others who would point an accusatory finger at Frank Pike. Among them was Caleb Andrews's daughter, a young woman whom Pike would not hurt for the world. As an image of her face came into his mind, he let out a gasp of pain.

'Forgive me, Madeleine!' he begged. 'It was not my fault.'

'What about the railway policemen who should have patrolled that line?' asked Victor Leeming. 'Why were they not on duty?'

'Because they were bound and gagged,' explained

Colbeck, brushing a speck of dust from his sleeve. 'Apparently, they were found behind some bushes in their underwear. The robbers had borrowed their uniforms.'

'What about their shoes?'

'Those, too, were missing.'

'Along with the shoes from all the people on board the train,' said Leeming. 'Are we looking for criminals with a passion for footwear?'

'No, Victor. We're searching for people who know that the simplest way to slow someone down is to make him walk in stockinged feet. By the time one of the guards reached the station to raise the alarm, the robbers were miles away.'

'With all that money and several pairs of shoes.'

'Don't forget the mail bags. They were a secondary target.'

'Were they?'

Sergeant Victor Leeming was puzzled. His brow wrinkled in concentration. He was a stocky man in his thirties, slightly older than Colbeck but with none of the Inspector's social graces or charm. Leeming's face had a benign ugliness that was not helped by his broken nose and his slight squint. Though he was not the most intelligent of detectives, he was always the first choice of Robert Colbeck, who valued his tenacity, his single-mindedness and his capacity for hard work. Leeming was a loyal colleague.

The two men were sitting in a first class carriage of a train that rumbled its way through Buckinghamshire.

When it passed Leighton Buzzard Junction, it slowed by prior arrangement so that it could drop the detectives near the scene of the crime. Colbeck peered through the window as the wrecked locomotive came into sight.

'They've repaired the line,' he said, pointing to the track that curved ahead of them, 'but I suspect it will take a lot longer to mend the engine and the carriage. They'll need a crane to lift them.'

'There's no shortage of railway policemen,' said Leeming, studying the knot of people beside the line. 'I can count a dozen or more.'

'All with their shoes on.'

'What sort of reception can we expect, Inspector?'

'A hostile one. They resent our interference.'

'But we're here to solve the crime.'

'They probably feel that it's their job to do that.'

Colbeck waited until the train shuddered to a halt then opened the door of the carriage. Taking care not to snag the tails of his coat, he jumped down nimbly onto the track. Leeming descended more slowly. Having deposited two of its passengers, the train chugged slowly off towards the Linslade Tunnel.

The newcomers took stock of the situation. Several people were gathered around the stricken engine and carriage. Others were standing in forlorn groups. Colbeck sought out the man whose name has been given to him as the person in charge. Inspector Rory McTurk of the railway police was a huge individual with a black beard and shaggy eyebrows. When he was introduced to them,

McTurk was patently unimpressed by Colbeck's tailored elegance and by Leeming's unsightly features. He put a note of disapproval into his gruff voice.

'So you've come at last, have you?' he said.

'Yes,' replied Colbeck, weighing him up. 'I trust that we can count on your full cooperation, Mr McTurk.'

'*Inspector* McTurk,' corrected the other.

'I beg your pardon.'

'We'll give you all the help you need – and some guidance.'

'Do you think that we'll need guidance, Inspector?'

'Yes,' said McTurk, brusquely. 'Railway lore is a complicated thing. You'll need someone to take you through it. As for the robbery,' he continued with an air of complacency, 'I've already made preliminary enquiries among those who were on board the train, and I'm in a position to tell you exactly what happened.'

'I'd prefer to hear it from the lips of the witnesses,' insisted Colbeck. 'That way we eliminate any narrative flourishes you might feel impelled to introduce.'

McTurk was indignant. 'I'll tell you the plain facts. Nothing else.'

'After we've spoken to those who actually travelled on the train, if you don't mind. Second-hand evidence is always suspect, as you know.' Colbeck looked around. 'Where are they?'

'The mail guards are there,' said McTurk, sourly, indicating the men who wore scarlet uniforms. 'The two railway policemen who were aboard are at the station along with Fireman Pike and the guard.'

'What about the driver, Caleb Andrews?'

'He's at Leighton Buzzard as well, Inspector. They took him to the station and sent for a doctor. Driver Andrews was badly hurt.'

'How badly?'

McTurk was blunt. 'This may turn into a murder investigation.'

'Does he have a family?'

'Only a daughter, according to his fireman. We've sent word to her. She'll have heard the worst by now.'

'I hope that tact and consideration were shown,' said Colbeck, glad that McTurk himself had not imparted the distressing news. Discretion did not appear to be one of the Scotsman's virtues. 'Victor?'

'Yes, Inspector?' said Leeming, stepping forward.

'Take full statements from the mail guards.'

'Yes, sir.'

'We'll speak to the others later.'

Leeming went off to interview the men who were sitting on the grass without any shoes and feeling very sorry for themselves. Colbeck was left to survey the scene. After looking up and down the line, he climbed the embankment and walked slowly along the ridge. McTurk felt obliged to follow him, scrambling up the incline and cursing when he lost his footing. The detective eventually paused beside some divots that had been gouged out of the turf. He knelt down to examine them.

'They brought the money this way,' he decided.

'What makes you think that?'

'The sovereigns were in bags that were packed into wooden boxes, Inspector. They were very heavy. It would have taken two men to carry each box and that meant that they had to dig their feet in as they climbed the embankment.' He glanced down at the line. 'What happened to the mail coach, the luggage van and the guard's van?'

'They were towed back to Leighton Buzzard and put in a siding.'

'They should have been left here,' said Colbeck, sharply, 'where the robbery actually took place. It would have made it easier for me to reconstruct events.'

'Railways run on timetables, Inspector Colbeck,' the Scotsman told him. 'As long as that rolling stock remained on the line, no down trains could get beyond this point.' He curled a derisive lip. 'Do you know what a down train is?'

'Of course, Inspector McTurk. I travel by rail frequently.' He looked back in the direction of Leighton Buzzard. 'We'll need to examine them. They may yield valuable clues.'

'We've already searched the mail coach and the luggage van.'

'That's what troubles me,' said Colbeck, meeting his gaze. 'If you and your men have trampled all over them, evidence may unwittingly have been destroyed. Please ensure that nobody else has access to that rolling stock until we've had the chance to inspect it.' McTurk glowered at him. 'It's not a request,' warned Colbeck. 'It's an order.'

McTurk turned away and waved an arm at the cluster of railway policemen gathered below. One of them scampered up the embankment to be given a curt order by his superior. The man then went back down the incline and trotted in the direction of the station. Having asserted his authority, Colbeck gave his companion a disarming smile.

'Thank you, Inspector,' he said, suavely. 'Your willing cooperation makes my job so much easier.'

McTurk remained silent but his eyes smouldered. He was much more accustomed to giving orders rather than receiving them. Colbeck swung on his heel and followed the marks in the grass. McTurk went after him. After picking their way through the undergrowth, they came to a narrow track that twisted its way off through a stand of trees. Colbeck noticed the fresh manure.

'This is where they left their horses,' he said, 'and the boxes must have been loaded onto a carriage. They chose their spot with care. It's hidden by the trees and only a short distance from the railway.'

'Wait till I get my hands on the rogues!'

'They'll face due process in a court of law, Inspector.'

'I want a word with them first,' growled McTurk, grinding his teeth. 'They stripped two of my men and trussed them up like turkeys.'

'With respect,' said Colbeck, reprovingly, 'there are more serious issues here than the humiliation of two railway policeman. We are dealing with an armed robbery during which the driver of the train was so badly injured that he may not survive.'

'I'd not forgotten that – and I want revenge.'

'Don't take it personally, Inspector McTurk. That will only cloud your judgement. Our job is to apprehend those responsible for this crime, and, if possible, to reclaim the stolen money and mail bags. Revenge has no place in that scheme of things.'

'It does for me,' affirmed McTurk. 'Look what they did,' he added, jabbing a finger at the wreckage below. 'They destroyed railway property. That's the worst crime of all to me.'

'Caleb Andrews is railway property,' Colbeck reminded him. 'His life is in the balance. When they're hauled off to Crewe, the locomotive and the carriage can be repaired, but I don't think that your engineering works runs to spare parts for injured drivers.' He raised his eyes to a sky that was slowly darkening. 'I need to make best use of the light I still have,' he announced. 'Excuse me, Inspector. I want to take a look at the rolling stock that was foolishly moved from the scene of the crime.'

'We only followed instructions,' complained McTurk.

'Do you always do as you're told?'

'Yes, Inspector.'

'Then here's another instruction for you,' said Colbeck, pointedly. 'Keep out of my way. The last thing I want at this moment is some over-obedient railway policeman getting under my feet. Is that understood?'

'You need my help.'

'Then I'll call upon it, as and when necessary.'

'You won't get far without me,' cautioned McTurk.

'I fancy that I will,' said Colbeck, easing him gently aside. 'You cast a long shadow, Inspector. And I want all the light that I can get.'

On the walk back to the station, Sergeant Leeming gave his superior an edited version of the statements he had taken from the mail guards. Not wishing to be left out, Inspector McTurk trailed in their wake. Colbeck was sceptical about what he heard.

'Something is missing, Victor,' he concluded.

'Is it?'

'Every man tells the same tale, using almost identical language. That means they've had time to rehearse their story in order to cover their blushes.'

'What blushes?'

'They were at fault. They were on duty in a locked carriage, yet they were caught napping by the ambush. How? Their assailants were quick but they still had to smash their way into the mail coach.'

'It was all over in a matter of seconds,' said Leeming. 'At least, that's what they told me.'

'Did they tell you why nobody fired a shot in anger?'

'No, Inspector.'

'Then that's what we need to establish,' said Colbeck. 'The train was stopped over a mile from the station but a gunshot would have been heard from here. It's the reason that the robbers took care not to fire themselves. They didn't wish to give themselves away.'

'I never thought of that.'

'They did – and the mail guards should have done so as well. The very least they should have managed was a warning shot. Help would have come from the station.'

'Now that you mention it,' recalled Leeming, scratching his chin, 'they did seem a little embarrassed when I questioned them. I put it down to the fact that they had no shoes on.'

'They're hiding something, Victor.'

'Do you think they might be in league with the robbers?'

'No,' said Colbeck. 'If that had been the case, they'd have fled when the crime was committed. My guess is that they helped the robbers in another way – by being lax in their duties.'

Light was starting to fade noticeably so the Inspector lengthened his stride. Leeming increased his own speed, but Inspector McTurk was panting audibly as he tried to keep pace with them. When they reached Leighton Buzzard Station, they saw that there was a sizeable crowd on the platform. Colbeck ignored them and led the way to the rolling stock that was standing in a siding. The railway policeman who had been dispatched by McTurk was standing officiously beside the guard's van.

Handing his top hat to Leeming, Colbeck first clambered up into the luggage van to examine the huge safe in which the money had been locked. Designed and built at the factory of one of England's most reputable locksmiths, John Chubb, the safe was made of inch thick steel plate. It was three feet high, wide and deep, with a door formed by the hinged lid that swung back on a guard-chain. On the front wall of the safe were keyholes to twin locks, whose interior mechanism was almost six inches deep.

Colbeck admired the quality of construction. The positioning of the locks, and the need for a combination number, confronted any burglar with almost insurmountable problems. Cracksmen whom he had arrested in the past had always admitted how difficult it was to open a Chubb safe. Yet, in this case, the doors of the safe were gaping. Colbeck made a quick search of the van but found nothing that could be construed as a clue. He left the van, dropped to the ground, and moved across to inspect the broken handles on the doors of the mail coach. One blow from a sledgehammer was all that had been required. Opening a door, Colbeck hauled himself up into the coach.

'You're wasting your time,' called McTurk.

'Am I?' he replied.

'I searched it thoroughly myself.'

'I'm sure that I'll see your footprints, Inspector.'

'You'll find nothing, I can tell you that.'

Colbeck beamed at him. 'Thank you for your encouragement,' he said. 'It's heartening to know we have your sage counsel to call upon.'

McTurk replied with a snort but Colbeck did not

even hear it. He had already stepped into the coach to begin his search. Instead of being divided into separate compartments, the carriage consisted of one long space that had been adapted to enable mail to be sorted in transit. A table ran the length of one wall, and above that was a series of wooden pigeonholes into which letters and parcels could be slotted. There were no signs of a struggle.

Robert Colbeck was meticulous. Beginning at one end of the coach, he made his way slowly forward and combed every inch. The search was painstaking and it produced no evidence at first, but he pressed on nevertheless, bending low to peer into every corner. It was when he was almost finished that he saw something that appeared to have fallen down behind the table. It was a small white object, resting against the side of the coach. Colbeck had to get on his knees and stretch an arm to its fullest extent to retrieve the object. When he saw what it was, he gave a smile of satisfaction and went across to the door.

Inspector McTurk and Sergeant Leeming waited beside the track.

'I told you there was nothing to see,' said McTurk, triumphantly.

'But there was,' Colbeck told him. 'You missed something.'

'What?'

'This, Inspector.' He held up the card that he had found. 'Now we know why the mail guards were taken unawares, Victor,' he went on. 'They were too busy playing cards to do their job properly.'

'No wonder they kept their mouths shut,' said Leeming.

'My guess is that the policemen were in there with them. Instead of staying at their post in the luggage van, they preferred to pass the time with a game of cards.' Colbeck leapt down to stand beside McTurk. 'I fear that some of your men are unable to follow your excellent example, Inspector,' he declared. 'Unlike you, they do not know how to obey instructions.'

CHAPTER THREE

It took some while to persuade Frank Pike to abandon his bedside vigil. Consumed with grief, he seemed to feel that it was his bounden duty to remain beside the injured driver, as if his physical presence in the stationmaster's office were the only hope of ensuring recovery. Having instructed his sergeant to take statements from the other people involved, Robert Colbeck turned his attention to Pike, and, with a mixture of patience, sympathy and cool reason, eventually coaxed him into another room, where they could talk alone.

'What about Caleb?' asked Pike, nervously.

'Mr Hayton, the stationmaster, will sit with him,' explained Colbeck, putting his hat on the table. 'If there's any change in his condition, we'll be called immediately.'

'I should have done more to help him, sir.'

'Let me be the judge of that, Mr Pike.'

'When that man hit Caleb, I just went numb. I couldn't move.'

'It's been a very distressing experience for you,' said Colbeck, taking the chair behind the table. 'I daresay that you're still suffering from the shock of it all. Why don't you sit down and rest?'

'I feel that I should be in there with Caleb.'

'Think of the man who attacked him. Do you want him caught?'

'Yes, Inspector,' said Pike with sudden urgency. 'I do.'

'Then you'll have to help us. Every detail you can provide may be of value.' He indicated the bench and the fireman slowly lowered himself on to it. 'That's better,' he said, producing a pencil and pad from his inside pocket. 'Now, in your own time, tell me what happened from the moment that the train was flagged down.'

Pike licked his lips with apprehension. He clearly did not wish to recount a story in which he felt his own conduct had been grievously at fault, but he accepted that it had to be done. On the other side of the wall, Caleb Andrews was fighting for his life. Even if it meant some personal discomfort for Pike, he knew that he had to be honest. It was the only way that he could help in the search for the men who had robbed the train and forced him to drive the locomotive off the track.

'When was your suspicion first aroused?' asked Colbeck.

'Not until the signalman threw his flag aside and drew a pistol.'

41

'Can you describe the fellow?'

'Oh, yes,' said Pike with feeling. 'He was as close as you are, Inspector. I looked him right in the face. He was a big man, around my own height, and with ginger whiskers. But it was his eyes I remember most clearly, sir. They was cold as death.'

Notwithstanding the fact that he was still badly shaken, Frank Pike gave a full and lucid account of the robbery, albeit punctuated with apologies for the way that he felt he had let the driver down. Noting down everything in his pad, Colbeck prodded him gently with questions until he elicited all the details. The fireman's deep respect and affection for Caleb Andrews was obvious. Colbeck was touched. He tried to offer a modicum of reassurance.

'From what you tell me,' he said, 'Mr Andrews was a plucky man.'

'Caleb would stand up to anybody.'

'Even when he was threatened with a loaded pistol.'

'Yes,' said Pike with a note of pride. 'He was fearless.'

'That courage will stand him in good stead now. He has a strong will to live and it should help him through. When his condition is more stable, I'll arrange for him to be taken home. Meanwhile, I'll make sure that's he's moved to a proper bed.'

'Thank you, Inspector.'

'I believe that he has a daughter.'

'That's true,' replied the other. 'Madeleine worships her father. This will be a terrible blow to her. It is to us all, of course, but Madeleine is the person who'll suffer most. Caleb is everything to her.'

'What about you, Mr Pike?'

'Me, sir?'

'Do you have someone who can help you through this ordeal?'

'I've a wife and child, Inspector. Heaven knows what Rose will say when she hears what happened today. She worries enough about me, as it is,' he said with a sheepish smile. 'My wife thinks that working on the railway is dangerous.'

'You may find it difficult to convince her otherwise, Mr Pike.'

The fireman sat upright. 'I like my job, sir,' he attested. 'It's the only thing I ever wanted to do. The robbery won't change that.'

'I admire your devotion to duty.' Colbeck glanced down at his notes. 'Let me just read through your statement, if I may, in case there's anything you wish to change or add.'

'There won't be, Inspector.'

'You never know. Please bear with me.'

Referring to his notes, Colbeck repeated the story that he had been told. Pike was astounded by the accuracy with which his words had been recorded and, in hearing them again, his memory was jogged.

'There *was* one more thing,' he said.

'Go on.'

'It may not be important but it struck me as odd at the time.'

'Odd?'

'Yes, Inspector. The man who climbed up onto the footplate called Caleb by his name. He *knew* who was driving that train.'

'I wonder how,' said Colbeck, making another entry in his notebook. He flipped it shut. 'Thank you, Mr Pike. That information is very pertinent. I'm glad that I double-checked your story.'

There was a tap on the door and it opened to admit Hayton, the stationmaster, a stooping man in his forties. His sad expression made Pike leap to his feet in alarm. He grabbed the newcomer by the shoulder.

'Has something happened to Caleb?' he demanded.

'Calm down, Mr Pike,' soothed Colbeck, rising from his chair.

'I want to know the truth.'

'Leave go of me and you shall,' said the stationmaster, detaching the fireman's hand. 'There's no need to be so anxious, Mr Pike. The news is good. I came to tell you that the patient has rallied slightly. Mr Andrews even took a sip of water.'

Sergeant Victor Leeming had not been idle. He was working in a little room that was used for storage. Having first taken a statement from the guard on the ambushed train, he interviewed the two railway policemen whose task was to protect the money in the safes. Initially, they denied having left the luggage van and insisted that they had not been playing cards in the mail coach. When

Leeming told them that the guard had given evidence to the contrary, they blustered, prevaricated, then, under close questioning, they caved in. One of the railway policemen, a surly individual with a walrus moustache, even tried to justify their actions.

'Sitting in a luggage van is very boring,' he said.

'You were not there to be entertained,' observed Leeming.

'We often slip into the mail van on such occasions. Nothing ever happens when we carry money. The train has never been under threat before. Ask yourself this, Sergeant. Who would even think of trying to rob us? It's impossible to open those two safes.'

'Not if you have the keys and the combination. What would have made it more difficult for them, of course,' said Leeming, 'is that they'd met stout resistance from two railway policemen hired to guard that money.'

'We didn't believe that it could ever happen, Sergeant.'

'That's no excuse.'

'It was *their* fault,' said the man, searching desperately for a way to redeem himself. 'We were led astray. The mail guards pleaded with us to join them in their coach. They should carry the blame.'

'If you wanted to play cards,' said Leeming, reasonably, 'you could have done that in the luggage van with your colleague.'

'It's not the same with only two players.'

'Tell that to Inspector McTurk.'

The two policemen quailed. They had already given accounts of the robbery to their superior, carefully omitting any mention of their visit to the mail coach. Thanks to the detective, they would now have to confess that they had lied to McTurk. It was a daunting prospect. In the event, it was Leeming who first informed the Scotsman that he had been misled. When he left the storeroom, he found McTurk lurking outside and told him what had transpired.

'Hell and damnation!' exclaimed McTurk. 'They'll swing for this.'

'They pulled the wool over your eyes, Inspector.'

'I'll make them regret that they did that.'

'You owe a debt to Inspector Colbeck,' said Leeming, enjoying the other's discomfort. 'Had he not searched the mail van, this dereliction of duty may not have come to light. It explains why those employed to look after the mail and the money were caught off guard.'

'I'll see them crucified,' vowed McTurk.

'You need to review your safety procedures.'

'Don't presume to tell me my job, Sergeant.'

'Your men were blatantly at fault.'

'Then they'll be punished accordingly,' said McTurk, nettled by the criticism. 'We have high standards to maintain. But I'll thank you not to pass comments on our police force. Might I remind you that we've been in existence a lot longer than the Detective Department at Scotland Yard?'

'Perhaps that's why complacency has set in.'

'We are not complacent, Sergeant Leeming!'

'Patently, some of your men are.'

'Isolated examples,' argued the Scotsman, barely able to contain his fury. 'And whatever their shortcomings, at least they *look* like policemen. I can't say that about you and Inspector Colbeck.'

'We belong to the Plain Clothes Detail.'

McTurk sniffed. 'There's nothing plain about your colleague's attire. He struts around like a peacock.'

'The Inspector puts a high premium on smartness.'

'Then he'd be more at home in fashionable society.'

'I agree with you there,' said Colbeck, coming into the room in time to hear McTurk's comment. 'Fashionable society is often the place where serious crimes are hatched. Were we to wear police uniform, we would disclose our identity at once and that would be fatal. Being able to move invisibly in society gives us an enormous advantage. It's one of the principles on which we operate.'

'It's not one that appeals to me,' said McTurk, tapping his chest. 'I'm proud to wear a uniform. It shows who I am and what I stand for.'

'But it also warns any criminals that you represent danger.'

'And what do *you* represent, Inspector Colbeck?'

'The veiled sarcasm in your voice suggests that you've already supplied your own answer to that question,' said Colbeck, tolerantly, 'so I'll not confuse you by giving you my reply. I simply came to thank you for your help and to tell you that we'll be leaving for London soon.' He could not resist a smile. 'On what, I believe, you call an up train.'

'What about the others?'

'They're free to leave, Inspector – with the exception of the patient, that is. The stationmaster has very kindly offered a bed in his house to Mr Andrews, who seems to have made a slight improvement.'

'That's cheering news,' said Leeming.

'Yes,' added McTurk. 'The station can get back to normal.'

'Normality will not be completely restored,' said Colbeck, 'until this crime has been solved and the villains are securely behind bars. Sergeant Leeming and I have done all that we can here. We move on to the next stage of the investigation.'

'May one ask where that might be?'

'Of course, Inspector. We're going to pay a visit to the Post Office.' He hovered in the doorway. 'Now, please excuse me while I speak to Fireman Pike. He insists on staying with the driver even though there's nothing that he can do.' He waved to McTurk. 'Goodbye.'

'And good riddance!' muttered the other as Colbeck went out. He turned on Leeming. 'A Detective-Inspector, is he? And how did he get that title?'

'Strictly on merit,' said the other.

'The merit of knowing the right people?'

'Not at all. He achieved his promotion by dint of hard work and exceptional talent. Inspector Colbeck is highly educated.'

'I knew that there was something wrong with him.'

'Don't you believe in education, Inspector McTurk?'

'Only in small doses,' retorted the other. 'Otherwise, it can get in your way. Book-learning is useless in this job. All that a good policeman really needs is a sharp eye and a good nose.'

'Is that what you have?' asked Leeming.

'Naturally.'

'Then they let you down, Inspector. Your sharp eye didn't help you to spot that playing card in the mail coach, and your good nose failed to pick up the smell of deception when you questioned the two policemen who travelled on the train.'

'That's immaterial.'

'Not to me. I put my trust in Inspector Colbeck's education.'

'You'd never get me working for that fop,' sneered McTurk.

'I can see that you don't know him very well,' said Leeming with a short laugh. 'He's no fop, I can assure you of that. But you're quite safe from him. He'd never even consider employing you.'

'Why not?'

'Because you are what you are, Inspector McTurk. Criminals can see you coming a mile away. Let's be frank about it, shall we? Even if you were stark naked, everyone would know that you were a policeman.'

Herbert Shipperley was a short, thin, harassed man in his fifties with a bald head that was dotted with freckles and a face that was a mass of wrinkles. His responsibilities at the Post Office included supervision of the mail coaches that were run on various lines. News of the train robbery had struck him with the force of a blow and he was quick to see all the implications. Shipperley knew that he would be in the line of fire. Even though it was quite late, he was still in his office when the detectives called on him and introduced themselves. He backed away as if they had come to arrest him.

'We just wish to ask you a few questions,' explained Colbeck.

'I've been bombarded with questions ever since people caught wind of the robbery,' moaned Shipperley. 'It's only a matter of time before I have newspaper reporters banging on my door. They'll blame me as well, whereas it's the railway company that's really at fault.'

'We're not here to apportion blame, Mr Shipperley. We merely wish to establish certain facts. Sergeant Leeming and I have just returned from the scene of the crime.'

'What did you learn?'

'Enough to see that we have a difficult case on our hands.'

'But you will recover everything, won't you?' bleated Shipperley. 'I need to be able to reassure the Royal Mint and the bank – not to mention my own superiors. The loss of that mail is a tragedy,' he cried. 'It threatens the integrity of our service. Imagine how people will feel when they discover that their correspondence has gone astray. Help me, Inspector Colbeck,' he implored. 'Give me your word. You do expect to catch the robbers, don't you?'

'We hope so.'

'I need more than hope to revive me.'

'It's all that I can offer at the moment.'

'You might try a glass of whisky,' advised Leeming. 'It will calm your nerves. We're not miracle-workers, I fear. We'll do our best but we can give you no firm promises.'

Shipperley sagged visibly. 'Oh, I see.'

'We're dealing with a premeditated crime,' said Colbeck. 'It was conceived and planned with great care, and couldn't possibly have been committed in the way that it was without the direct assistance of insiders.'

'You're surely not accusing *me*?' gasped the other, clutching at his throat. 'I've worked for the Post Office all my life, Inspector. My reputation is spotless.'

'I'm sure that it is, Mr Shipperley, and I can say now that you're not under any suspicion.' He signalled to Leeming, who took out his notepad and pencil. 'We simply want a few details from you, please.'

'About what?'

'The procedure for carrying money on the mail train.'

'We go to great lengths to maintain secrecy.'

'Word obviously got out on this occasion,' said Colbeck. 'We need to know how. Perhaps you can tell me how often you liaise with the Royal Mint or with the Bank of England to carry money on their behalf on the mail train. We'd also like to hear how many of your employees know the exact dates of each transfer.'

'Very few, Inspector.'

'Let's start with the frequency of such deliveries, shall we?'

Herbert Shipperley took a deep breath and launched into what turned out to be a prolonged lecture on how the mail trains operated, giving far more detail than was actually required. Colbeck did not interrupt him. In talking about his work, the man gradually relaxed and some of his facial corrugations began to disappear. The longer he went on, the more enthusiastic he got, as if initiating some new recruits into the mysteries of the Post Office. It was only when he had finished that his eyes regained their hunted look and the anxious furrows returned.

'As you see, gentlemen,' he said, stroking his pate with a sweaty palm, 'our system is virtually foolproof.'

'Until today,' commented Leeming.

'The Post Office was not in error.'

'That remains to be seen.'

'The information must have been leaked by the Royal Mint.'

'Let's consider the names that you've given us, Mr Shipperley,' said Colbeck, thoughtfully. 'Apart from yourself, only three other people here had foreknowledge of the transfer of money by means of mail train.'

'Yes, Inspector, and I can vouch for all of them.'

'But even they – if I understood you right – wouldn't necessarily be able to say what was being carried on any particular day.'

'That's correct,' said Shipperley. 'It's an extra safeguard.

Only I would know for certain if the consignment were coming from the Royal Mint or the Bank of England. Coin, bank notes and gold bullion are sent to assorted destinations around the country. Some gold is periodically exported to France from one of the Channel ports.'

'Of the three names you gave us,' said Leeming, glancing at his notebook, 'which employee would you trust least – Mr Dyer, Mr Ings or Mr Finlayson?'

'I have equal faith in all of them,' said the other, loyally.

'Then let me put the question a different way,' suggested Colbeck, taking over. 'Which of the three has the lowest wage?'

'I don't see that that has any relevance, Inspector.'

'It could do.'

'Then the answer is William Ings. He's the most junior of the three in terms of position. However,' Shipperley went on, 'there's not a blemish on his character. Mr Ings has always been strongly committed to the Post Office. He's been with us longer than either Mr Dyer or Mr Finlayson.'

'We'll need to speak to all three of them.'

'Is that necessary, Inspector?'

'I think so,' said Colbeck. 'What time will they arrive for work tomorrow morning?' The other man looked uncomfortable. Colbeck took a step closer. 'Is there a problem, Mr Shipperley?'

'Yes,' he confessed. 'Mr Dyer and Mr Finlayson will definitely be here but I can't guarantee that Mr Ings will turn up.'

'Oh? Why is that, pray?'

'He's been sick all week and unable to work.'

Leeming put a tick against one of the names in his notebook.

When she heard the knock on the front door, Maud Ings rushed to open it, first drawing back the heavy bolts. Her expectation changed instantly to disappointment when she saw, by the light of her lamp, that the caller was a complete stranger. Inspector Robert Colbeck touched the brim of his hat politely then explained who he was. Mrs Ings was alarmed to hear of his occupation.

'Has something happened to William?' she asked.

'Not that I know of, Mrs Ings.'

'That's a relief!'

'My understanding was that your husband was at home.'

She shifted her feet uneasily. 'I'm afraid not, sir.'

'His employer told me that he was ill.'

'Why?' she said in surprise. 'Has he not been to work?'

'I wonder if I might come in,' said Colbeck, quietly.

The house was at the end of a terrace not far from Euston Station. It was small and neat with a presentable exterior. Once inside, however, Colbeck saw signs of sustained neglect. Wallpaper was starting to peel on some walls and the paint work was in a poor condition. There was a distinct smell of damp. The room into which he was conducted had no more than a few sticks of furniture in it and a threadbare carpet. There was an air of neglect about

Maud Ings as well. She was a slim, shapeless woman in her late thirties with a haggard face and unkempt hair. He could see from the red-rimmed eyes that she had been crying. A moist handkerchief protruded from the sleeve of her dress.

Embarrassed by her appearance, she took off her apron then adjusted her hair with a hand. She gave him an apologetic smile.

'Excuse me, Inspector,' she said. 'I was not expecting company.'

'But you were expecting someone, Mrs Ings. I could tell that by the alacrity with which you opened the door. Did you think that I might be your husband?'

'Yes.'

'Does he not have a key to his own front door?'

'Of course.'

'Then why did you bolt it against him?'

She shook her head. 'I don't know.'

'Perhaps you should sit down,' he suggested, seeing her distress. 'I'm sorry that I called at such an inopportune hour but I had no choice. It's imperative that I speak to Mr Ings.'

'Why?' she asked, sitting down.

'It's a matter that relates to his work at the Post Office.'

'Is he in trouble, Inspector?'

'I'm not sure.'

'What has he done?'

'Well,' he replied, taking the chair opposite her, 'Mr

Ings failed to report for work this week. He sent word to say that he was sick.'

'But there's nothing wrong with him.'

'So why did he lie to his employers?'

Maud Ings bit her lip. 'William has never let them down before,' she said with vestigial affection for her husband. 'He works long hours at the Post Office. They don't appreciate what he does.' She gave a shrug. 'It may be that he *is* unwell. That's the only thing that would keep him away. The truth is that I haven't seen him this week.'

'And why is that, Mrs Ings?'

'My husband is . . . staying elsewhere.'

'Do you have an address for him?'

'No,' she said, bitterly, 'and I don't really want it.'

Colbeck took a swift inventory of the room then looked at her more closely. Maud Ings was evidently a woman who was at the end of her tether. Apparently abandoned by her husband, she was still hoping that he might come back to her even though he had caused her obvious suffering. The remains of her youthful prettiness were all but obscured now. Colbeck treated her with great sympathy.

'I regret that I have to ask you about your private life,' he said, 'but it's germane to my investigation. Mrs Ings, it's not difficult to see that you and your husband were short of money.'

'I did my best,' she said, defensively. 'I always managed on what he gave me, however little it was.'

'Yet Mr Ings earned a reasonable wage at the Post Office.'

'Earned it and threw it away, Inspector.'

'Was he a drinking man?'

'No,' she replied, as another flicker of affection showed, 'William was no drunkard. I can clear him of that charge. He was a good man at heart – kind and considerate.' Her voice darkened. 'At least, he was for a time. That was before he caught the disease.'

'What disease?'

'Gambling. It ruined our marriage, Inspector.'

'I take it that he was not a successful gambler.'

'Only now and then,' she said, wistfully. 'That was the trouble, sir. William had a run of luck at the start and he thought that it would last. He bought me a new coat with his winnings and some lovely furniture.' She shook her head sadly. 'Then his luck changed. We had to sell the furniture last month.'

'Yet he still went on gambling?'

'Yes, Inspector.'

'Do you know where he went to play cards?'

'I do now,' she said, vengefully. 'I got it out of him in the end. I mean, I had a right to know. I'm his wife, Inspector. Sometimes, he'd be away all night at this place. I had a right to be told where it was.'

'And where was it, Mrs Ings?'

'Devil's Acre.'

'I see.'

Colbeck knew the area only too well. It was a

favoured haunt of the criminal fraternity and notorious for its brothels and gambling dens. If her husband were a regular visitor to the Devil's Acre, then Maud Ings had been right to describe his addiction as a disease. No decent or sensible man would even dare to venture into such a hazardous district. Colbeck was seeing an aspect of William Ings that had been carefully hidden from his employer. Herbert Shipperley might believe that Ings had an unblemished character but the man consorted regularly with criminals around a card table.

Colbeck was certain that he had picked up a scent at last.

'Is that where your husband is now?' he asked. 'Playing cards?'

'Probably.'

'Can you be a little more precise, Mrs Ings?'

'No,' she replied. 'He wouldn't tell me exactly where he went in case I tried to follow him there. And I would have, Inspector,' she went on with an edge of desperation. 'William left us with no money.'

'He left you with a roof over your head.'

'That's true, Inspector. I've still got a home for myself and the children. It's one consolation. And he did promise that he'd send me something when the money came through.'

'From his wages, you mean?'

'Well, I don't think it would be from his winnings at a card table,' she said, 'because he always seemed to lose.' She peered at Colbeck. 'Why are you so interested in my husband? I still don't understand why you came here looking for him.'

'Earlier today,' he explained, 'there was a train robbery.'

'He'd never get involved in anything like that,' she protested.

'Not directly, perhaps, but the mail train that was ambushed was carrying a consignment of money. Mr Ings was one of the few men who knew that the money would be in transit today.'

'That doesn't mean he betrayed the secret.'

'No,' he conceded, 'and it may well be that your husband is completely innocent. What I need to do is to establish that innocence as soon as is possible so that we can eliminate him from our inquiries. Now,' he said, softly, 'I realise that this is a difficult time for you but I must press you on the matter of his whereabouts.'

'I told you, Inspector. I don't know where he is.'

'You must have some idea, Mrs Ings.'

'None at all.'

'When did he leave?'

'Last weekend.'

'Did he offer you no explanation?'

'William simply packed a bag and walked out of the house.'

'He must have had somewhere to go to,' insisted Colbeck, watching her carefully. 'Somewhere – or someone.'

Her cheeks reddened. 'I don't know what you mean, Inspector.'

'I think that you do.'

'William is not that sort of man.'

'Your husband is a trusted employee at the Post Office,' he told her, calmly, 'a man with access to important information. On the eve of a serious crime that may be linked to his place of work, Mr Ings not only pleads illness and stays away, he leaves his wife and children to fend for themselves while he goes elsewhere.' He fixed her with a piercing stare. 'I think that we have rather more than a curious coincidence here, Mrs Ings. Don't you?'

Maud Ings was in a quandary. Wanting to protect her husband, she was deeply hurt by his treatment of her. Refusing to accept that he could be involved in a crime, she came to see that the evidence was pointing against him. She wrestled with her conscience for a long time but Colbeck did not rush her, recognising that her situation was already exerting almost unbearable pressure upon the woman. She was the discarded wife of a man who might turn out to be involved in a major crime. It took time for her to adjust to the full horror of her predicament.

Eventually, she capitulated and gabbled the information.

'I don't know the woman's name,' she said with rancour, 'but I think that she lives in the Devil's Acre.'

CHAPTER FOUR

Superintendent Edward Tallis was just finishing another cigar when there was a knock on the door of his office. It was late, but he rarely left his desk before ten o'clock at night, believing that long hours and continual vigilance were required to police a city as large and volatile as London. He cleared his throat noisily.

'Come in,' he called, stubbing out his cigar in an ashtray.

Robert Colbeck entered. 'Good evening, sir,' he said.

'I was wondering when you'd deign to put in an appearance.'

'Sergeant Leeming and I have been very busy.'

'To what effect?'

'I believe that we've made slight headway, Superintendent.'

'Is that all?'

'There's still a lot of intelligence to gather,' said Colbeck, 'but I wanted to keep you abreast of developments. Is this a convenient time?'

'No,' said Tallis, grumpily, 'it most definitely is not. My head is pounding, my bad tooth is aching and I'm extremely tired. This is a highly inconvenient time, Inspector, but I'll endure it with good grace. Take a seat and tell me what you have to report.'

Colbeck chose a leather armchair and settled back into it. Relying solely on his memory, he gave a concise account of the progress of the investigation and drew a periodic grunt of approval from the other man. He took it as a good sign that Tallis did not even try to interrupt him. Colbeck just wished that the cigar smoke were not quite so acrid, mingling, as it did, with the stink from the gas lighting to produce a foul compound.

'Where is Sergeant Leeming now?' asked Tallis.

'Questioning senior figures at the railway company,' said Colbeck. 'I left him to do that while I called at the home of William Ings.'

'But the cupboard was bare.'

'The man himself may not have been there, Superintendent, but I feel that I gathered some valuable clues. I strongly advise that we keep the house under surveillance in case Mr Ings should chance to return.'

'Why should he do that?'

'To give his wife money and to see his children.'

'The complications of marriage!' sighed Tallis, sitting back in his chair. 'The more I see of holy matrimony, the more grateful I am that I never got embroiled in it myself. I daresay that you feel the same.'

'Not exactly, sir.'

'Then why have you remained single?'

'It was not a conscious decision,' explained Colbeck, unwilling to go into any detail about his private life. 'I suppose the truth is that I have yet to meet the lady with whom I feel impelled to share my life, but I have every hope of doing so one day.'

'Even if it might impede your career as a detective?'

'Unlike you, sir, I don't see marriage as an impediment.'

'Anything that prevents a man from devoting himself to his work is a handicap,' announced Tallis. 'That's why I limit my social life so strictly. We have an enormous amount to do, Inspector. London is a veritable sewer of crime. Our job is to sluice it regularly.'

'I have a feeling that this case will take us much further afield than the capital, Superintendent,' said Colbeck. 'The robbery occurred in a rural location in Buckinghamshire and that county is hardly a hive of criminal activity. On the other hand, the crucial information about the mail train was doubtless supplied by someone in London.'

'William Ings?'

'I reserve judgement until we get conclusive proof.'

'It sounds to me as if we already have it.'

'The evidence is only circumstantial,' Colbeck pointed out. 'Do I have your permission to arrange for the house to be watched?'

'No, Inspector.'

'Why not, sir?'

'Only a fool would dare to go back there again.'

'Only a fool would run up gambling debts.'

'I can't spare the men.'

'You said that I could have unlimited resources.'

'Within reason,' Tallis reminded him, 'and I don't happen to think that keeping this house under observation is a reasonable use of police time. Ings has obviously gone to ground somewhere else. I doubt if his wife will ever see the rogue again.'

Colbeck was far too used to having his suggestions blocked by his superior to be irritated. It was something he had learnt to accept. Edward Tallis seemed to take pleasure from frustrating any initiatives that the other man put forward. It was one of the reasons why the antipathy between them had deepened over the years.

'It's your decision, sir,' said Colbeck with exaggerated civility.

'Abide by it.'

'What else can I do?'

'Invent some hare-brained scheme of your own to subvert me,' said Tallis with vehemence, 'and I'll not stand for that. It's happened before, as I know to my cost.'

'I only took what I felt were the appropriate steps.'

'You resorted to untried, unauthorised methods. And, yes,' he admitted, raising a hand, 'they did achieve a measure of success, I grant you. But they also left me to face a reprimand from the Commissioners. Never again, Inspector – do you hear me?'

'Loud and clear, sir.'

'Good. You must follow procedure to the letter.'

'Yes, Superintendent.'

'So what's your next step?'

'To meet up with Victor Leeming and hear what he found out at the railway company. He acquitted himself well when he talked to the people who were on board the train. He asked all the right questions.'

'I'll want to know what he gleaned from the railway company.'

'Of course, sir.'

'What are your plans for tomorrow?'

'I intend to catch the earliest possible train to Birmingham.'

'Why?' demanded Tallis.

'Because I need to speak to the manager of the bank to which that money was being sent. He has a key to open that safe. I'd like to know how it came into the possession of the robbers.'

'So you suspect treachery at that end as well?'

'I'm certain of it, Superintendent,' said Colbeck. 'I believe that we're looking at a much wider conspiracy than might at first appear. There was inside help at the Post Office, the bank and, possibly, at the Mint. The robbers might also have had a confederate inside the London and North Western Railway Company,' he argued. 'I don't believe that William Ings is the only man implicated.'

Tallis grimaced. 'In other words,' he said, tartly, 'this case will take a long time to solve.'

'I'm afraid so.'

'Then I'll have to endure even more harassment from all sides.'

'Your back is broad, sir.'

'That's the trouble,' complained Tallis. 'It presents a big target for anybody with a whip in his hand. If we fail to make swift progress in this investigation, I'll be flayed alive. I've already had to fight off the so-called gentlemen of the press. Tomorrow's headlines will not make pleasant reading, Inspector. My bad tooth is throbbing at the prospect.'

'There's a way to solve that problem, Superintendent.'

'Is there?'

'Yes,' said Colbeck, cheerfully. 'Don't buy a newspaper.'

Caleb Andrews had never known such fierce and unremitting pain. He felt as if his skull were about to split apart. The only escape from the agony was to lapse back into unconsciousness. Every so often, however, he recovered enough, if only fleetingly, to remember something of what had happened and he felt the savage blows being administered by the butt of the pistol again and again. When that torment eased slightly with the passage of time, he became more acutely aware of the pain in his body and limbs. He ached all over and one of his legs seemed to be on fire. What frightened him was that he was unable to move it.

As his mind slowly cleared, he hovered for an age between sleep and waking, conscious of the presence of others, but unable to open his eyes to see whom they might be. There was movement at his bedside and he heard whispers, but, before he could identify the voices, he always drifted off again. It was infuriating. He was desperate to reach out, to make contact, to beg for help, to share his suffering with others. Yet somehow he could not break through the invisible barrier between his private anguish and the public world. And then, just as he despaired of ever waking up again, he had a momentary surge of energy, strong enough for him to be able to separate his eyelids at last.

Faces swam in front of him then one of them swooped in close. He felt a kiss on his cheek and his hand was squeezed very gently. A soft female voice caressed his ear.

'Hello, Father,' said Madeleine Andrews. 'I'm here with you.'

Victor Leeming was weary. After conducting a long and taxing series of interviews at the offices of the London and North Western Railway Company, he was grateful that his duties were almost over for the day. All that he had to do was to repair to Colbeck's house in order to compare notes with the Inspector. He hoped that the latter had had a more productive evening than he had managed.

As a cab took him to the house in John Islip Street, he listened to the clacking of the horse's hooves on the hard surface and mused on the seductive simplicity of a cab driver's life. Ferrying passengers to and fro across London was an interesting, practical and undemanding way of life, free from the dangers of police work or from the tedium that often accompanied it. One could even count on generous tips, something that was unheard of among those who toiled at Scotland Yard. By the time he reached his destination, Leeming had come to envy the virtues of a less onerous occupation.

Once inside the house, however, he dismissed such thoughts from his mind. Robert Colbeck had a warm welcome and a bottle of Scotch whisky waiting for him. The two men sat down in a study that was lined with books on all manner of subjects. Neat piles of newspapers and magazines stood on a beautiful mahogany cabinet. Framed silhouettes occupied most of the mantelpiece. Above them, on the wall, in a large, rectangular gilt frame, was a portrait of a handsome middle-aged woman.

'How did you fare?' asked Colbeck, sipping his drink.

'Not very well, Inspector.'

'Did the railway company close ranks on you?'

'That's what it amounted to,' said Leeming, taking a first, much-needed taste of whisky. 'They denied that any of their employees could have leaked information to the robbers and boasted about their record of carrying money safely by rail. I spoke to four different people, and each one told me the same thing. We must search elsewhere.'

'We'll certainly do that, Victor, but I still think that we should take a closer look at the way the company operates its mail trains. We've already exposed the shortcomings of railway policemen.'

'They were rather upset when I told them about that.'

'Understandably.'

'Though not as irate as Inspector McTurk,' recalled Leeming with a broad grin. 'He was in a frenzy. McTurk was such a bad advertisement for Scotland.' He raised his glass. 'Unlike this excellent malt whisky.'

'Yes,' said Colbeck with amusement. 'The good Inspector was not the most prepossessing individual, was he? But I'm sorry that you found the railway company itself in an uncooperative mood. I had a much more profitable time at the home of William Ings.'

'What sort of man is he?'

'An absent one.'

Colbeck told him in detail about the visit to Maud Ings and how his request for the house to be watched had been summarily turned down. Leeming rolled his eyes.

'If only Superintendent Tallis was on *our* side for once.'

'Now, now, Victor,' said Colbeck with mock reproof. 'Do I hear a murmur of insubordination?'

'He's supposed to put handcuffs on the villains, not on us.'

'He does hamper us now and then, I agree, but we must contrive to work around him. One of the things I want you to do in the morning is to find out who patrols the beat that includes the house. Ask the officers in question to keep an eye out for Mr Ings.'

'Yes, Inspector. What else am I to do tomorrow?'

'Report to Superintendent Tallis first thing,' said Colbeck. 'He wishes to know exactly what you found out at the offices of the London and North Western Railway Company.'

'Precious little.'

'That's rather perplexing, I must say. People with nothing to hide are usually more open and helpful.'

'They were neither.'

'Then we must find out why. When you've delivered your report, I want you to go to the Royal Mint to see if there was any breach of security there. I fancy there are more names to unearth than that of William Ings.'

'What if he doesn't make the mistake of returning to his house?'

'We'll have to go looking for him.'

'In the Devil's Acre?' asked Leeming with disbelief. 'You'd be searching for a needle in a haystack. Besides, we couldn't venture in there without a dozen or more uniformed constables at our back.'

'Oh,' said Colbeck, casually, 'that won't be necessary.'

He finished his drink and put his glass on the mahogany desk. He looked at ease in the elegant surroundings. Leeming was making a rare visit to the house and he felt privileged to be there. Colbeck was a private man who invited few colleagues to his home. It was so much larger and more comfortable than the one in which Leeming and his family lived. He gazed at the well-stocked shelves.

'Have you read all these books, Inspector?' he asked.

'Most of them,' replied the other. 'And the ones I haven't read, I've probably referred to. A good library is an asset for a detective. If you're interested, I have a few books here on the development of the steam locomotive.'

'No, thank you. I barely have time to read a newspaper.'

'That's a pity.'

'There's no such thing as leisure when you have a family.'

'I'll take your word for it, Victor.'

Leeming admired the mahogany cabinet beside him. 'My wife would covet some of this lovely furniture,' he said, stroking the wood.

'It's not for sale, I fear,' warned Colbeck with a fond smile. 'I inherited it with the house. My father was a cabinetmaker. Most of the things in here are examples of his handiwork.'

'He must have been a fine craftsman.'

'He was, Victor, but he never wanted his son to follow in his footsteps. My father had boundless faith in the powers of education. That's why I was packed off to school at such an early age.'

The clock on the desk began to strike and Leeming realised how late it was. It was time to go home. He downed the last of the whisky in one gulp then rose to his feet.

'What will *you* be doing tomorrow, sir?' he asked.

'Going to Birmingham. I need to speak to the bank manager.'

'Better you than me. I hate long train journeys. They unsettle my stomach. To be honest, I don't like travelling by rail at all.'

'Really? I love it. Believe it or not, there was a time in my youth when I toyed with the notion of being an engine driver.'

'The life of a cab driver has more attraction for me.'

'You prefer the horse to the steam locomotive?'

'I do, Inspector.'

'Then you're behind the times, Victor,' said Colbeck. 'The railways are here to stay. In any race between them, a steam train will always beat a horse and carriage.'

'That's not what happened today, sir.'

'What do you mean?'

'The mail train came a poor second,' argued Leeming. 'It was put out of action completely while the robbers escaped overland by horse. I think that there's a message in that.'

Colbeck pondered. 'Thank you, Victor,' he said at length. 'I do believe that you're right. There was indeed a message.'

The fight was over almost as soon as it had begun. After exchanging loud threats and colourful expletives, the two men leapt to their feet and squared up to each other. But before either of them could land a telling blow, they were grabbed by the scruff of their necks, marched to the door and thrown out into the alleyway with such force that they tumbled into accumulated filth on the ground.

Rubbing his hands together, the giant Irishman who had ejected them sauntered back to the crowded bar.

'I see that you haven't lost your touch,' said a voice in the gloom.

'Who are you?' growled Brendan Mulryne, turning to the man.

'I was waiting for you to remember.'

Mulryne blinked. 'Haven't I heard that voice before somewhere?'

'You should have. It gave you a roasting often enough.'

'Holy Mary!' exclaimed the other, moving him closer to one of the oil lamps so that he could see the stranger more clearly. 'It's never Mr Colbeck, is it?'

'The very same.'

Mulryne stared at him in the amazement. The Black Dog was one of the largest and most insalubrious public houses in Devil's Acre and the last place where the Irishman would have expected to find someone as refined as Robert Colbeck. The detective had taken trouble to blend in. Forsaking his usual attire, he looked like a costermonger down on his luck. His clothes were torn and shabby, his cap pulled down over his forehead. Colbeck had even grimed his face by way of disguise and adopted a slouch. He had been standing next to Mulryne for minutes and evaded recognition. The Irishman was baffled.

'What, in God's sacred name, are you doing here?' he said.

'Looking for you, Brendan.'

'I've done nothing illegal. Well,' he added with a chuckle, 'nothing that I'd own up to in a court of law. The Devil's Acre is a world apart. We have our own rules here.'

'I've just seen one of them being enforced.'

Colbeck bought his friend a pint of beer, then the two of them adjourned to a table in the corner. It was some time since the detective had seen Mulryne but the man had not changed. Standing well over six feet tall, he had the physique of a wrestler and massive hands. His gnarled face looked as if it had been inexpertly carved out of rock, but it was shining with a mixture of pleasure and surprise now. During his years in the Metropolitan Police, Mulryne had been the ideal person to break up a tavern brawl or to arrest a violent offender. The problem was that he had been too eager in the exercise of his duties and was eventually dismissed from the service. The Irishman never forgot that it was Robert Colbeck who had spoken up on his behalf and tried to save his job for him.

A pall of tobacco smoke combined with the dim lighting to make it difficult for them to see each other properly. The place was full and the hubbub loud. They had to raise their voices to be heard.

'How is life treating you, Brendan?' asked Colbeck.

'Very well, sir.'

'You don't have to show any deference to me now.'

'No,' said Mulryne with a grin that revealed several missing teeth. 'I suppose not. Especially when you're dressed like that. But, yes, I'm happy here at The Black

74

Dog. I keep the customers in order and help behind the bar now and then.'

'What do you get in return?'

'Bed, board and all the beer I can drink. Then, of course, there's the privileges.'

'Privileges?'

'We've new barmaids coming here all the time,' said Mulryne with a twinkle in his eye. 'I help them to settle in.'

'Would you be interested in doing some work for me?'

Mulryne was hesitant. 'That depends.'

'I'd pay you well,' said Colbeck.

'It's not a question of money. The Devil's Acre is my home now. I've lots of friends here. If you're wanting help to put any of them in jail, then you've come to the wrong shop.'

'The man I'm after is no friend of yours, Brendan.'

'How do you know?'

'Because he doesn't really belong in this seventh circle of hell,' said Colbeck. 'He's an outsider, who's taken refuge here. A gambler who drifted in here to play cards and to lose his money.'

'We've lots of idiots like that,' said Mulryne. 'They always lose. There's not an honest game of cards in the whole of the Devil's Acre.'

'He still hasn't realised that.'

'Why do you want him?'

'It's in connection with a serious crime that was committed earlier today – a train robbery.'

'Train robbery!' echoed the other with disgust. 'Jesus, what will they think of next? There was never anything like that in my time. The only people I ever arrested were beggars, footpads, cracksmen, flimps, doxies, screevers and murderers – all good, decent, straightforward villains. But now they're robbing trains, are they? That's shameful!'

'It was a mail train,' said Colbeck. 'A substantial amount of money was also being carried. They got away with everything.'

'How does this gambler fit into it?'

'That's what I need to ask him, Brendan – with your help.'

'Ah, no. My days as a bobby are over.'

'I accept that. What I'm asking you is a personal favour.'

'Is it that important, Mr Colbeck?'

'It is,' said the other. 'I'd not be here otherwise. It's been a long day and walking through the Devil's Acre in the dark is not how I'd choose to spend my nights. No offence, Brendan,' he added, glancing around at some of the sinister faces nearby, 'but the company in The Black Dog is a little too primitive for my taste.'

Mulryne laughed. 'That's why I like it here,' he said. 'The place is alive. The sweepings of London come in through that door, looking for a drink, a woman and a fight in that order. I keep very busy.'

'Could you not spare some time to assist me?'

'I'm not sure that I can, Mr Colbeck. I've no idea what this man looks like and not a clue where to start looking.'

'I can help you on both counts,' said the detective. 'When I finally persuaded his wife that I needed to track him down, she gave me a good description of William Ings. He's living with a woman somewhere. But the place to start is among the moneylenders.'

'Why – did he borrow from them?'

'He must have Brendan. He lost so much at the card table that he had to sell or pawn most of the furniture in his house. The only way he could have carried on gambling was to borrow money – probably at an exorbitant rate of interest.'

'There are no philanthropists in the Devil's Acre.'

Colbeck leant in closer. 'I need to locate this man.'

'So I see. But tell me this – does that black-hearted devil, Superintendent Tallis, know that you're here?'

'Of course not.'

'What about Sergeant Leeming?'

'There's no need for Victor to be told,' said Colbeck. 'That way, he can't get into trouble with Mr Tallis. This is my project, Brendan. You'll only be answerable to me.'

'And there's money in it?'

'If you can root out William Ings.'

Mulryne pondered. Before he could reach a decision, however, he saw a drunk trying to molest one of the prostitutes who lounged against the bar. When she pushed the man away, he slapped her hard across the face and produced a squeal of outrage. Mulryne was out of his seat in a flash. He stunned the troublemaker with a solid punch on the side of his head before catching him as he fell. The man was lifted bodily and hurled out of the door into the alleyway, where he lay in a pool of his own vomit. The Irishman returned to his table.

'I'm sorry about the interruption,' he said, sitting down.

'You have a living to earn, Brendan.'

'I do, Mr Colbeck. Mind you, I can always do with extra money. Since I became forty, my charm is no longer enough for some of the girls. They expect me to buy them things as well – as a mark of my affection, you understand.'

'I don't care how you spend what I give you.'

'That's just as well,' said Mulryne. 'Before I agree, promise me there'll be no questions about any friends of mine here who might accidentally have strayed from the straight and narrow.' His eyes glinted. 'I'm not an informer, Mr Colbeck.'

'The only man I'm interested in is William Ings. Will you help me?'

'As long as my name never reaches Mr Tallis.'

'It won't,' said Colbeck, 'I can assure you of that.'

'Then I'm your man.'

'Thank you, Brendan. I appreciate it. Though I'm afraid it won't be easy to find Ings in this rabbit warren.'

Mulryne was confident. 'If he's here – I'll find the bastard!'

Polly Roach was much older than she looked. By dyeing her hair and using cosmetics artfully, she lost over a decade, but her body was more difficult to disguise. She had therefore placed the oil lamp where the spill of its light did not give too much away. As she lay naked in his flabby arms, she made sure that the bed sheet covered her sagging breasts, her spindly legs and the mottled skin on her protruding belly. She nestled against his shoulder.

'When are you going to take me away from here?' she asked.

'All in good time.'

'You said that we'd have a home together.'

'We will, Polly. One day.'

'And when will that be?'

'When it's safe for me to leave here,' he said, unwilling to commit himself to a date. 'Until then, I'll stay with you.'

'But you told me that I didn't belong in the Devil's Acre.'

'You don't, Poll.'

'You promised that we'd live together properly.'

'That's what we are doing,' he said, fondling a breast and kissing her on the lips. 'I left a wife and children for you, remember.'

'I know, Bill.'

'I changed my whole life just to be with you.'

'I simply want you to get me out of the Devil's Acre.'

'Be patient.'

William Ings was a plump man in his forties with large, round eyes that made him look as if he was in a state of constant surprise, and a tiny mouth that was out of proportion with the rest of his facial features. It was lust rather than love that had drawn him to Polly Roach. She offered him the kind of sexual excitement that was unimaginable with his prudish and conventional wife and, once she had a hold on him, she slowly tightened her grasp. During the first few days when he moved in with her, he was in a state of euphoria, enjoying a freedom he had never known before and luxuriating in sheer decadence. It was worlds away from the humdrum routine of the Post Office.

The shortcomings of his situation then became more apparent. Instead of having his own house, he was now sharing two small rooms in a fetid tenement whose thin walls concealed no sounds from the rest of the building. Ings soon learnt that his immediate neighbours, an elderly man and his wife, had ear-splitting arguments several times a day and he had been shocked when he heard the prostitute in the room above them being beaten into silence by one of her more brutal customers. In the room below, a couple had made love to the accompaniment of such vile language that it made his ears burn. In the past, paying an occasional brief visit to Polly Roach had been exhilarating. Living with her in a place of menace was beginning to have distinct drawbacks.

'What are you thinking, Bill?' she asked, gently rubbing his chest.

He sat up. 'I've decided to go out again.'

'*Now*? It must be almost midnight.'

'There are places that never close.'

'You don't want to play cards again, surely?'

'Yes, Poll,' he said, easing her away from him. 'I feel lucky.'

'You always say that,' she complained, jabbing him with a finger, 'yet you always manage to lose somehow.'

'I won this week, didn't I?' he said, peevishly.

'That's what you told me, anyway.'

'Don't you believe me?'

'I'm not sure that I do.'

Anger stirred. 'Where else would I have got so much money from?' he said. 'You should be grateful, Polly. It enabled me to leave my job and move in here with you. Isn't that what you wanted?'

'Yes, Bill. Of course.'

'Then why are you pestering me like this?'

'I just wanted to know where the money came from,' she said, putting a conciliatory hand on his arm. 'Please don't go out again. I know that you feel lucky, but I'd hate you to throw away what you've already earned at the card table. That would be terrible.'

'I only play to win more,' he insisted, getting up and reaching for his clothes. 'This is my chance, don't you see? I can play for higher stakes.'

'Not tonight.'

'I must. I have this feeling inside me.'

Her voice hardened. 'How much have you given to *her*?' she asked, coldly. 'I don't want you wasting any of our money on your wife.'

'That's a matter between me and Maud.'

'No, it isn't, Bill.'

'I have responsibilities.'

'*I'm* your only responsibility now,' she said, climbing out of bed to confront him in the half-dark. 'Have you forgotten what you promised? You swore that I was the only person who mattered in your life.'

'You are, Poll.'

'Then prove it.'

'Leave me be,' he said, fumbling for his trousers.

'Prove it.'

'I've already done that.'

'Not to my satisfaction.'

'What more do you want of me?' he demanded, rounding on her. 'Because of you, I walked out on my wife and children, I gave up my job and I started a whole new life. I tried my best to make you happy.'

'Then take me away from here.'

'I will – in due course.'

'Why the delay?' she challenged. 'What are you hiding from?'

'Nothing.'

'Then why this talk about it not being safe to leave here?'

He pulled on his trousers. 'We'll talk about this in the morning,' he said, evasively. 'I have other things on my mind now.'

She glared at him. 'Are you lying to me, Bill?'

'No!'

'There's something you're not telling me.'

'You've been told everything you need to know, Poll.'

'I'm your woman. There should be no secrets between us.'

'There *are* none,' he said, irritably. 'Now stand out of my way and let me get dressed. I have to go out.'

Polly Roach had played the submissive lover for too long now. She decided that it was time to assert herself. When she got involved with William Ings, she had seen him as her passport out of the squalor and degradation that she had endured for so many years. He represented a last chance for her to escape from the Devil's Acre and its attendant miseries. The thought that he might be deceiving her in some way made her simmer with fury. As he tried to do up the buttons on his shirt, she took him by the shoulders.

'Stay here with me,' she ordered.

'No, Polly. I'm going out.'

'I won't let you. Your place is beside me.'

'Don't you *want* me to make more money, you silly woman?'

'Not that way, Bill. It's too dangerous.'

'Take your hands off me,' he warned.

'Only if you promise to stay here tonight.'

'Don't make me lose my temper.'

'I have a temper as well,' she snarled, digging her nails into his flesh. 'I fight for what's mine. I'm not going to let you sit at a card table and lose money that could be spent on me. I've been in this jungle far too long, Bill. I want to live somewhere *respectable*.'

'Get off me!' he yelled.

'No!'

'Get off!'

Stung by the pain and annoyed by her resistance, he pushed her away and lashed out wildly with a fist, catching her on the chin and sending her sprawling on to the floor. Her head hit the bare wood with a dull thud and she lost consciousness. Ings felt a pang of guilt as he realised what he had done but it soon passed. When he looked down at her, he was repelled by her sudden ugliness. Her mouth was wide open, her snaggly teeth were revealed and he could see the deep wrinkles around her scrawny neck for the first time. Her powdered cheeks were hollow. Ings turned away.

He had never hit a woman before and expected to be horrified at his own behaviour. Yet he felt no remorse. If anything, he felt strangely empowered. He finished dressing as quickly as he could. Polly Roach could do nothing to stop him when he retrieved his belongings from a corner and stuffed them into a leather bag. After taking a farewell look around the tawdry bedroom, he stepped over her body as if it were not there and went out with a swagger.

CHAPTER FIVE

Madeleine Andrews had refused the kind offer of accommodation in the neighbouring house, preferring instead to spend the night beside her father's bed. With a blanket around her shoulders and a velvet cushion beneath her, she sat on an upright wooden chair that was not designed to encourage slumber. Every time she fell asleep, she was awake again within minutes, fearful that she might fall off the chair or miss any sign of recovery by the patient. In fact, Caleb Andrews did not stir throughout the night, lying motionless on his back in the single bed, lost to the world and looking in a pitiful condition. It was only his mild but persistent snore that convinced Madeleine that he was still alive.

She loved her father dearly. In the five years since her mother's death, she had been running their home, taking on full responsibility and treating her father with the kind of affectionate cajolery that was needed. Madeleine was an attractive, alert, self-possessed young woman in her early twenties with an oval face framed by wavy auburn hair and set off by dimpled cheeks. She was calm and strong-willed. Instead of showing panic when told of the attack on her father, she had simply abandoned what she was doing and made her way to Leighton Buzzard as soon as she could.

By the time that she arrived, her father had been moved to the spare bedroom in the stationmaster's house and a penitent Frank Pike was seated beside him. It took her over an hour to convince the fireman that he needed to go home to his wife in order to reassure her that he had not been injured during the robbery. Still troubled in his mind, Pike had finally departed, given some hope by the brief moment when his friend and workmate seemed to rally. He accepted that it was Madeleine's place to keep watch over her father. Both she and the fireman prayed earnestly that she was not sitting beside a deathbed.

It was well after dawn when Caleb Andrews started to wake from his long sleep. Eyes still shut, he rocked from side to side as if trying to shake himself free of something, and a stream of unintelligible words began to tumble from his mouth. Madeleine bent solicitously over him.

'Can you hear me?' she asked.

He puckered his face as he fought to concentrate. When he tried to move the arm that was in a sling, he let out a cry of pain then became silent again. Madeleine thought he had fallen asleep and made no effort to rouse him. She simply sat there and gazed at him by the light that was slanting in through a gap in the curtains. The room was small and featureless, but the bed was a marked improvement on the table in the stationmaster's office. Greater comfort had allowed the patient to rest properly and regain some strength. When his daughter least expected it, Caleb Andrews forced his eyes open and squinted at the ceiling.

'Where am I?' he whispered.

'You're somewhere safe, Father,' she replied.

He recognised her voice. 'Maddy? Is that you?'

He turned his head towards her and let out another yelp of pain.

'Keep still, Father.'

'What's wrong with me?'

'You were badly injured,' she explained, putting a delicate hand on his chest. 'The train was robbed and you were attacked.'

'Where's Frank? Why isn't my fireman here?'

'I sent him home.'

Andrews was bewildered. 'Home? Why?' His eyes darted wildly. 'Where are we, Maddy?'

'In the stationmaster's house at Leighton Buzzard.'

'What am I doing here? I should be at work.'

'You need rest,' she told him, putting her face close to his. 'You took some blows to the head and you fractured a leg when you fell from the footplate. Your arm is in a sling because you have a broken collarbone. Be very careful how you move.'

His face was puce with rage. 'Who *did* this to me?'

'There's no need to worry about that now.'

'Tell me. I want to know.'

'Calm down. You must not get excited.'

'Frank Pike shouldn't have deserted his post. He'll be reported.'

'Forget him, Father,' she advised. 'All we have to think about is how to get you better. It's a miracle that you're alive and able to talk again. I thought I might have lost you.'

She brushed his lips with a tender kiss. Though his face was contorted with pain, he managed a faint smile of thanks and reached up with his free hand to touch her arm. Still hazy, torn between fatigue and anger, puzzled and comforted by his daughter's presence, he struggled to piece together what had happened to him but his memory was hopelessly clouded. All that he could remember was who he was and what he did for a living. When he heard a train steaming through the nearby station, a sense of duty swelled up in him.

'I must get out of here,' he decided, attempting to move.

'No, Father,' she said, using both hands to restrain him gently.

'Frank and I have to take the mail train to Birmingham.'

'It was robbed yesterday. You were assaulted.'

'Help me up, Maddy. We have to get there on time.'

'There *is* no mail train,' she said, trying to break the news to him as softly as she could. 'The men who robbed you removed a section of the track. When you were knocked unconscious, Frank Pike was forced to drive the engine off the rails. He told me that it's lying on its side until they can get a crane to it.'

Andrews was appalled. 'My engine came off the track?' Madeleine nodded sadly. 'Oh, no! That's a terrible thing to hear. She was such a lovely piece of engineering. Mr Allan designed her and I looked after her as if she was my own daughter – as if she was *you*, Maddy.' His eyes moistened. 'I don't care what happened to me. It's her that I worry about. I loved her like a father. She was *mine*.'

Caleb Andrews sobbed as if he had just lost the dearest thing in his life. All that Madeleine could do was to use her handkerchief to wipe away the tears that rolled down his cheeks.

The train that had sped through Leighton Buzzard Station continued on its journey to Birmingham, passing the spot where the robbery had occurred and allowing its passengers a fleeting view of the scene of the crime before taking them on into the Linslade Tunnel. Among those in one of the first class compartments was Inspector Robert Colbeck, who took a keen interest in the sight of the wrecked locomotive that still lay beside the line. He spared a thought for its unfortunate driver.

Though it had given him a very late night, he felt that his visit to the Devil's Acre had been worthwhile and he had been struck once again by the fact that one of the most hideous rookeries in London was cheek by jowl with the uplifting beauty of Westminster Abbey. Rising early the next day, he had travelled by cab to Euston Station where he bought two different newspapers to compare their treatment of the story.

Edward Tallis had been right in his prediction. For anyone involved in law enforcement, reports of the robbery did not make happy reading. The stunning novelty of the crime and the sheer size of the amount stolen – over £3,000 in gold sovereigns – encouraged the newspapers to inject a note of hysteria into their accounts, stressing the ease with which the robbery had been carried out and the apparent inability of either the mail guards or the railway policemen to offer anything but token resistance. The Detective Department at Scotland Yard, they told their readers, had never mounted an investigation of this kind before and were therefore operating in the dark.

Robert Colbeck was mentioned as being in charge of the case and he was surprised to read a quotation from Superintendent Tallis, who referred to him as 'an experienced, reliable and gifted detective'. When he remembered some of the less flattering things that his superior had called him in private, he gave a wry smile. One point made by both newspapers was incontrovertible. No crime of this nature had ever before confronted a Detective Department that, formed only nine years earlier, was still very much in its infancy. They were in uncharted waters.

While the newspapers used this fact as a stick with

which to beat the men at Scotland Yard, the Inspector in charge of the investigation saw it as a welcome challenge. He was thrilled by the notion of pitting himself against a man who had organised a crime of such magnitude and audacity. Most of the offenders he had arrested were poor, downtrodden, uneducated men who had turned to crime because there was no honest way for them to make a living. London had its share of seasoned villains, desperate characters who would stop at nothing to achieve their ends, but the majority who trooped through the courts were pathetic figures for whom Colbeck felt a sneaking sympathy.

This time, however, it was different. They were up against a man of clear intelligence, a natural leader who could train and control a gang of almost a dozen accomplices. Instead of fearing him, as the reporters were inclined to do, Colbeck saw him as a worthy adversary, someone who would test his skills of detection and who would stretch the resources of Scotland Yard in a way that had never occurred before. Solving the crime would be an adventure for the mind. However long it might take, Colbeck looked forward to meeting the man behind the train robbery.

Meanwhile, he decided to catch up on some lost sleep. The train was moving along at a comfortable speed, but there were stops to make and it would be hours before it reached Birmingham. He settled back in his upholstered seat and closed his eyes. It was a noisy journey. The chugging of the locomotive combined with the rattling of the carriages and the clicking of the wheels on the rails to produce a cacophony that tried to defy slumber. There was also a lurching motion to contend with as the train powered its way along the standard gauge track.

Because it offered more stability, Colbeck preferred the wider gauge of the Great Western Railway and the greater space in its carriages but he had no choice in the matter on this occasion. The company whose mail train had been robbed was the one taking him to Birmingham, and he was interested to see how it treated its passengers. His compartment was almost full and sleep would offer him a refuge from conversation with any of his companions. Two of them, both elderly men, were scandalised by what they had read in their newspapers.

'A train robbery!' protested one of them. 'It's unthinkable.'

'I agree,' said the other. 'If this kind of thing is allowed to go on, we'll all be in danger. Any passenger train would run the risk of being ambushed and we would be forced to hand over everything we are carrying of value.'

'What a ghastly prospect!'

'It might come to that.'

'Not if this gang is caught, convicted and sent to prison.'

'What chance is there of that?' said the other, sceptically.

'Detectives have already begun an investigation.'

'I find it hard to put much faith in them, sir.'

'Why?'

'Because they have almost no clues to help them. According to *The Times*, these devils came out of nowhere, stole what they wanted, then vanished into thin air. The detectives are chasing phantoms.'

'Yet they claim that this Inspector Colbeck is a gifted policeman.'

'It will need more than a gifted policeman to solve this crime.'

'I agree with you there, my friend.'

'My guess is that this Inspector will not even know where to start.'

On that vote of confidence in his ability, Colbeck fell asleep.

The Devil's Acre was almost as menacing by day as by night. Danger lurked everywhere in its narrow streets, its twisting lanes and its dark alleyways. There was a pervading stink that never seemed to go away and an unrelenting clamour. Bawling adults and screaming children joined in a mass choir whose repertory consisted solely of a sustained and discordant din that assaulted the eardrums. Scavenging dogs and fighting tomcats added their own descant. Smoke-blackened tenements were built around small shadowed courtyards, thick with assorted refuse and animal excrement. In every sense, it was a most unhealthy place to live.

Brendan Mulryne, however, loved the district. Indeed, he was sad that parts of it had recently been pulled down during the building of Victoria Street, thereby limiting its size and increasing the population of the area that was left, as those who had been evicted moved into houses that were already crowded with occupants. What the Irishman enjoyed about the Devil's Acre was its raucous life and its sense of freedom. It was a private place, set apart from the rest of London, a swirling underworld that offered sanctuary to criminals of every kind in its brothels, its tenements, its opium dens, its gambling haunts and its seedy public houses.

Mulryne felt at home. People he had once hounded as a policeman were now his neighbours and he tolerated their misdemeanours with ease. It was only when a defenceless woman was being beaten, or when a child was in distress, that he felt obliged to intervene. Otherwise, he let the mayhem continue unabated. It was his natural milieu. Unlike strangers who came into the Acre, he could walk its streets without fear of assault or of attracting any of the pickpockets who cruised up and down in search of targets. Mulryne's size and strength bought him respect from almost everyone.

Isadore Vout was the exception to the rule. When the Irishman found him that morning, the moneylender was at his lodging, enjoying a breakfast of stale bread and dripping that he first dipped into a mug of black, brackish tea. Rich by comparison with most people in the area, Vout led a miserly existence, wearing tattered clothes and eating poor food. He was a short, skinny weasel of a man in his fifties, with long grey hair that reached his shoulders and a mean face that was forever set in an expression of distaste. He was not pleased when the landlady showed in his visitor. His voice betrayed no hint of respect.

'Wor d'yer want, Mulryne?' he said through a mouthful of food.

'First of all,' replied the other, standing over him, 'I'd like a little politeness from that arsehole you call a mouth. Unless, that is, you'd like me to pour the rest of that tea over your head.'

'Yer got no right to threaten me.'

'I'm giving you friendly advice.' Pulling up a stool, Mulryne sat beside him at the table and saw what he was eating. 'Bread and dripping, is it?' he noted with disgust. 'And you, able to dine off the finest plate and eat like a lord.'

'It's been a bad month, ain't it?'

'You never have a bad month, you leech. There's always plenty of blood for you to suck out of people who can't afford to lose it. That's why I'm here, Isadore. I want to talk about debts.'

Vout was surprised. 'Yer want to borrow money?'

'I wouldn't borrow a penny from a creeping Shylock like you.'

'Yer'd get a good rate of interest, Mulryne.' He nudged his visitor. 'Friends of mine have special terms, see?'

'I'm no friend of yours, you old skinflint. Special terms?' repeated Mulryne with derision. 'I don't give a fiddler's fart for your special terms.'

'Then why are yer botherin' me?'

'Because I need information from you. There's a man who probably turned to you for a loan – God help him! I want to know where he is.'

'I can't tell yer,' said Vout, guzzling his tea.

'You haven't heard his name yet.'

'Meks no diff'rence, Mulryne. I never discusses business matters. Them's confeedential.' He jerked his thumb over his shoulder. 'Shut the door when yer leaves – and don't come back.'

'I'm going nowhere until I get an answer,' warned Mulryne.

'Sling yer 'ook, you big, Irish numbskull. Yer wasting yer time.'

'Now you're insulting my nation as well as trying my patience.'

'I wants to finish my grub, that's all.'

'Then let a big, Irish numbskull offer you some assistance,' said Mulryne, grabbing the remainder of the food to stuff into his mouth. 'Like more tea to wash it down, would you?'

Holding the moneylender's hair, he pulled his head back and poured the remaining tea all over his face until Vout was squealing in pain and spluttering with indignation. Mulryne felt that more persuasion was still needed. He got up, pushed the other man to the floor, took him by the heels and lifted him up so that he could shake him vigorously. A waterfall of coins came pouring out of his pockets. Isadore Vout shrieked in alarm and tried to gather up his scattered money. Without any effort,

Mulryne held him a foot higher so that he could not reach the floor.

'Put me down, yer madman!' wailed Vout.

'Only when you tell me what I want to know.'

'I'll 'ave yer locked away fer this!'

'Shut up and listen,' Mulryne ordered, 'or I'll bounce your head on the floor until all your hair falls out.'

By way of demonstration, he lowered his captive hard until Vout's head met the carpet with such a bang that it sent up a cloud of dust. The moneylender yelled in agony.

'Stop it!' he pleaded. 'Yer'll crack my skull open.'

'Will you do as you're told, then?'

'No, Mulryne. I never talks about my clients.' His head hit the floor once again. 'No, no!' he cried. 'Yer'll kill me if you do that again.'

'Then I'd be doing the Devil's Acre a favour,' said Mulryne, hoisting him high once more. 'We can do without vultures like you. Now then, you snivelling rogue, what's it to be? Shall I ask my question or would you rather I beat your brains out on the floor?'

It was no idle threat. Seeing that he had no alternative, Vout agreed to help and he was promptly dropped in a heap on the carpet. He immediately began to collect up all the coins he had lost. Mulryne brought a large foot down to imprison one of his hands.

'Yer'll break my fingers!' howled Vout.

'Then leave your money until you've dealt with me.'

Removing his foot, the Irishman took him by the

lapels of his coat and lifted him back into his chair. He put his face intimidatingly close. Vout cowered before him.

'Who's this man yer knows?' he asked in a quavering voice.

'His name is William Ings.'

'Never 'eard of 'im.'

'Don't lie to me, Isadore.'

'It's the truth. I never met anyone called that.'

'There's an easy way to prove that, isn't there?' said Mulryne, looking around the dingy room. 'I can check your account book.'

'No!'

'You keep the names of all your victims in there, don't you? If I find that William Ings is among them, I'll know that you're lying to me. Now, where do you keep that book?'

'It's private. Yer can't touch it.'

'I can do anything I like, Isadore,' said Mulryne, walking across to a chest of drawers. 'Who's to stop me?'

As if to prove his point, he pulled out the top drawer and emptied its contents all over the floor. Vout leapt up from his seat and rushed across to grab his arm.

'No, no,' he shouted. 'Leave my things alone.'

'Then tell me about William Ings.'

The moneylender backed away. 'Maybe I *can* help yer,' he said.

'Ah, I've jogged your memory, have I?'

'It was the name that confused me, see? I did business

with a Bill Ings, but I can't say for certain that 'e's the same man. Wor does this William Ings look like?'

'I've never seen him myself,' admitted Mulryne, 'but I'm told he's a fat man in his forties who can't resist a game of cards. Since he lost so much, he'd turn to someone like you to borrow. Did he?'

'Yes,' confessed Vout.

'How much does he owe you?'

'Nothing.'

'*Nothing*?'

'He paid off his debt,' said the other. 'In full. Ings told me that 'e 'ad a big win at cards and wanted to settle up. Shame, really. I likes clients of 'is type. They're easy to squeeze.'

'Where can I find him?'

'Who knows?'

'You do, Isadore,' insisted Mulryne. 'You'd never lend a farthing unless you had an address so that you could chase the borrower for repayment. Find your account book. Tell me where this man lives.'

'I can't, Mulryne. I took 'im on trust, see? Someone I knew was ready to vouch for 'im and that was good enough for me.' He gave a sly grin. 'Polly has done a favour or two for me in the past. If 'e's with 'er, Bill Ings is a lucky man, I can tell yer. I knew I could always get to my client through Polly.'

'Polly who? Does she live in the Devil's Acre?'

'Born and bred 'ere. Apprenticed to the trade at thirteen. 'Er name is Polly Roach,' he said, grateful to be getting rid of Mulryne at last. 'Ask for 'er in Hangman's Lane. You may well find Mr Ings there.'

Robert Colbeck woke up as the train was approaching Birmingham and he was able to look through the window at the mass of brick factories and tall chimneys that comprised the outskirts. It was a depressing sight, but, having been there before, he knew that the drab industrial town also boasted some fine architecture and some spacious parks. What made it famous, however, were its manufacturing skills and Colbeck read the names of engineers, toolmakers, potters, metalworkers, builders and arms manufacturers emblazoned across the rear walls of their respective premises. Through the open window, he could smell the breweries.

Arriving at the terminus, he climbed into a cab and issued directions to the driver. During the short ride from Curzon Street to the bank, he was reminded that Joseph Hansom, inventor and architect, had not only built the arresting Town Hall with its Classical colonnade, he had also registered the Patent Safety Cab, creating a model for horse-drawn transport that had been copied down the years. Birmingham was therefore an appropriate place in which to travel in such a vehicle.

Spurling's Bank, one of the biggest in the Midlands, was in the main street between a hotel and an office building of daunting solidity. When he heard that a detective had come to see him, the manager, Ernest Kitson, invited Colbeck into his office at once and plied

100

him with refreshments. A tall, round-faced, fleshy man in his fifties, Kitson was wearing a black frock coat and trousers with a light green waistcoat. He could not have been more willing to help.

'The stolen money must be recovered, Inspector,' he said.

'That's why I'm here, sir. Before we can find it, however, I must first know how it went astray in the first place. Inside help was utilised.'

'Not from Spurling's Bank, of that you can rest assured.'

'Have you questioned the relevant staff?'

'It was the first thing I did when I heard of the robbery,' said Kitson, straightening his cravat. 'Apart from myself, only two other people here have access to the key that would open the safe containing the money. I spoke to them both at length and am satisfied that neither would even consider betraying a trust. Do not take my word for it. You may talk to them yourself, if you wish.'

'That will not be necessary,' decided Colbeck, impressed by his manner and bearing. 'I simply need to examine the key in question.'

'It is locked in the safe, Inspector.'

'Before you take it out, perhaps you could explain to me why the mail train was carrying such a large amount of money in gold coin.'

'Of course,' replied Kitson. 'We abide by the spirit of the Bank Charter Act of 1844. Does that mean anything to you, Inspector?'

'No, Mr Kitson.'

'Then let me enlighten you. Currency crises are the bane of banking and we have suffered them on a recurring basis. When he was Prime Minister, the late Mr Peel sought to end the cycle by imposing certain restrictions. Strict limits were placed on the issue of notes by individual banks and the fiduciary note issue of the Bank of England was set at £14,000,000. Any notes issued above this sum were to be covered by coin or gold bullion.'

'That sounds like a sensible precaution.'

'It is one that Spurling's Bank took to heart,' explained Kitson. 'We stick to that same principle and ensure that notes in all our banks are balanced by a supply of gold coin or bullion. A bank note, after all, is only a piece of paper that bears promise of payment. In the event of a sudden demand for real money, we are in a position to cope. Other banks have collapsed in such situations because they over-extended themselves with loans and had inadequate reserves.'

'How much of the money stolen was destined for this branch?'

'Over a half of it. The rest was to be shared between some of our smaller branches. None of us,' he emphasized, 'can afford to lose that money.' Taking a key from his waistcoat pocket, he crossed to the safe in the corner. 'Let me show you what you came to see.'

'What about the combination number of the safe on the train?'

'That, too, is kept in here.'

'Have you not memorised it, Mr Kitson?'

'I'm a banker, Inspector,' he said. 'I keep a record of everything.'

He opened the safe and took out a metal box that had a separate lock on it. After using a second key to open it, he handed the box to Colbeck. Inside was a slip of paper and a large key on a ring. Colbeck took them out and studied them carefully. Kitson watched in surprise when the detective produced a magnifying glass from his inside pocket to scrutinise the key more carefully. He even held it to his nose and sniffed it.

'May I ask what you are doing?' said Kitson, intrigued.

'Looking for traces of wax, sir. That's the way that duplicates are made. A mould is taken so that it can be used to produce an identical key. Not all locksmiths are as law-abiding as they should be, alas.'

'And this key?'

'It has not been tampered with,' said Colbeck.

'That is what I told you.'

'I needed to check for myself.'

'The only other set of keys is at the Royal Mint.'

'My colleague, Sergeant Leeming, will be visiting the Mint this very day, but I doubt if he will find a lapse in security there. Their procedures are usually faultless. That leaves only a third option.'

'And what is that, Inspector?'

'A visit to the factory where the safe was made,' said Colbeck, handing the key back to him. 'Please excuse me, Mr Kitson. I have to catch a train to Wolverhampton.'

* * *

Victor Leeming's day had had an abrasive start to it. When he reported to Tallis, he had found the Superintendent at his most irascible as he read the accounts of the train robbery in the morning newspapers. Seeing himself mocked, and misquoted, Tallis had taken out his anger on the Sergeant and left him feeling as if he had just been mauled by a Bengal tiger. Leeming was glad to escape to the Royal Mint where he could lick his wounds. His guide was a far less truculent companion.

'As you see, Sergeant Leeming,' he said, 'security has absolute priority here. Nobody has sole access to the keys to that safe. There are always two of us present, so it would be impossible for anybody to take a wax impression of the key.'

'I accept that, Mr Omber.'

'There has been a mint here on Tower Hill since Roman times. Methods of guarding the supply of coin thus have a long and honourable history. Having learnt from our predecessors, we feel that we have turned the Royal Mint into an impregnable stronghold.'

'There is no question of that,' conceded Leeming.

He was fascinated by all he had seen, particularly by the thick steel doors that seemed to be fitted everywhere. Once locked, they were almost airtight, and would not buckle before a barrel of gunpowder. Charles Omber took a justifiable pride in their security arrangements. He was a short, stout, middle-aged man whose paunch erupted out of his body and tested the buttons on his trousers to their limit. Having been subjected to Tallis's bellow, Leeming was grateful for Omber's quiet, friendly, helpful voice.

'What else can I show you, Sergeant?' he asked.

'While I'm here, I'd be interested to see the whole process.'

'It will be a pleasure to show you.'

'Thank you.'

Omber waddled off and Leeming fell in beside him. After passing the weighing room, where the amounts of bullion were carefully recorded, they went through some steel doors into the hot metallic atmosphere of the refining shop. Leeming brought up a hand to shield his eyes from the startling brilliance of the furnaces where molten gold was simmering in crucibles like over-heated soup. With long-handled dipping cups, refiners stood in their shirtsleeves before the furnaces to scoop out the liquid gold and pour it into zinc vats of water. Even those who were used to the heat and the noise had to use their bare forearms to wipe the sweat from their faces. Leeming was loosening his collar with a finger within seconds.

Charles Omber took him on to the corroding shop, where they were met with billowing steam from the porcelain vats in which the golden granules sizzled in hot nitric acid. It was like walking into a golden fog. When his eyes grew accustomed to the haze, Leeming watched the muscular men in their leather aprons and noticed that they all wore hats to protect them from the fumes. Interested to see every stage of the process, he was nevertheless relieved when they moved out of the room, enabling him to breathe more easily.

In the casting shop, with its arched furnace bricked into a wall, he saw the gold being melted again before being poured with utmost care into the moulds of the ingots. Standing at his shoulder, Omber explained what was happening then took his visitor on into the rolling room, the largest and most deafening part of the establishment. The massive steam-driven mill, powered by iron wheels on each side, thundered ceaselessly on, enabling the brick-like ingots to be pressed into long strips from which coins could be punched.

It was when they moved into the coining shop that Leeming suddenly realised something. He had to shout above the metallic chatter of the machines.

'I think I know why the robbers stole coin from that train,' he yelled. 'What is the melting point of gold?'

'That depends on its source and composition,' replied Omber, 'but it is usually between 1,200 and 1,420 degrees centigrade. Why do you ask, Sergeant Leeming?'

'They would need a furnace to handle gold bullion so the robbers let the Royal Mint do their work for them and waited until a shipment of coin was being made. They chose carefully,' he said, watching the blank discs being cut out of the metal. 'Had the train been carrying an issue of notes from the Bank of England, they would have ignored them because they might be traced by their serial numbers. Gold sovereigns are more easily disposed of, Mr Omber.'

'That is certainly true.'

'Then how did they know that you were only sending

106

gold coin yesterday?' wondered Leeming. 'I have an uncomfortable feeling that someone found a way to get past all these steel doors of yours.'

The journey to Wolverhampton obliged Colbeck to travel second class on the Birmingham, Lancaster and Carlisle Railway. It took him through the heart of the Black Country and he looked out with dismay at the forges, mills, foundries, nail factories, coal mines and ironstone pits that stretched for miles beneath the curling dark smoke that spewed from a thousand brick chimneys. Cutting through the smoke, filling the sky with a fierce glare, were lurid flames from countless burning heaps of rubbish. Those who laboured for long hours in heavy industry were unacquainted with the light of day and vulnerable to hideous accidents or cruel diseases. Above the thunder of his train, Colbeck could hear the pounding of hammers and the booming explosion of a blast furnace.

Wolverhampton was a large, dirty, sprawling industrial town that was celebrated for the manufacture of locks, brass, tin, japanned wares, tools and nails. The immaculate detective looked rather incongruous in its workaday atmosphere. Given directions by the stationmaster, he elected to walk to his destination so that he could take a closer look at the people and place. By the time that he arrived at the Chubb Factory, he felt that he had the measure of Wolverhampton.

Silas Harcutt, the manager at the factory, could not

understand why someone had come all the way from London to question him. He was a slim individual of middle height with the look of a man who had worked his way up to his position with a slowness that had left a residual resentment. Harcutt was abrupt.

'Your visit is pointless, Inspector,' he declared.

'Not at all,' said Colbeck. 'I've always been curious to see the inside of the Chubb factory. I once had the privilege of a visit to the Bramah Works and it was a revelation.'

'Bramah locks are nothing compared to ours.'

'Your competitors would disagree. At the forthcoming Great Exhibition, they are to display a lock that is impossible to pick.'

'We, too, will have our best lock on show,' boasted Harcutt, 'and we will challenge anyone to open it. I can tell you now that nobody will.'

'You obviously have faith in your product.'

'The Chubb name is a guarantee of quality.'

'Nobody disputes that, Mr Harcutt,' said Colbeck, ignoring the man's brusque manner. 'For professional reasons, I try to keep abreast of developments in the locksmith's trade and I'm always interested to read about your progress. The railway safe that you devised was a marvel of its kind. Even so,' he went on, 'I fear that it was not able to prevent a consignment of money from being stolen.'

'The locks were not picked,' insisted the manager, huffily. 'The safe is specifically designed so that a burglar has nothing to work upon but the keyholes with their protective internal barrels and the steel curtain at their mouths. Do not dare to blame us, Inspector. We were not at fault.'

'I hope that turns out to be the case, sir.'

'It *is* the case, Inspector. Let me show you why.'

Opening the door of his office, he led Colbeck down a corridor to a room that housed dozens of safes and locks. Harcutt walked across to a replica of the safe that the detective had seen on board the train.

'You see?' said the manager, patting the safe. 'Far too heavy to lift without the aid of a crane and resistant to any amount of gunpowder. It is solid and commodious, able to carry a quarter of a ton of gold, coin, or a mixture of both.'

'The robbers showed due respect for the Chubb name,' said Colbeck. 'Instead of trying to pick the locks, they opened them with the keys and the combination number. I am certain that they got neither from Spurling's Bank and security at the Royal Mint is very tight.'

Harcutt was offended. 'Are you suggesting that the keys came from *here*?' he said, drawing himself up to his full height. 'I regard that as an insult, Inspector.'

'It was not meant to be. If I may examine the keys to this safe, I can tell you at once whether there has been subterfuge in your factory.'

'That is inconceivable.'

'I must press you on this point,' said Colbeck, meaningfully.

Lips pursed, Harcutt turned away and strode back to his office with the detective at his heels. He had to use two keys and a combination number to open the wall safe, making sure that he kept his back to his visitor so that Colbeck could see nothing of the operation. Extracting a metal box, the manager unlocked it with a third key and handed it over.

Colbeck took out the keys. Unable to detect anything suspicious with the naked eye, he brought his magnifying glass out again. He saw exactly what he had expected to find.

'Minute traces of wax,' he noted, offering the glass to the other man. 'Would you care to confirm that, Mr Harcutt?'

The manager took the magnifying glass and peered through it with disbelief. Both keys had discernible specks of wax still attached to them.

'Who else was authorised to open your safe?' asked Colbeck.

'Only two people. Mr Dunworth, my deputy, is one of them.'

'And the other?'

'Daniel Slender.'

'I need to speak to both of them at once, Mr Harcutt.'

'Of course,' said the manager, grudgingly. 'Mr Dunworth is in the next office. But you'll have to wait until you get back to London before you question Mr Slender.'

'Oh?'

'He left some weeks ago to take up a new post there.' He saw the suspicion in Colbeck's eyes. 'You are quite wrong, Inspector,' he continued, shaking his head. 'Daniel Slender could not possibly be the culprit. He has been with us for decades. For the last few years, he has been looking after his sick mother in Willenhall. When she died, he felt that it was time to move out of the Midlands.' He thrust the magnifying glass at Colbeck. 'I have complete trust in Daniel Slender.'

The frock coat fitted perfectly. He preened himself in front of the mirror for minutes. Daniel Slender had finally fulfilled his ambition to wear clothing that had been tailored for him in Bond Street. Tall and well-proportioned, he looked as if he belonged in such fine apparel. When he had changed back into his other suit, he took a wad of five pounds notes from his wallet and began to peel them off. Years of self-denial were behind him now. He had enough money to change his appearance, his place in society and his whole life. He was content.

CHAPTER SIX

It was early evening before Robert Colbeck finally got back to his office in Scotland Yard. Victor Leeming was waiting to tell him about his visit to the Royal Mint and to voice his suspicion that someone there might have warned the train robbers when gold coin was actually being dispatched to Birmingham. He took a positive delight in describing the processes by which gold bullion was transformed into coinage.

'I have never seen such a large amount of money,' he said.

'No, Victor,' remarked Colbeck. 'The irony is that the men who sweat and strain to make the money probably get little of it in their wages. It is a cruel paradox. Workers who are surrounded by gold every day remain relatively poor. It must be a vexing occupation.'

'A dangerous one as well, sir. Had I stayed in the refining shop any longer, the heat from those furnaces would have given me blisters. As it is, I can still smell those terrible fumes.'

'I had my own share of fumes in the Midlands.'

'Was the visit a useful one?' asked Leeming.

'Extremely useful. While you were learning about the mysteries of the Royal Mint, I was being taught sensible banking practices and given an insight into the art of the locksmith.'

Colbeck related the events of his day and explained why he had enjoyed travelling by rail so much. Leeming was not convinced that train rides of well over a hundred miles each way were anything but purgatory. He was happy to have missed the ordeal.

'We now know where the keys were obtained,' he said.

'And the combination number, Victor. That, too, was essential.'

'This man, Daniel Slender, must be responsible.'

'Not according to the manager,' said Colbeck, remembering the protestations of Silas Harcutt. 'He claims that the fellow is innocent even though he is the only possible suspect. He set great store by the fact that Slender was a dutiful son who looked after an ailing mother.'

'That certainly shows kindness on his part.'

'It might well have led to frustration. Caring for a sick parent meant that he had no real life of his own. When he was not at the Chubb factory, he was fetching and carrying for his mother. I find it significant that, the moment she died, Daniel Slender sold the house.'

'If he was moving to another post, he would have to do that.'

'I doubt very much if that post exists, Victor.'

'Do you know what it was?'

'Yes,' said Colbeck. 'I even have the address of the factory to which he is supposed to have gone. But I'll wager that we won't find anyone of his name employed there.'

'So why did he come to London?'

Colbeck raised an eyebrow. 'I can see that you've never visited the Black Country. On the journey to Wolverhampton, I saw what the poet meant when he talked about 'dark, satanic mills'.'

'Poet?'

'William Blake.'

'The name means nothing to me, sir,' admitted Leeming, scratching a pimple on his chin. 'I never had much interest in poetry and such things. I know a few nursery rhymes to sing to the children but that's all.'

'It's a start, Victor,' said Colbeck without irony, 'it's a start. Suffice it to say that – with all its faults – London is a much more attractive place to live than Willenhall. Also, of course, Daniel Slender had to get well away from the town where he committed the crime.' He nodded in the direction of the next office. 'What sort of a mood is Mr Tallis in today?'

'A vicious one.'

'I told him not to read the newspapers.'

'They obviously touched him on a raw spot. When I

saw the Superintendent this morning, he was breathing fire.'

'I need to report to him myself,' said Colbeck, moving to the door. 'Hopefully, I can dampen down the flames a little. At least we now have the name of the man who made it possible for the robbers to open that safe with such ease.'

'That means we have two suspects.'

'Daniel Slender and William Ings.'

'I did as you told me, Inspector,' said Leeming. 'I asked the men on that beat to keep watch on Mr Ings's house, though I still think that he's unlikely to go back there. It would be too risky.'

'Then we'll have to smoke him out of the Devil's Acre.'

'How on earth could you do that?'

Colbeck suppressed a smile. 'I'll think of a way,' he said.

Work had kept Brendan Mulryne too busy throughout most of the day to continue his search. That evening, however, he took a break from The Black Dog and strode along to Hangman's Lane. The name was apposite. Most of the people he saw loitering there looked if they had just been cut down from the gallows. The man who told him where Polly Roach lived was a typical denizen of the area. Eyes staring, cheeks hollow and face drawn, he spoke in a hoarse whisper as if a noose were tightening around his neck.

Entering the tenement, Mulryne went up the stairs

and along a narrow passageway. It was difficult to read the numbers in the gloom so he banged on every door he passed. At the fourth attempt, he came face to face with the woman he was after.

'Polly Roach?' he inquired.

'Who's asking?'

'My name is Brendan Mulryne. I wanted a word with you, darling.'

'You've come to the wrong place,' she said, curtly. 'I don't entertain guests any more.'

'It's not entertainment I want, Polly – it's information.' He looked past her into the room. 'Do you have company, by any chance?'

'No, Mr Mulryne.'

'Would you mind if I came in to look?'

'Yes,' she cautioned, lifting her skirt to remove the knife from the sheath strapped to her thigh. 'I mind very much.'

Mulryne grinned benignly. 'In that case, we'll talk here.'

'Who sent you?'

'Isadore Vout.'

'That mangy cur! If you're a friend of his, away with you!'

'Oh, I'm no friend of Isadore's,' promised Mulryne, 'especially since I lifted him up by the feet and made him dance a jig on his head. He'd probably describe me as his worst enemy.'

'So why have you come to me?'

'I'm looking for someone called William Ings – Billy Ings to you.'

'He's not here,' she snapped.

'So you do know him?'

'I did. I thought I knew him well.'

'So where is he now?'

Polly was bitter. 'You tell me, Mr Mulryne.'

'Is he not coming to see you?'

'Not any more.'

There was enough light from the oil lamp just inside the door for him to see her face clearly. Polly Roach looked hurt and jaded. The thick powder failed to conceal the dark bruise on her chin. Mulryne sensed that she had been crying.

'Did you and Mr Ings fall out, by any chance?' he asked.

'That's my business.'

'It happens to be mine as well.'

'Why – what's Bill to you?'

'A week's wages. That's what I get when I find him.'

'His wife!' she cried, brandishing the knife. 'That bitch sent you after him, didn't she?'

'No, Polly,' replied Mulryne, holding up both hands in a gesture of surrender. 'I swear it. Sure, I've never met the lady and that's the honest truth. Now, why don't you put that knife away before someone gets hurt?' She lowered the weapon to her side. 'That's better. If you were hospitable, you'd invite me in.'

She held her ground. 'Say what you have to say here.'

'A friend of mine is anxious to meet this Billy Ings,' he explained, 'and he's paying me to find him. I'm not a man who turns away the chance of an honest penny and, in any case, I owe this man a favour.'

'What's his name?'

'There's no need for you to know that, darling.'

'Then why is he after Billy?'

'There was a train robbery yesterday and it looks as if Mr Ings may have been involved. His job at the Post Office meant that he had valuable information to sell.'

'So *that's* where he got the money from,' she said. 'He told me that he won it at the card table.'

'Isadore Vout heard the same tale from him.'

'He lied to me!'

'Then you have no reason to protect him.'

Polly Roach became suspicious. She eyed him with disgust.

'Are you a policeman?' she said.

Mulryne laughed. 'Do I *look* like a policeman, my sweetheart?'

'No, you don't.'

'I work at The Black Dog, making sure that our customers don't get out of hand. Policeman, eh? What policeman would dare to live in the Devil's Acre?' He summoned up his most endearing smile. 'Come on now, Polly. Why not lend me a little assistance here?'

'How can I?' she said with a shrug. 'I've no idea where he is.'

'But you could guess where he's likely to be.'

'Sitting at a card table, throwing his money away.'

'And where did he usually go to find a game?'

'Two or three different places.'

'I'll need their names,' he said. 'There's no chance that he'll have sneaked back to his wife then?'

'No, Mr Mulryne. He said that it wouldn't be safe to leave the Acre and I can see why now. He's here somewhere,' she decided, grimly. 'Billy liked his pleasures. That's how we met each other. If he's not gambling, then he's probably lying between the legs of some doxy while he tells her what his troubles are.'

The long day had done nothing to curb Superintendent Tallis's temper or to weaken his conviction that the newspapers were trying to make a scapegoat of him. Even though he brought news of progress, Colbeck still found himself on the receiving end of a torrent of vituperation. He left his superior's office with his ears ringing. Victor Leeming was in the corridor.

'How did you get on, Inspector?' he asked.

'Superintendent Tallis and I have had quieter conversations,' said Colbeck with a weary smile. 'He seemed to believe that he was back on the parade ground and had to bark orders at me.'

'That problem will not arise with your visitor.'

'Visitor?'

'Yes, sir. I just showed her into your office. The young lady was desperate to see you and would speak to nobody else.'

119

'Did she give a name?'

'Madeleine Andrews, sir. Her father was the driver of the train.'

'Then I'll see her at once.'

Colbeck opened the door of his office and went in. Madeleine Andrews leapt up from the chair on which she had perched. She was wearing a pretty, burgundy-coloured dress with a full skirt, and a poke bonnet whose pink ribbons were tied under her chin. She had a shawl over her arm. Introductions were made then Colbeck indicated the chair.

'Do sit down again, Miss Andrews,' he said, courteously.

'Thank you, Inspector.'

Colbeck sat opposite her. 'How is your father?'

'He's still in great pain,' she said, 'but he felt well enough to be brought home this afternoon. My father hates to impose on anyone else. He did not wish to spend another night at the stationmaster's house in Leighton Buzzard. It will be more comfortable for both of us at home.'

'You went to Leighton Buzzard, then?'

'I sat beside his bed all night, Inspector.'

'Indeed?' He was amazed. 'You look remarkably well for someone who must have had very little sleep.'

She acknowledged the compliment with a smile and her dimples came into prominence. Given her concern for her father, only something of importance could have made her leave him to come to Scotland Yard. Colbeck wondered what it was and why it made her seem so uneasy and tentative. But he did not press her. He waited until she was ready to confide in him.

'Inspector Colbeck,' she began at length, 'I have a confession to make on behalf of my father. He told me something earlier that I felt duty bound to report to you.'

'And what is that, Miss Andrews?'

'My father loves his work. There's not a more dedicated or respected driver in the whole company. However . . .' She lowered her head as if trying to gather strength. He saw her bite her lip. 'However,' she went on, looking at him again, 'he is inclined to be boastful when he has had a drink or two.'

'There's no harm in that,' said Colbeck. 'Most people become a little more expansive when alcohol is consumed.'

'Father was very careless.'

'Oh?'

'At the end of the working day,' she said, squirming slightly with embarrassment, 'he sometimes enjoys a pint of beer with his fireman, Frank Pike, at a public house near Euston. It's a place that is frequented by railwaymen.'

'In my opinion, they're fully entitled to a drink for what they do. I travelled to the Midlands by train today, Miss Andrews, and am deeply grateful for the engine drivers who got me there and back. I'd have been happy to buy any of them a glass of beer.'

'Not if it made them talkative.'

'Talkative?'

'Let me frank with you,' she said, blurting it out. 'My father blames himself for the robbery yesterday. He thinks that he may have been drinking with his friends one evening and let slip the information that money was being carried on the mail trains.' She held out her hands in supplication. 'It was an accident, Inspector,' she said, defensively. 'He would never willingly betray the company. You may ask Frank Pike. My father stood up to the robbers.'

'I know, Miss Andrews,' said Colbeck, 'and I admire him for it. I also admire you for coming here like this.'

'I felt that you should know the truth.'

'Most people in your situation would have concealed it.'

'Father made me promise that I would tell you the terrible thing that he did,' she said, bravely. 'He feels so ashamed. Even though it will mean his dismissal from the company, he insisted.' She sat forward on her chair. 'Will you have to arrest him, Inspector?'

'Of course not.'

'But he gave away confidential information.'

'Not deliberately,' said Colbeck. 'It popped out when he was in his cups. I doubt very much if that was how the robbers first learnt how money was being carried. They had only to keep watch at the station for a length of time and they would have seen boxes being loaded under armed guard on to the mail train. Such precautions would not be taken for a cargo of fruit or vegetables.'

Her face brightened. 'Then he is *not* to blame for the robbery?'

'No, Miss Andrews. What the villains needed to know was what a particular train was carrying and the exact time it was leaving Euston. That information was obtained elsewhere – along with the means to open the safe that was in the luggage van.'

Madeleine caught her breath. 'I'm so relieved, Inspector!'

'Tell your father that he's escaped arrest on this occasion.'

'It will be a huge load off his mind – and off mine.'

'I'm delighted that I've been able to give you some reassurance.'

Relaxed and happy, Madeleine Andrews looked like a completely different woman. A smile lit up her eyes and her dimples were expressive. She had come to Scotland Yard in trepidation and had feared the worst. Madeleine had not expected to meet such a considerate and well-spoken detective as Robert Colbeck. He did not fit her image of a policeman at all and she was profoundly grateful.

For his part, Colbeck warmed to her. It had taken courage to admit that her father had been at fault, especially when she feared dire consequences from the revelation. There was a quiet integrity about Madeleine Andrews that appealed to him and he was by no means immune to her physical charms. Now that she was no longer so tense, he could appreciate them to the full.

Pleased that she had come, he was glad to be able to put her mind at rest.

'Thank you, Inspector,' she said, getting to her feet. 'I must get back home to tell Father. He felt so dreadfully guilty about this.'

Colbeck rose at well. 'I think that some censure is in order,' he pointed out. 'Mr Andrews did speak out of turn about the mail train, that much is clear. On reflection, he will come to see how foolish that was and be more careful in future.'

'Oh, he will, he will.'

'I leave it to you to issue a stern warning.'

'Father needs to be kept in line at times. He can be wayward.'

'What he requires now,' suggested Colbeck, 'is a long rest. Far from dismissing him, the London and North Western Railway Company should be applauding him for trying to protect their train.' He smiled at her. 'When would it be possible for me to call on your father?'

'At home, you mean?'

'I hardly expect Mr Andrews to come hopping around here.'

'No, no,' she said with a laugh.

'Mr Pike has given me his version of events, of course, but I would like to hear what your father has to say. Is there any chance that I might question him tomorrow?'

'Yes, Inspector – if he continues to improve.'

'I'll delay my arrival until late morning.'

'We will expect you,' said Madeleine, glad that

she would be seeing him again. Their eyes locked for a moment. Both of them felt a mild *frisson*. It was she who eventually turned away. 'I've taken up too much of your time, Inspector. I look forward to seeing you tomorrow.'

'One moment,' he said, putting a hand on her arm to stop her. 'I may be a detective, but I find it much easier to visit a house when I know exactly where it is.' He took out his notebook. 'Could I trouble you for an address, Miss Andrews?'

She gave another laugh. 'Yes – how silly of me!'

He wrote down the address that she dictated then closed the notebook. When he looked up, she met his gaze once more and there was a blend of interest and regret in her eyes. Colbeck was intrigued.

'I hope that you catch these men soon, Inspector,' she said.

'We will make every effort to do so.'

'What they did to my father was unforgivable.'

'They will be justly punished, Miss Andrews.'

'He was heartbroken when he heard what happened to his locomotive. Father dotes on it. Why did they force it off the track? It seems so unnecessary.'

'It was. Unnecessary and gratuitous.'

'Do you have any idea who the train robbers might be?'

'We have identified two of their accomplices,' he told her, 'and we are searching for both men. One of them – a former employee of the Post Office – should be in custody before too long.'

* * *

125

William Ings was astounded by his good fortune. He never thought that he would meet any woman whose company he preferred to a game of cards but that is what had happened in the case of Kate Piercey. He had shared a night of madness with her and spent most of the next day in her arms. Kate was younger, livelier and more sensual than Polly Roach. Her breath was far sweeter, her body firmer. More to the point, she was not as calculating as the woman he had discarded on the previous night. Ings had bumped into her in the street as he fled from the clutches of Polly Roach. He knew that the collision was no accident – she had deliberately stepped out of the shadows into his path – but that did not matter. He felt that the encounter was fateful.

There was something about Kate that excited him from the start, an amalgam of boldness and vulnerability that he found irresistible. She was half-woman and half-child, mature yet nubile, experienced yet seemingly innocent. William Ings was a realist. He knew that he was not the first man to enjoy her favours and he had no qualms about paying for them, but he was soon overcome by the desire to be the last of her clients, to covet her, to protect her, to rescue her from the hazards of her profession and shape her into something better. Impossible as the dream might appear, he wanted to be both father and lover to Kate Piercey.

As he watched her dress that evening by the light of the lamp, he was enchanted. Polly Roach might have brought him to the Devil's Acre but she had been displaced from his mind completely.

'Where shall we go, Billy?' she asked.

'Wherever you wish,' he replied.

'We can eat well but cheaply at Flanagan's.'

'Then we'll go elsewhere. That place is not good enough for you.'

She giggled. 'You say the nicest things.'

'You deserve the best, Kate. Let me take you somewhere special.'

'You're so kind to me.'

'No, my love,' he said, slipping his arms around her, 'it's you who are kind to me.' He kissed her once more. 'I adore you.'

'But you've known me less than twenty-four hours, Billy.'

'That's long enough. Now, where can we dine together?'

'There's a new place in Victoria Street,' she told him, 'but they say that it's very expensive.'

He thrust his hand deep into his leather bag and brought out a fistful of bank notes. Ings held them proudly beneath her nose, as if offering them in tribute.

'Do you think that this would buy us a good meal?'

'Billy!' she cried with delight. 'Where did you get all that money?'

'I've been saving it up until I met you,' he said.

Madeleine Andrews was touched when Colbeck insisted on escorting her to the front door of the building. Light was beginning to fade and there was a gentle breeze. She turned to look up at him.

'Thank you, Inspector. You are very kind.'

'It must have taken an effort for you to come here.'

'It did,' she said. 'The worst of it was that I felt like a criminal.'

'You've done nothing wrong, Miss Andrews.'

'I shared my father's guilt.'

'All that he was guilty of was thoughtless indiscretion,' he said, 'and I'm sure that nobody could ever accuse you of that.' Her gaze was quizzical. 'What's the matter?'

'Oh, I'm sorry. I did not mean to stare like that.'

'You seem to be puzzled by something.'

'I suppose that I am.'

'Let me see if I can guess what it is, Miss Andrews,' he said with a warm smile. 'The question in your eyes is the one that I've asked myself from time to time. What is a man like me doing in this job?'

'You are so different to any policemen that I have ever met.'

'In what way?'

'They are much more like the man who showed me to your office.'

'That was Sergeant Leeming,' he explained. 'I'm afraid that Victor is not blessed with the most handsome face in London, though his wife loves him dearly nevertheless.'

'It was his manner, Inspector.'

'Polite but rough-edged. I know what you mean. Victor spent years, pounding his beat in uniform. It leaves

128

its mark on a man. My time in uniform was considerably shorter. However,' he went on, looking up Whitehall, 'you did not come here to be bored by my life story. Let me help you find a cab.'

'I had planned to walk some of the way, Inspector.'

'I'd advise against it, Miss Andrews. It is not always safe for an attractive woman to stroll unaccompanied at this time of day.'

'I am well able to look after myself.'

'It will be dark before long.'

'I am not afraid of the dark.'

'Why take any risks?'

Seeing a cab approach in the distance, he raised a hand.

'There is no risk involved,' she said with a show of spirit. 'Please do not stop the cab on my account. If I wished to take it, I am quite capable of hailing it myself.'

He lowered his hand. 'I beg your pardon.'

'You must not worry about me. I am much stronger than I may appear. After all, I did come here on foot.'

He was taken aback. 'You *walked* from Camden Town?'

'It was good exercise,' she replied. 'Goodbye, Inspector Colbeck.'

'Goodbye, Miss Andrews. It was a pleasure to meet you.'

'Thank you.'

'I will see you again tomorrow,' he said, relishing the thought. 'I hope that you'll forgive me if I arrive by Hansom cab.'

She gave him a faint smile before walking off up Whitehall. Colbeck stood for a moment to watch her then he went back into the building. As soon as the detective had disappeared, a figure stepped out from the doorway in which he had been hiding. He was a dark-eyed young man of medium height in an ill-fitting brown suit. Pulling his cap down, he set off in pursuit of Madeleine Andrews.

By the time he got back to The Black Dog, the fight had already started. Several people were involved and they had reached the stage of hurling chairs at each other or defending themselves with a broken bottle. Brendan Mulryne did not hesitate. Hurling himself into the middle of the fray, he banged heads together, kicked one man in the groin and felled a second with an uppercut. But even he could not stop the brawl. When it spilt out into the street, he was carried along with it, flailing away with both fists and inflicting indiscriminate punishment.

Mulryne did not go unscathed. He took some heavy blows himself and the brick that was thrown at him opened a gash above his eye. Blood streamed down his face. It only served to enrage him and to make him more determined to flatten every man within reach. Roaring with anger, he punched, kicked, grappled, gouged and even sank his teeth into a forearm that was wrapped unwisely across his face. Well over a dozen people had been involved in the fracas but, apart from the Irishman, only three were left standing.

As he bore down on them, they took to their heels and Mulryne went after the trio, resolved to teach them to stay away from The Black Dog in future. One of them tripped and fell headlong. Mulryne was on him at once, heaving him to his feet and slamming him against a wall until he heard bones crack. The next moment, a length of iron pipe struck the back of Mulryne's head and sent him to his knees. The two friends of the man who had fallen had come back to rescue him. Hurt by the blow, the Irishman had the presence of mind to roll over quickly so that he dodged a second murderous swipe.

He was on his feet in an instant, grabbing the pipe and wresting it from the man holding it. Mulryne used it to club him to the ground. When the second man started to belabour him, he tossed the pipe away, lifted his assailant up and hurled him through a window. Yells of protest came from the occupants of the house. Dazed by the blow to his head and exhausted by the fight, Mulryne swayed unsteadily on his feet, both hands to his wounds to stem the bleeding. He did not even hear the sound of the police whistles.

Robert Colbeck sat in his office and reviewed the evidence with Victor Leeming. While no arrests had yet been made, they felt that they had a clear picture of how the robbery had taken place, and what help had been given to the gang responsible by employees in the Post Office and the lock industry. The Sergeant still believed that someone from the Royal Mint was implicated as well. Colbeck told him about the interview with Madeleine Andrews and how he had been able to still her fears.

'The young lady was well-dressed for a railwayman's daughter.'

'Did you think that she'd be wearing rags and walking barefoot?'

'She looked so neat and tidy, sir.'

'Engine drivers are the best-paid men on the railway,' said Colbeck, 'and quite rightly. They have to be able to read, write and understand the mechanism of the locomotive. That's why so many of them begin as fitters before becoming firemen. Caleb Andrews earns enough to bring up his daughter properly.'

'I could tell from her voice that she'd had schooling.'

'I think that she's an intelligent woman.'

'And a very fetching one,' said Leeming with a grin.

'She thought that you were a typical policeman, Victor.'

'Is that good or bad, sir?'

Colbeck was tactful. 'You'll have to ask the young lady herself.' There was a tap on the door. 'Come in!' he said.

The door opened and a policeman entered in uniform.

'I was asked to give this to you, Inspector Colbeck,' he said, handing over the envelope that he was carrying.

'I'm told that it's quite urgent. I'm to wait for a reply.'

'Very well.' Colbeck opened the envelope and read the note inside. He scrunched up the paper in his hand. 'There's no reply,' he said. 'I'll come with you myself.'

'Right, sir.'

'Bad news, Inspector?' wondered Leeming.

'No, Victor,' said Colbeck, smoothly. 'A slight problem has arisen, that's all. It will not take me long to sort it out. Excuse me.'

The only time that Brendan Mulryne had seen the inside of a police cell was when he had thrown the people he had arrested into one. It was different being on the other side of the law. When the door had slammed shut upon him, he was locked in a small, bare, cheerless room that was no more than a brick rectangle. The tiny window, high in the back wall, was simply a ventilation slit with thick iron bars in it. The place reeked of stale vomit and urine.

The bed was a hard wooden bench with no mattress or blankets. Sitting on the edge of it, Mulryne wished that his head would stop aching. His wounds had been tended, and the blood wiped from his face, but it was obvious that he had been in a fight. His craggy face was covered with cuts and abrasions, his knuckles were raw. His black eye and split lip would both take time to heal. It had been a savage brawl yet he was not sorry to have been in it. His only regret was that he had been arrested as a result. It meant that he would lose money and leave The Black Dog unguarded for some time.

When a key scraped in the lock, he hoped that someone was bringing him a cup of tea to revive him. But it was not the custody sergeant who stepped into the cell. Instead, Inspector Robert Colbeck came in and looked down at the offender with more disappointment than sympathy. His voice was uncharacteristically harsh.

'Why ever did you get yourself locked up in here, Brendan?'

'It was a mistake,' argued Mulryne.

'Police records do not lie,' said Colbeck. 'According to the book, you have been charged with taking part in an affray, causing criminal damage, inflicting grievous bodily harm and – shocking for someone who used to wear a police uniform – resisting arrest.'

'Do you think that I *wanted* to be shut away here?'

'Why make things worse for yourself?'

'Because I was goaded,' said Mulryne. 'Two of the bobbies that tried to put cuffs on me recognised who I was and had a laugh at my expense. They thought it was great fun to arrest an old colleague of theirs. I'll not stand for mockery, Mr Colbeck.'

'Look at the state of you, man. Your shirt is stained with blood.'

Mulryne grinned. 'Don't worry. Most of it is not mine.'

'I do worry,' said Colbeck, sharply. 'I asked for help and you promised to give it. How can you do that when you're stuck in here?'

'The man to blame is the one who started the fight.'

'You should have kept out of it.'

'Sure, isn't keeping the peace what I'm paid to do?' asked Mulryne, earnestly. 'I'm a sort of policeman at The Black Dog, excepting that I don't wear a uniform. All I did was to try to calm things down.'

'With your fists.'

'They were not in the mood to listen to a sermon.'

Colbeck heaved a sigh. 'No, I suppose not.'

'Is there anything you can do for me?' said Mulryne, hopefully. 'Ask at The Black Dog. They'll tell that I didn't start the affray. I just got caught up in it. As for criminal damage, the person at fault is the one who dived head first through that window. On my word of honour, I did my best to stop him.'

'I know you too well, Brendan. I've seen you fight.'

'Well, at least get them to drop the charge of grievous bodily harm. Jesus! You should feel the lump on the back of my head. It's the size of an egg, so it is. I was the *victim* of grievous bodily harm.' He got up from the bed. 'Please, Mr Colbeck. I'm a wronged man.'

'Are you?'

'I'm such a peaceable fellow by nature.'

'Tell that to the policeman whose teeth you knocked out.'

'I did apologise to him afterwards.'

'What use is that?' demanded Colbeck. 'And what use are you to me while you're cooling your heels in here?'

'None at all, I admit. That's why you must get me out.'

'So that you can create more havoc?'

'No, Mr Colbeck,' said Mulryne, 'so that I can find out where Billy Ings is hiding. He's within my grasp, I know it. I did as you told me. I spoke to Isadore Vout, the bloodsucker who loaned him money when he lost at the card table.'

'Did he know where Ings could be found?'

'With a doxy named Polly Roach who lives in Hangman's Lane.'

'And?'

'I paid her a call. When I asked her about Billy Ings, she spat out his name like it was a dog turd. They had a disagreement, you see, and he walked out on her. I fancy that he knocked her about before he went. He told Polly that he'd won a lot of money playing cards but she knows better now. It made her livid.'

'I'm the one who is livid,' asserted Colbeck. 'You let me down.'

'I could never walk away from a fight.' He took his visitor by the arms. 'Help me, please. If you don't get me released, it will be too late.'

'What do you mean?'

'Polly Roach has gone looking for Ings as well,' said Mulryne, 'and it's not to give him her best wishes. There's only one thing on her mind.'

'Is there?'

'Revenge.'

The Devil's Acre was a comparatively small district but it was teeming with inhabitants, packed into its houses and tenements until their walls were about to burst. Tracking someone down in its labyrinthine interior was not a simple task, even for someone like Polly Roach who had lived there since birth. It had such a shifting population. She first tried the various gambling dens where William

Ings was known but he had not been seen at any of them that day. Polly reasoned that he must have found himself a bed for the night and that meant he paid someone to share it with him.

There was no shortage of prostitutes in the Acre. Clients could pick anyone from young girls to old women. Polly Roach knew from personal experience the sordid acts that they were called upon to perform. It was what set William Ings apart from all the other men who had paid for her services. He had made no demands on her. He came in search of a friend rather than a nameless whore who would simply satisfy his urges and send him on his way. Ings wanted a confidante, a source of sympathy, someone who would listen patiently to his bitter complaints about his private life and offer him succour.

Polly Roach felt that she had done just that. Over a period of several months, she had soothed his wounded pride. She had lost count of the number of times he talked about his unhappy marriage, his problems at work and his disputes with his neighbours. Until he met her, his life had had no joy or purpose. Polly had given him direction. Seeing how she could benefit herself, she had flattered him, advised him, supported him, even pretended that she loved him. If he had come into some money, she had earned her share of it and was determined to get it. William Ings was going to pay for all the time she had devoted to him.

Hours of searching for him eventually paid off. After

questioning almost anybody she encountered, Polly met an old acquaintance who recognised the description of William Ings and said that he had seen him in the company of Kate Piercey. He was even able to give her an address. Incensed that she had been replaced by a younger woman, Polly fingered the knife under her skirt and went off to confront the man who had cast her aside so unfairly.

When she reached the tenement, she hastened up the stairs to the attic room and saw the light under the door. It was no time for social niceties. She kicked the timber hard.

'Come out of there, Billy!' she shouted.

To her surprise, the door swung back on its hinges to reveal the hazy outline of a small, dirty, cluttered room with bare rafters. What hit her nostrils was a smell of damp mixed with the aroma of cheap perfume, a kind that she herself had used in the past. There was an oil lamp in the corner but it had been turned down so that it gave only the faintest glow. Polly turned up the flame in order to see more clearly. A hideous sight was suddenly conjured out of the dark. When she realised that she was not alone in the room, she let out a cry of horror. On a bed in the corner, lying side by side as if they were asleep, were William Ings and Kate Piercey. Their throats had been cut.

Polly began to retch and her first instinct was to run from the scene. Self-interest then slowly got the better of fear. Though Ings was dead, she might still get what she wanted. She breathed in deeply as she tried to compose herself. Averting her gaze from the bed, she used the lamp to illumine the corners of the room as she looked for Ings's leather bag so that she could take the money that she felt was hers. But she was too late. His belongings were scattered all over the floor and the bag was empty. In desperation, she grabbed his jacket and felt in the inside pocket but his wallet was no longer there. Not a penny of his money was left. Whoever had murdered them, had known exactly where to look. She gazed ruefully at William Ings. Her hopes of escape had bled to death. Polly Roach was condemned to stay in the Devil's Acre forever.

CHAPTER SEVEN

When word of the crime reached him, Inspector Robert Colbeck took an immediate interest. Murder was not a rare phenomenon in the Devil's Acre, and ordinarily, he would have been content to let someone else lead the investigation. But the fact that one of the victims was a middle-aged man alerted him and he persuaded Superintendent Tallis to let him look into the case. After collecting Victor Leeming, he left Scotland Yard and took a cab to the scene of the crime.

Policemen were already on duty, guarding the room where the victims lay and questioning other occupants of the building. There was no sign of Polly Roach. Additional lamps had been brought in so that the attic room was ablaze with light. When the detectives entered, the grisly scene was all too visible. In spite of the number of times he had seen murder victims, Leeming was inclined to be squeamish but Colbeck had no qualms about examining the dead bodies at close range. Both were partly clothed, their garments spattered with blood. The sheets and pillows were also speckled.

After inspecting the corpses for some time, Colbeck stood up.

'At least, they did not suffer too much,' he observed.

'How do you know that?' asked Leeming.

'Both of them have wounds on the back of their heads, Victor. I think that they were knocked unconscious before their throats were cut. One neat incision was all that it took. The killer knew his trade.'

'So I see, Inspector.' He looked at the face of the dead man and quailed slightly. 'Do you think it's William Ings?'

'Yes,' said Colbeck, sifting through the items on the floor. 'He matches the description that Mrs Ings gave me and nobody who lives in the Acre dresses quite as smartly as he did. This man is an outsider.' Picking up a jacket, he searched the pockets and found a small brown envelope. 'This confirms it,' he said.

'What is it?'

'An empty pay packet from the Post Office. His very last wages.'

'Does he have a wallet on him?'

'That appears to have been taken,' said Colbeck, putting the jacket aside. 'It must have contained money. Judging by the way that it was emptied all over the floor, so did that bag.'

Leeming was annoyed. 'We've lost one of our suspects to a thief.'

141

'This was not the work of a thief, Victor.'

'It must have been. They were obviously killed for the money.'

'Not at all,' contradicted the other. 'The young lady died because she had the misfortune to be with Mr Ings at the time. *He* was the target. In my opinion, the murder was directly connected to the train robbery. He was silenced because he knew too much. Since Ings no longer had any need of it, his paymaster took the opportunity to repossess the hefty bribe that must have been paid to him.'

'These men are more dangerous than I thought,' said Leeming.

'They'll go to any lengths to cover their tracks.'

'Does that mean the other accomplice is at risk?'

'Yes, Victor,' said Colbeck. 'Unless we can find him first.'

'And how do we do that?'

'To be honest, I'm not sure.' He glanced at the policeman by the door. 'Who discovered the body?'

'A woman named Polly Roach, sir,' replied the man.

'I'll need to speak to her,' said Colbeck, recalling that Mulryne had mentioned her name. 'I've reason to believe that she knew at least one of the victims. Where is she?'

'Being held at the station, Inspector. I must warn you that she's very jittery. Walking in on this has upset her badly.'

'I daresay that it has. A lot of people are going to be upset when they learn what happened here tonight. The

142

person I feel sorry for is the man's wife,' said Colbeck with a sigh. 'I'm not looking forward to breaking the news to Mrs Ings.'

Maud Ings was about to retire to bed when she heard the click of her letterbox. Taking the lamp, she went to the front door to investigate and saw a small package lying on the doormat. Puzzled as to what it might contain, she picked it up and read the bold capitals that ran across the front of it – FROM YOUR HUSBAND. She was even more mystified. She put her lamp on the hall table so that she could use both hands to open the package. As she peeled back the brown paper, she found, to her utter astonishment, that it was covering a sizeable wad of five pound notes. The arrival of such unexpected bounty was too much for her. Overcome with emotion, she burst into tears.

'I want results, Inspector,' shouted Tallis, rising angrily to his feet. 'I want progress, not this incessant litany of excuses.'

'We could not foresee that William Ings would be murdered.'

'Perhaps not, but you could have prevented the crime by reaching him before anyone else did.'

'That's what I attempted to do, sir,' said Colbeck.

'Yes,' snarled Tallis, 'by employing that Irish maniac, Mulryne. Whatever possessed you to do that? The fellow is a confounded menace. When he was in the police force, his notion of making an arrest was to beat the offender to a pulp.'

'Brendan was simply too zealous in the execution of his duties.'

'Zealous! He was uncontrollable. I'm told that it took four officers to subdue him this evening. Was that another example of his zeal?' asked Tallis with heavy sarcasm. 'Why ever did you turn to him?'

'Because he knows the Devil's Acre from the inside.'

'He'll know a prison cell from the inside before I'm done with him.'

'There were extenuating circumstances about the brawl,' said Colbeck, 'and, when the time is ripe, I'd like to speak up on Mulryne's behalf. The reason that I engaged him is that he's a good bloodhound. He did, after all, find the woman with whom William Ings had been living. Her name was Polly Roach. She was the person who raised the alarm tonight.'

'What did she have to say for herself?'

'She was very bitter when I questioned her earlier. Mr Ings had promised to take her away from the Acre to start a new life with him. Polly Roach offered him something that he could not find at home.'

'I was in the army, Inspector,' said Tallis, darkly. 'You don't need to tell me why married men visit whores. Our doctor was the busiest man in the regiment, trying to cure them of their folly.' He sat down again behind his desk. 'Now, tell me in detail what this Polly Roach said.'

Standing in front of him, Robert Colbeck gave him a terse account of his interview with the woman who had found the dead bodies and who had provided confirmation that one of the victims was William Ings. Wreathed in cigar smoke, Tallis listened in stony silence. His eye occasionally drifted to the newspapers that lay on his desk. When Colbeck finished, the Superintendent fired questions at him.

'Do you believe this woman?'

'Yes, sir.'

'Did you find any witnesses?'

'None, sir.'

'How many people live in that tenement?'

'Dozens.'

'Yet not one of them saw or heard a stranger entering or leaving the premises? Is the place a home for the blind and deaf?'

'People in the Devil's Acre do not like assisting the police.'

'So why did you rely on someone like Mulryne?'

'Brendan is the exception to the rule.'

'He's a liability,' said Tallis, acidly. 'Whatever you do, make sure that the newspapers don't get hold of the fact that you sought his help. I'll have enough trouble keeping those reporters at bay when they ask me about the murder.'

'Would you rather I spoke to them, sir?'

'No, it's my duty.'

'Of course.'

'Yours is to find these villains before they commit any more crimes. What's your plan of campaign?'

'Courtesy must come before anything else, Superintendent.'

'In what way?'

'Mrs Ings has a right to be informed of the death of her husband,' said Colbeck. 'It was far too late to call on her tonight. It would only have given her additional distress if she'd been hauled out of bed to be told that her husband had been murdered.'

'While lying between foul sheets beside some pox-ridden whore.'

'I'll try to put it a little more diplomatically than that, sir.'

'And then what?'

'It seems that the driver of the train has recovered somewhat, sir, so I intend to visit him to see if he can give us any useful information.' Colbeck remembered that he would be seeing Madeleine Andrews again. 'I think that it's very important for me to question the man.'

Tallis narrowed his eyes to peer at him through the cigar smoke.

'We are dealing with armed robbery and brutal murder, Inspector,' he reminded him. 'What the devil are you *smiling* about?'

Caleb Andrews was well enough to sit up in bed and sip tea from the cup that his daughter had brought him. Still in pain, he moved his limbs very gingerly. His pugnacity,

146

however, had been restored in full. Now that his mind had cleared, he had vivid memories of the moment when his train was ambushed, and he was anxious to confront the man who had knocked him down with a pistol butt. Madeleine came into the room to see how he was and, as they talked, she tidied the place up.

'Why are you wearing your best dress?' he wondered.

'I always like to look smart, Father.'

'But you usually save that one for church. Is it Sunday?'

'You know that it isn't,' she said, repositioning the two china dogs on the mantelpiece. 'Are you sure that you're well enough to speak to Inspector Colbeck?'

'Yes, I think so.'

'I can always send word to Scotland Yard to ask him to postpone the visit. Would you like me to do that?'

'No, Maddy. I want to see him today. Apart from anything, I want to know if he's caught anybody yet. Those men deserve to be strung up for what they did to my locomotive.'

'Frank Pike still has nightmares about that.'

'I don't hold it against him.'

'His wife told me that he's racked with guilt.'

'Frank always was a sensitive lad,' said Andrews, fondly. 'None of us likes to go off the road like that. It's the thing a driver hates most.'

'You forget about your fireman,' she said, adjusting his pillows to make him more comfortable. 'All you have to worry about is getting better. Have you finished your tea?'

'Yes, Maddy.'

'Then I'll take the cup downstairs with me.'

'What time is Her Majesty due to arrive?'

Madeleine was baffled. 'Her Majesty?'

'That's what all of this in aid of, isn't it?'

'All what?'

'Your best dress, tidying up my room, clearing my cup away, putting on something of a show. At the very least, I expect a visit from Queen Victoria.'

'Stop teasing me, Father.'

'Then tell me why you're making such an effort,' he said with a lopsided grin. 'You even changed the bandaging on my wounds so that I looked a little better. Why did you do that? Are you going to put me on display at the Great Exhibition?'

Seated in her armchair, Maud Ings received the news without flinching. It was almost as if she had expected it. Colbeck spoke as gently as he could be but he did not disguise any of the salient details from her. It was only when he told her the name of the other murder victim that she winced visibly.

'And how old was this Kate Piercey?' she asked.

'Somewhat younger than your husband.'

'Is that why he ran off with her?'

'Does that matter, Mrs Ings?'

'What was she like?'

'I did not exactly see her at her best,' he said.

Colbeck saw no point in telling her that the woman to

148

whom William Ings had first gone was Polly Roach. The widow had enough to contend with as it was. To explain that he had abandoned one prostitute and immediately shared a bed with another would only be adding further to her misery. Bitter and bereaved, Maud Ings nevertheless had some sympathy for the man who had betrayed her. Colbeck did not wish to poison any last, lingering, pleasant memories of their marriage.

'I'm sorry to be the bearer of such sad tidings,' he said.

'It was kind of you to come, Inspector.'

'This has been a shock for you, Mrs Ings. Would you like me to ask one of the neighbours to come in and sit with you?'

'No, no. I prefer to be alone. Besides,' she said, 'our neighbours were never fond of William. I don't think many tears will be shed for him in this street.'

'As long as you are not left alone to brood.'

'I have the children. They are my life now.'

'Family is so important at a time like this, Mrs Ings. Well,' he said, relieved that there had been no outpouring of grief, 'I'll intrude no longer. You'll be informed when the body is ready to be released.'

'Wait!' she said, getting up. 'Before you go, Inspector, I need your advice. I can see that I've been living on false hope.'

'False hope?'

'Yes. Last night, before I went to bed, a package was put through my letterbox. Inside it was almost two hundred pounds.'

'Really?' Colbeck was curious. 'Was there any note enclosed?'

'No,' she said, 'but there was something written on the paper. I still have it, if you'd like to see it.'

'I would, Mrs Ings.' He waited as she lifted the cushion of her chair to take out the brown paper in which the money had been wrapped. When she handed it to him, he read the words on the front. 'At what time did this arrive?' he asked.

'It must have been close to eleven o'clock,' she replied. 'I thought at first that William had brought it. But, by the time I had unbolted the door and opened it, there was nobody to be seen in the street. Having the money gave me the best night's sleep I've had since he left.' Her face went blank. 'I was misled. From what you've told me, it obviously could not have been delivered by my husband.'

'I fear not. By that time, his body had already been discovered.'

'Then who could have brought the money?'

'The person who stole it from Mr Ings.'

She was bewildered. 'I do not understand, Inspector.'

'I'm not certain that I do,' he said, 'but I can see no other explanation. That money was paid to your husband in return for vital information about the mail train. Somebody was clearly aware of his domestic situation. When your husband was killed, this person somehow felt that his widow was entitled to the money.'

'So it is not really mine at all.'

'Why not?'

'It is money that was made from crime. I'll have to surrender it.'

'That's the last thing you should do,' advised Colbeck. 'It was money that your husband earned from a source that has yet to be identified. It was not part of the haul from the train robbery so there is no onus on you to return it. In view of the situation,' he went on, 'I believe that you are fully entitled to hold on to that money. Nobody need know how it came into your hands.'

'Then I am not breaking the law?'

'No, Mrs Ings. You are simply inheriting something that belonged to your husband. Look upon it as a welcome gift. It may not bring Mr Ings back to you, but it may help to console you in your grief.'

'I'll not deny that we *need* the money,' she said, looking balefully around the bare room. 'But I find it hard to accept that the man who murdered my husband and stole money from him should bring it to me.'

'It is an unusual situation, I grant you.'

'Why did he do it, Inspector?'

'It may have been an act of atonement.'

'Atonement?'

'Even the most evil men sometimes have a spark of goodness.'

Maud Ings fell silent as she thought about the life she had shared with her husband. It was a painful exercise. She remembered how they had met, married and set off together with such high expectations. Few of them had been fulfilled. Yet, soured as her memories were by his recent treatment of her, she could still think of the dead man with a distant kindness.

'You are right,' she said, coming out of her reverie. 'Evil men sometimes do good deeds. The problem is,' she added with tears at last threatening to come, 'that good men – and William was the soul of goodness when I first knew him – sometimes do evil.'

With his arm in a sling, it was impossible for Caleb Andrews to hold the newspaper properly so he had to rely on his daughter to fold it over in such a way that he could grasp it with one hand to read it. It had gone to press too early to carry news of the murder in the Devil's Acre but there was an article about the train robbery and it was critical both of the railway policemen on duty that day, and of the Detective Department of the Metropolitan Police. Andrews saw his own name mentioned.

'Have you read this, Maddy?' he asked, petulantly. 'It says that Driver Andrews is still unable to remember what happened during the ambush. I can recall *exactly* what happened.'

'I know, Father,' said Madeleine.

'So why do they make me sound like an invalid?'

'Because you *are* an invalid.'

'My body may be injured but there's nothing wrong with my mind. This article says that I'm still in a complete daze.'

'That was my doing.'

'What do you mean?'

'Some reporters came knocking on our door this morning,' she explained. 'They wanted to interview you about the robbery. I told them that you were in no fit state to speak to anyone and that your mind was still very hazy. I was trying to protect you, Father.'

'By telling everyone in London that I cannot think straight.'

'I had to get rid of the reporters somehow. I was not going to have them pestering you when you need rest.'

'Yet you let this Inspector Colbeck pester me,' he argued.

'He is trying to solve the crime,' she said. 'Inspector Colbeck wants to catch the men who ambushed the train and did this to you. He knows that you were badly injured and will be very considerate.'

Andrews tossed the newspaper aside. 'If he reads this first, he'll think that he's coming to speak to a distracted fool who's unable to tell what day of the week it is.'

'The Inspector will not think that at all, Father.'

Gathering up the newspaper, Madeleine put it on the table beside the bed. The sound of an approaching horse took her to the window and she looked down to see a cab pulling up outside the house. After a quick glance around the room, she adjusted her dress and went quickly out. Caleb Andrews gave a tired smile.

'Ah!' he said. 'I think that Queen Victoria has arrived at last.'

Two minutes later, Robert Colbeck was being shown

into the bedroom to be introduced to the wounded railwayman.

'Can I offer you any refreshment, Inspector?' said Madeleine.

'No, thank you, Miss Andrews.'

'In that case, I'll leave you alone with Father.'

'There's no need to do that,' said Colbeck, enjoying her company too much to lose it. 'I'm quite happy for you to stay while we talk and, in any case, there's something that you need to know.'

Madeleine was cheered. 'You've arrested someone?'

'Not exactly,' he replied, 'but we have caught up with one of the accomplices who was involved. His name was William Ings.'

'Let me get my hands on the devil,' said Andrews.

'That's not possible, I fear. Mr Ings was killed last night.'

'Killed?' echoed Madeleine, shocked at the news.

'Yes, Miss Andrews,' said Colbeck. 'It means that we are no longer merely investigating a train robbery. This is now a murder case as well.'

'Do you have any clue who the killer might be?'

'Someone employed to make sure that Mr Ings's tongue would tell no tales. Once we discovered that he was implicated, we were very close to apprehending him. The assassin got to him first.'

'I wish that I had!' said Andrews, truculently. 'If he helped that gang to ambush my train, I'd have throttled him.'

154

'Father!' reproached his daughter.

'I would have, I swear it.'

'You are hardly in a position to throttle anyone, Mr Andrews,' noted Colbeck with a sympathetic smile. 'Mr Ings, alas, was not alone when he was attacked. The young lady with him also had her throat cut.'

'How horrible!' exclaimed Madeleine.

'It shows you the sort of men we are up against.'

'The worst kind,' said Andrews. 'They destroyed my locomotive. They made Frank Pike drive it off the track.' He indicated the chair beside the bed and Colbeck sat down. 'Do you know anything about the railway, Inspector?'

'I travel by train regularly, Mr Andrews.'

'But do you know anything about the locomotive that pulls it?'

'A little,' replied Colbeck. 'I'm familiar with the engines designed by Mr Bury; four-wheeled, bar-framed locomotives with haystack fireboxes, and tight coupling between locomotive and tender to give more stability.'

Andrews was impressed. 'You obviously know far more than most passengers,' he said. 'They have no clue how a steam locomotive works. Like many others, I began driving Bury locomotives, but they had too little power. We had to use two, three, sometimes four locomotives to pull a heavy train. If there were steep gradients to go up, we might need as many as six to give us enough traction power.'

'The mail train that you were taking to Birmingham

was pulled by a Crampton locomotive – at least, that's what it looked like to me.'

'It was very similar to a Crampton, I agree, but it was designed by Mr Allan at the Crewe Works. He's the foreman there and assistant to Mr Trevithick. Allan locomotives have double frames that extend the whole length of the engine with the cylinders located between the inside and outside frames.'

'Inspector Colbeck does not want a lecture,' warned Madeleine.

'I'm always ready to learn from an expert,' said Colbeck.

'There you are, Maddy,' said Andrews, happily. 'The Inspector is really interested in the railways.' He turned to Colbeck. 'When we used inside cylinders, we were always having crank-axle breakages. Mr Allan was one of the men who began to develop horizontal outside cylinders. He may not be as famous as Mr Bury or Mr Crampton but I'd drive any locomotive that Alexander Allan built.'

'Why is that?' prompted Colbeck.

Caleb Andrews was in his element. He got so carried away describing the technicalities of locomotive construction that he forgot all about the nagging pain in his broken leg and the dull ache in one shoulder. Colbeck's interest was genuine but that was not the only reason he had asked for instruction. He wanted the driver to relax, to feel at ease with him, to trust him. Watching from the other side of the room, Madeleine was struck by the way that the detective gently guided her father around to the subject of the train robbery and coaxed far more detail out of him about the event than she had managed to do. During the interview, Colbeck jotted down a few things in his notebook.

'Would you recognise the man who attacked you?' asked Colbeck.

'I'll never forget that face of his,' replied Andrews.

'Mr Pike gave us a good description.'

'If my daughter were not present, Inspector, then I'd give you a good description of him – in one word.'

'We do not wish to hear it, Father,' scolded Madeleine.

'That's what he was, Maddy.'

'Forgive him, Inspector.'

'There's nothing to forgive, Miss Andrews,' said Colbeck, getting up and putting his notebook away. 'In view of what happened, your father has been remarkably restrained. He's also added some new details for me and that was very useful. One last question,' he said, looking at the driver once more. 'Is the London and North Western Railway a good company to work for, Mr Andrews?'

'The best, Inspector.'

'Are you saying that out of loyalty?'

'No, Inspector Colbeck – I speak from experience. I hope to see out my time working for the London and North Western. And my link with the company will not end there.'

'Oh?'

'I have every hope that my son-in-law will be a driver one day.'

Madeleine blushed instantly. 'Father!' she cried.

'Gideon would make a good husband.'

'This is not the place to bring up the subject.'

'The two of you were made for each other.'

'That is not true at all,' she asserted, 'and you know it.'

'Gideon loves you.'

'Perhaps I ought to withdraw,' volunteered Colbeck, seeing Madeleine's patent discomfort. 'Thank you for talking to me, Mr Andrews. Meeting you has been an education.'

'Let me know when you catch up with those villains.'

'I will, I promise you.' He moved to the door. 'Goodbye, Miss Andrews. I can see myself out.'

'Wait,' she said. 'Let me come to the front door with you.'

'But you clearly have something to discuss with your father.'

'High time that she discussed it with Gideon Little,' said Andrews.

Madeleine shot him a look of reproof and followed Colbeck down the stairs. Before she could apologise to him, the detective retrieved his silk hat from the table and opened the front door.

'Goodbye, Miss Andrews,' he said, masking his disappointment behind a smile. 'Allow me congratulate you on your forthcoming engagement.'

* * *

It was Victor Leeming's turn to face the wrath of Superintendent Tallis once more. A night's sleep had not improved the older man's temper. He was pacing up and down his room like a caged animal. When Leeming came in, Tallis rounded on him accusingly.

'Where have you been, man?' he demanded.

'Making inquiries, sir.'

'That is exactly what those jackals from the press have been doing. They almost drove me insane by making their damned inquiries. I had a dozen of them in here this morning,' he complained, 'wanting to know why we had made no progress with our investigation into the robbery, and why Inspector Colbeck was also in charge of this latest murder case.'

'The two crimes are connected, Superintendent.'

'They could not understand how.'

'Why not let the Inspector deal with the newspapers in future?'

'I'd never countenance that,' affirmed Tallis. 'My seniority obliges me to take on that particular duty and I have never been one to shun the cares of office. Besides, I want you and the Inspector out there, solving the crime, not getting distracted by a bevy of reporters.'

'What did you tell them?' asked Leeming.

'Enough to give them a story but no more. The information we feed to the press has to be carefully controlled. Give too much away and we alert the very people we are trying to apprehend.'

'I agree with you there, sir.'

'The main thing was,' said Tallis, 'to ensure that they did not get wind of Mulryne's role in this whole sorry affair. It was reckless of Inspector Colbeck to use that Irish blockhead in the way that he did.' He confronted the Sergeant. 'I presume that you condoned his decision.'

'Not entirely,' admitted Leeming, uneasily.

Tallis blenched. 'You mean that he did not even have the grace to tell you what he was proposing? That is unpardonable.'

'The Inspector did raise the matter,' said the other, lying to protect his colleague, 'and I could see the advantage of using Brendan Mulryne.'

'What advantage?'

'He knew where to look for William Ings.'

'So did the killer.'

'That's why we're making efforts to track down the other suspect, sir. Inspector Colbeck gave me an address that was passed on to him at the Chubb factory in Wolverhampton. It was a locksmith's where a man called Daniel Slender was supposed to have worked.' He put a hand in his pocket. 'I have just returned from the factory.'

'But this Daniel Slender was not employed there?'

'No, sir.'

'I daresay that they never heard of him.'

'That's not true,' said Leeming, taking out a letter to pass to him. 'When they advertised a post, Daniel Slender was among those who applied for it, as you will see from that letter.' Tallis began to read the missive. 'His qualifications are good and he could have expected a strong recommendation from the Chubb factory. Mr Slender was invited to come for an interview.'

'But?'

'He never turned up.'

'Then why apply for the post?'

'So that he would have written evidence to show to his employers that the position he was after did exist. They believed that he went for that interview,' said Leeming, 'and secured the appointment. It meant that his departure aroused no suspicion.'

'Where is Daniel Slender now?'

'Here in London, sir.'

'How do you know that?'

'Because he had always had an ambition to work here. According to the manager at the Chubb factory, he talked of little else. But he was tied to the Midlands by the need to look after his sick mother.'

'If the woman had stayed alive,' moaned Tallis, 'her son would never have got drawn into this conspiracy.' He waved the letter in front of Leeming. 'Look at the fellow's work record. It is admirable.'

'Those who bribed him must have caught him at a weak moment.'

'We need to get to him while he is still alive.'

'Inspector Colbeck feels that we should put out a wanted poster. He came back from Wolverhampton with a good description of Daniel Slender. We should circulate it at once.'

'Yes,' agreed Tallis. 'Have the poster drawn up,

Sergeant Leeming. And – quickly! The last thing we need is for this man to finish up on a slab next to William Ings.'

The dog made the discovery. Scampering along the river-bank with his master, he went sniffing at a heap that lay up against a wall. It was covered with sacking and most people had walked past without even noticing it. The little terrier made sure that nobody would ignore it now. With the sacking gripped in his teeth, he pulled hard and exposed a pair of legs, then a body, then a head that was split grotesquely open and crowned with dried blood.

When she saw the corpse, a female passer-by screamed and clutched at her chest, the dog's owner ran to put the animal on his lead and another man went off in search of help. By the time that he returned, with two policemen in tow, he saw that a small crowd was standing around the body with ghoulish curiosity. The policemen ordered everyone to stand back while they checked for vital signs and, finding none, felt in the dead man's pockets for clues as to his identity.

The pockets of his immaculate suit were empty but that did not matter. Sewn into the silk lining of the jacket was the owner's name.

'Daniel Slender,' noted one of the policemen. 'Poor man!'

Inspector Robert Colbeck responded swiftly. The moment he heard about the second murder, he visited the scene of the crime, examined the body and gave permission for it to be moved. Half an hour later, Daniel Slender had been deprived of his new suit, as well as the remainder of his apparel, washed and laid out, beneath a shroud, on a cold slab at the morgue. Victor Leeming joined his colleague to look down at the corpse.

'Those wanted posters will not be needed now,' he said.

'No, Victor.'

'They closed his mouth for good.'

'Mr Slender will never enjoy wearing that new suit of his.'

Leeming was thoroughly perplexed. 'How did they know where to find him, Inspector?' he asked. 'That's what I fail to see. And how did they know where to get hold of William Ings, for that matter?'

'By using an insurance policy.'

'Insurance policy?'

'Yes,' said Colbeck. 'The person behind the robbery realised from the start that both these men would have to be killed. They knew too much and, in the event of arrest, lacked the guile to conceal their secrets. My guess is that he paid them some of the money for services rendered, and promised to give them the balance when the crime was successfully committed. To do that,' he pointed out, 'Mr Ings and Mr Slender would have had to disclose their whereabouts.'

'What if there's a third accomplice?'

'Then he, too, is likely to be silenced.'

'My feeling is that he works for the Royal Mint.'

'Yet there's no breath of suspicion against anyone there.'

'Someone told the robbers when gold coin was being moved by train. The only person outside the Mint who knew the relevant date was Mr Shipperley at the Post Office and, as we found out when we spoke to him, he is certainly not involved.' Leeming gave a mirthless laugh. 'He'd sooner sell his grandmother to a brothel-keeper.'

'You have a point, Victor.'

'The information must have originated from the Royal Mint.'

'Perhaps you should pay a second visit there.'

'Yes, Inspector.'

'I, meanwhile, will visit Bond Street to speak to Daniel Slender's tailor. He will be able to tell me precisely when the suit was ordered and give me some idea of what manner of man his customer was.'

'A foolish one.'

'Mr Slender was offered a large amount of money to create a new life for himself,' said Colbeck, tolerantly. 'That would be a temptation for anyone in his position. It was too much for William Ings to resist as well.'

'Did you speak to his wife, sir?'

'First thing this morning.'

'How did she receive the news that she was now a widow?'

'Very bravely,' replied Colbeck. 'Mark you, Mrs Ings does have something to console her in her bereavement.'

'And what's that?'

'The best part of two hundred pounds, Victor. The money was put through her letterbox last night by an anonymous hand.'

'Two hundred pounds?' said Leeming in astonishment. 'That's a substantial amount. Who is her benefactor?'

'William Ings.'

'Her husband?'

'Indirectly,' said Colbeck. 'My feeling is that the money paid to him for providing information was given to his wife after his death. The man who authorised payment clearly knew that Maud Ings would be left destitute by her husband's demise. He sought to help her.'

'Murdering her husband is hardly a way to help.'

'Perhaps he is trying to make amends. Do you see what we have here, Victor? A ruthless killer with a conscience. That's a weakness.'

'What about the money paid to Daniel Slender?'

'That has doubtless been repossessed,' said Colbeck, 'because he had no family to whom it could be left. Mr Ings did. However, when I told her where her gift came from, his wife was not at all sure that she should keep it.'

'Why not?'

'She thought that it was tainted money.'

'It could not have come from the proceeds of the robbery.'

'That's what I said to her. In the end, I persuaded her that she had every right to keep the money. Incidentally,' he went on, lowering his voice, 'this is not something that needs to come to the ears of Mr Tallis. He would be certain to misunderstand and might even argue that the money should be taken from the widow.'

'That would be unfair.'

'Then say nothing, Victor. I speak to you in confidence.'

'It would have been very helpful had you done that before,' said Leeming, as he recalled his bruising encounter with the Superintendent. 'You should have told me that you were thinking of employing Mulryne.'

'You would only have tried to talk me out of it.'

'I would, Inspector. No question about that.'

'Brendan has his uses.'

'With respect, sir, that's beside the point. You kept me ignorant.'

'Only as a means of defending you from Mr Tallis.'

'You did the opposite,' protested Leeming. 'You exposed me to his anger. He demanded to know if you'd discussed your intentions with me and I was forced to lie in order to cover for you.'

'Thank you, Victor. I appreciate that.'

'I can't say that I appreciated being put in that position, sir.'

'You have my profound apologies,' said Colbeck. 'I may have expected too much of Brendan Mulryne. I accept the blame for that. But,' he continued, glancing down at the body once more, 'let us put that mistake behind us. So far, we have a train robbery and two murders to investigate. What we must try to do is to anticipate their next move.'

'To kill their source at the Royal Mint?'

'If there is such a person.'

'There is, Inspector. I feel it in my bones.'

'What I believe is that they will not just sit back and enjoy the fruits of their crime. They want more than the money they stole.'

Leeming pointed a finger. 'Those mail bags.'

'Exactly,' said Colbeck. 'Why go to the trouble of stealing them if there was no profit to be made from their contents? Yes, Victor. I think that it's only a matter of time before we hear about some of the mail that went astray.'

After luncheon at his club, Lord Holcroft decided to take a walk in Hyde Park for the benefit of his constitution. Accompanied by a friend, he set out at a brisk pace and gave his views on the political affairs of the day. His friend concurred with all that he said. Lord Holcroft was an imposing figure in his dark frock coat, light trousers and silk hat. Now almost sixty, he had the energy of a much younger man and a zest for debate that was indefatigable. He was expressing his reservations about the impending Great Exhibition when someone stepped out from behind a tree to accost him.

'Lord Holcroft?' he inquired.

'Who might you be, sir?' said the other, glaring at the newcomer.

'I'd like a quiet word with you about a certain person.'

'Stand aside, fellow. I never talk to strangers.'

'Even when he has news about Miss Grayle?'

whispered the other so that Holcroft's companion did not hear the name. 'Two minutes of your valuable time is all that I ask.'

Lord Holcroft studied the man. Tall, well-dressed and wearing a full beard, the stranger was in his thirties. He had a look in his eye that was politely menacing. Excusing himself from his friend, Holcroft stepped aside to speak to the newcomer. He tried to browbeat him.

'How dare you interrupt my walk like this!' he growled. 'Who are you and what's your business?'

'I came to save you from embarrassment,' said the man, calmly. 'A letter has fallen into our hands that casts an unflattering light on your character. It is written by you to a Miss Anna Grayle, who lives close to Birmingham, and it expresses sentiments that are quite improper for a married man such as yourself.'

'The letter is a forgery,' snapped Holcroft.

'We will let your wife be the judge of that, if you wish. Lady Holcroft knows your hand well enough to be able to tell us if you wrote the *billet-doux*.'

Holcroft reddened. 'My wife must *never* see that letter.'

'Even though it is a forgery?' teased the other.

'Miss Grayle's good name must be protected.'

'That will not happen if we release the letter to a scandal sheet. Her good name – and your own – would be in jeopardy. I should perhaps tell you, Lord Holcroft,' he lied, 'that we have already been offered a sizeable sum for the missive. We did not, of course, divulge your identity but we explained that you were a person of some importance.'

Lord Holcroft was squirming. His temples began to pound.

'How can I be sure that you have the letter?' he demanded.

'Because I brought a copy with me,' replied the other, taking a sheet of paper from his pocket to give to him. 'You have a colourful turn of phrase, Lord Holcroft. If what you say in the letter is correct, I also have to admire your stamina.'

After reading the copy, Holcroft swore under his breath and scrunched the paper in his hand. He was cornered. Were his wife to see the letter, his marriage would come to an abrupt end. If his disgrace reached a wider audience, he would never recover from the scandal. There was no point in trying to reason with the stranger. Lord Holcroft was forced into a sour capitulation.

'How much do you want?' he asked.

CHAPTER EIGHT

Having worked as a tailor in Bond Street for over thirty years, Ebenezer Trew was inclined to judge everyone by his own high sartorial standards. When he first set eyes on Robert Colbeck, therefore, he took note of the cut and colour of his apparel and saw that he was a man of discernment. Colbeck's height and well-proportioned frame were a gift to any tailor, and his attire served to enhance his air of distinction. Trew was somewhat nonplussed, therefore, to learn that the visitor to his shop that afternoon was a Detective Inspector, and dismayed that he had lost what he hoped would be a potential customer.

Further disappointment followed. Colbeck opened a bag to produce a jacket that the tailor recognised at once. When he saw the bloodstains on the material, Ebenezer Trew winced. He was a short, neat, fastidious man with the hunched shoulders of someone who spent most of his time bent over a work table.

'You know the jacket, I see,' observed Colbeck.

'I could pick out my handiwork anywhere, Inspector.'

'Do you remember the customer for whom you made the suit?'

'Very well. His name was Mr Slender.' He reached out to take the jacket and looked more closely at the stains on the shoulders. 'This will be almost impossible to remove,' he warned. 'Mr Slender was so proud of his suit. How did it come to be marked like this?'

'Daniel Slender was attacked on the embankment, Mr Trew.'

'Dear me! Was the assault a serious one?'

'Extremely serious,' said Colbeck, 'I fear that your customer was bludgeoned to death.' Trew turned pale. 'If you had not providentially sewn his name into the lining, we might not have identified him.'

'Mr Slender insisted on that. He told me that he had always wanted his name in a suit made by a Bond Street tailor.' He wrinkled his nose. 'The clothing he wore when he first came in here was of poor quality. Not to put too fine a point on it,' he said, 'it was very provincial – quite the wrong colour for him and made with such inferior material. Frankly, Inspector, I'd not have been seen dead in a suit like that.' He chewed his lip as he heard what he had just said. 'Oh, I do apologise,' he added, quickly. 'That was a rather tasteless remark.'

Colbeck studiously ignored it. 'What else can you tell me about Daniel Slender?' he asked.

'That he had obviously never been to a place like this before.'

'Was he shy and awkward?'

'On the contrary,' said Trew, 'he was full of confidence. I've never met anyone who enjoyed the experience of buying a suit from us so much. He gave me the impression that he had come into an appreciable amount of money that allowed him to indulge himself in a way that he had never been able to do before.'

'That fits in with what I know of the man,' said Colbeck. 'Until he came here, Daniel Slender worked as a locksmith in Wolverhampton.'

Trew wrinkled his nose again. 'Those dreadful Midlands vowels travelled with him to London,' he said with mild disgust. 'I could make him *look* like a gentleman, but he would never sound like one.'

'I trust that you concealed your prejudice from him, Mr Trew,' said Colbeck, irritated by the man's snobbery. 'None of us can choose the place where we are born or the accent that we inherit.'

'Quite so, quite so.'

'You, I suspect, hail from the West Country.'

'Yes, I do,' admitted the tailor, hurt that his attempts to remove the telltale burr from his voice had not been quite as successful as he thought. 'But I have lived in London since the age of ten.'

'How many times did you meet Mr Slender?'

'Three, Inspector. He came in to place the order and returned for a fitting. The third time was to collect the suit.'

'And to pay for it.'

'He did that with something of a flourish.'

'Did he ever tell you why he had moved to London?'

'Oh, yes,' said Trew, handing the jacket back to Colbeck. 'It was an ambition that he had nursed for years but domestic concerns kept him in the Midlands. At long last, he told me, he had a means of escape.'

'What else did he say?'

'That he was going to enjoy his retirement.'

'Not for very long, alas,' said Colbeck, sadly. He looked around at the various items of clothing on display. 'Being measured for a suit is usually an occasion for light conversation with one's tailor. Did you find Daniel Slender a talkative man?'

'To the point of garrulity, Inspector.'

'In what way?'

Ebenezer Trew needed no more encouragement. Feeling that he had aroused Colbeck's disapproval, he tried to atone by recalling snatches of the various conversations he had had with his customer. Most of it was irrelevant, but enough was of interest to the detective for him to let Trew ramble on. When the tailor's reminiscences came to an end, Colbeck seized on one remark made by Slender.

'He told you that he intended to move in society?'

'That is what I took him to mean, Inspector,' said Trew. 'I think that his exact words were that he would be "rubbing shoulders with a different class of person." It was one reason why he wanted a new suit.' He gave an ingratiating smile. 'Have I been of any assistance?'

173

'A little, Mr Trew.'

'Good. I aim to please.'

'Did your customer furnish you with an address?'

'Of course,' said Trew, seriously. 'I insisted on that. Had we not known where he lived, we would not have undertaken the work. We are very punctilious about such matters.' He opened a ledger and leafed through the pages. 'Here we are,' he said, stopping at a page and pointing a finger. 'Mr Slender had lodgings at 74, Delamere Street.' He offered the ledger to Colbeck. 'You may see for yourself, Inspector.'

'There is no need for that, Mr Trew,' said Colbeck, who knew the street well. 'It seems that you were not as punctilious as you imagined. The last time that I was in Delamere Street, it comprised no more than two dozen houses. In other words, Daniel Slender was residing at an address that does not exist.'

Trew was shocked. 'He *lied* to me?' he said with disbelief. 'But he seemed to be so honest and straightforward.'

'Never judge by appearances,' advised Colbeck, putting the jacket back into his bag. 'They can be very misleading.'

'So I see.'

'Goodbye, Mr Trew.'

'One moment, Inspector,' said the tailor. 'I am still trying to come to terms with the notion that one of my customers was murdered. Do you have any idea *why* Mr Slender was killed?'

'Of course.'

'May one know what it is?'

'Not at this stage,' said Colbeck, unwilling to discuss the details of the crime with a man he found increasingly annoying. 'Of something, however, I can assure you.'

'And what is that?'

'He was not killed for his new suit, Mr Trew,' said the detective, crisply. 'Or, for that matter, because he had an unfortunate accent.'

Leaving him thoroughly chastened, Colbeck went out of the shop.

On his second visit, Victor Leeming found the Royal Mint a much less welcoming place. Hoping that the detective had brought good news, Charles Omber was disturbed to hear that no significant progress had been made in the investigation and that suspicions were still harboured about his colleagues. He had defended them staunchly and said that he would take a Bible oath that there had been no breach of security at the Mint. An argument had developed. Omber was determined to win it. Leeming finally withdrew in some disarray.

When he got to Euston Station, he found that Colbeck was already in the waiting room. It was thronged with passengers. The Inspector had suggested they meet there for two reasons. It would not only keep them out of range of the simmering fury of Superintendent Tallis, it would, more importantly, take them back to the place from which the mail train had set out on its doomed journey.

Colbeck saw the jaded expression on the Sergeant's ugly face.

'I take it that you found nothing,' he said.

'Only that Mr Omber has a very nasty temper when his word is challenged. He refuses to accept that the Mint could be at fault.'

'Do you believe him, Victor?'

'No, sir,' said Leeming. 'I have this doubt at the back of my mind.'

'Was Mr Omber deceiving you, then?'

'Not at all. His sincerity is not in question. In fact, he spoke so passionately on behalf of his colleagues that I felt a bit embarrassed for even suggesting that one of them may have leaked information about the movement of gold coin.'

'Yet your instinct tells you otherwise.'

'Yes, Inspector.'

'Then rely on it, Victor. It rarely lets you down.'

'Thank you,' said Leeming. 'How did you get on in Bond Street?'

'I met a tailor whom I would never dare to employ.'

'Why not?'

'Which of the ten reasons would you care to hear first?'

Colbeck told him about his meeting with Ebenezer Trew and why he had disliked the man so much. He explained what the tailor had said about his erstwhile customer. On one point, Leeming wanted elucidation.

'Daniel Slender had *retired*?' he said.

'Apparently.'

'Could he afford to do so, Inspector?'

'He sold the house in Willenhall, remember, and he would have had a certain amount of savings. Then, of course, there is the money that he would have received from the train robbers.'

'More or less than William Ings?'

'More, I should imagine,' said Colbeck.

'Mr Ings got the best part of two hundred pounds.'

'Yet all he did was to tell them that money was being carried by train to Birmingham on a specific day. Mr Slender's contribution was far more critical,' he noted. 'Without those keys and that combination number, they could never have opened the safe so easily. That would have left them with two options – trying to blow it open with a charge of gunpowder or taking the whole safe with them.'

'That would have entailed the use of a crane,' said Leeming.

'And taken far too long. Speed was the essence of the operation and Daniel Slender's help was decisive. I think that he was paid handsomely in advance with a promise of more to come.'

'Much more, probably.'

'Yes,' said Colbeck. 'When you do not intend to part with another penny, you can afford to offer any amount by way of temptation. It may well be that Mr Slender was lured to the embankment last night in the hope of receiving the rest of his pay.'

'Instead of which, his head was smashed in.'

'They do not take prisoners, Victor.'

'Mr Slender must have wished that he had stayed in Willenhall.'

'The attack on him was so ferocious that he had no time to wish for anything. It was a gruesome but quick death. Come with me for a moment,' he said, putting a hand on Leeming's shoulder, 'I want to show you something.'

They walked out of the waiting room and picked their way through the milling crowd. Colbeck stopped when he reached the first platform. A train had just arrived and passengers were streaming off it. Friends were waiting to greet them. On the other platform, a train was about to depart, and dozens of people had come to wave off their friends or family members. Porters were everywhere, moving luggage on their trolleys, and several other railway employees were in evidence. The noise of a locomotive letting off steam rose above the tumult.

Colbeck nudged his colleague. 'What do you see, Victor?'

'Bedlam, sir.'

'No, you see a thriving industry. You are looking at visible proof of the way that the railways have transformed our lives. Euston Station is as busy as this every day of the week – and so is Paddington. Everybody has somewhere to get to,' said Colbeck, indicating the scene, 'and they choose to travel by rail in order to get there. Why is that?'

'Because they think it is quicker.'

'Demonstrably so.'

'If they travel second or third class, it is certainly cheaper as well.'

'You've missed out the real attraction of the railway.'

'Have I?' said Leeming.

'It is safe. At times, I grant you, it can also be noisy, smelly and a trifle uncomfortable but it is, as a rule, safe. It gets passengers to their appointed destinations in one piece. Railway companies met with great fear and opposition at first,' Colbeck reminded him, 'but the public has now come to trust them. This is the Railway Age.'

'I still prefer to travel by horse.'

'Then you are behind the times, Victor.'

'I am not ashamed of that, Inspector.'

'Nor should you be,' said Colbeck. 'But the point I am trying to make is this. The train robbery is a dangerous precedent. It imperils the safety record of the railway companies. If we do not catch and convict those responsible, then they will surely be emboldened to strike again.'

'And others might be inspired by their example.'

'Exactly. We must solve these crimes soon, Victor.'

'How can we when we have so little to go on?' asked Leeming with a gesture of despair. 'We still know nothing whatsoever about the man who organised the train robbery.'

'But we do,' said Colbeck. 'We know three crucial things.'

'Do we?'

'First, he is a gentleman.'

'Gentleman!' exclaimed Leeming. 'How can you describe someone who is behind such callous murders as a gentleman?'

'Think what else he did, Victor. He may have seen fit to have William Ings killed but he made sure that the widow inherited her husband's money. That was the act of a gentleman.'

'Not in my opinion.'

'Have you forgotten what the tailor told me about Daniel Slender?' asked Colbeck. 'Here was a man from a modest background in the Midlands, suddenly finding himself in London with money in his pockets. And what pleased him most was that he was about to rub shoulders with what he called a better class of person. In short, with gentlemen.'

'What's the second thing we know about this fellow?'

'He was in the army.'

Leeming was surprised. 'You sound very certain of that, sir.'

'I'd put money on it,' said Colbeck, 'and, as you know, I am not a betting man. The train robbery was no random attack. It was a military operation that was planned and, I daresay, rehearsed very carefully. Only someone who is used to commanding a body of men like that could have brought it off. So,' he went on, 'what do we have so far?'

'An officer and a gentleman.'

'Add the most telling thing about him, Victor.'

'He's a cold-blooded killer.'

'Cast your mind back to the robbery itself.'

'It's as you say,' conceded the other. 'He knew when and how to strike and, as a result, got away with the money and the mail bags.'

'What other part of his plan was put into action?'

Leeming needed a moment for consideration. 'The locomotive was deliberately run off the track,' he remembered.

'Yes,' said Colbeck, snapping his fingers. 'Severe damage was inflicted and Caleb Andrews's beloved engine was put out of action for a long time. What sort of person would do that, Victor?'

'Someone who hates trains.'

Sir Humphrey Gilzean sat in an open carriage on the Berkshire Downs and watched his racehorses being put through their paces. Bunched together, they thundered past and left a flurry of dust in their wake. Gilzean's eyes were on the black colt at the front of the group. As they galloped on, its rider used his whip to coax extra speed out of his mount and the colt surged ahead of the others to establish a lead of several lengths. Gilzean slapped his thigh in delight. He turned to his trainer, a big, sturdy man, who sat astride a chestnut mare beside him.

'*That's* what I want from him,' he declared.

'Starlight is a fine horse, Sir Humphrey,' said the trainer.

'Good enough to win the Derby?'

'If he loses, it will not be for want of trying. Starlight has a turn of foot to leave most colts and fillies behind. The secret is to bring him to a peak at just the right time.'

'I rely on you to do that, Welsby.'

'Yes, Sir Humphrey.'

'Starlight was certainly expensive enough to win the Derby,' said Gilzean, as the horses ended their race and trotted back in his direction. 'I expect a return on my investment.'

'Naturally.'

'Make sure that I get it.'

He was about to give some more instructions to his trainer when the distant sound of a train whistle distracted him. Gilzean's eyes flashed and his jaw tightened. He dispatched the trainer with a dismissive flick of his hand then spoke to the driver of the carriage.

'Take me home.'

'Yes, Sir Humphrey.'

'By way of the church.'

The coachman cracked his whip and the two horses pulled the carriage in a semicircle before setting off across the Downs at a steady trot. It was a large estate, parts of which were farmed by tenants. Some of the land was arable but most was given over to herds of dairy cattle and flocks of sheep. Gilzean found the sight of so many animals grazing in the fields strangely reassuring. There was a timelessness about the scene that appealed to him, an unspoilt, unhurried, natural quality that he had known and loved since he was a small child. It was the English countryside at its best.

Sitting erect in the carriage, Sir Humphrey Gilzean was a striking figure in his late thirties, tall, slim, swarthy of complexion and with finely chiselled features. Dressed in the most fashionable attire, he had the unmistakable air of an aristocrat, allied to the physique and disposition of a soldier. Even at his most relaxed, he exuded a sense of authority. As he was driven past the labourers in the fields, he collected an endless sequence of servile nods or obsequious salutes.

The Norman church stood at the edge of the village. Built of local stone, it was a small but solid structure that had withstood the unruly elements for centuries. Its square tower was surmounted by a little steeple with a weathervane at its apex. The churchyard was enclosed by a low and irregular stone wall, pierced by a wooden lychgate. Members of the Gilzean family had been buried there for generations, and it was their money that had kept the church in a state of good repair. When the carriage drew up outside the lychgate, Gilzean got out and tossed a curt command over his shoulder.

'Wait here,' he said to the coachman. 'I may be some time.'

During an investigation, leisure did not exist for Robert Colbeck. Having worked until late, he was back at his desk early the following morning so that he could collate all the evidence that had so far been gathered and address his mind to it when there was little chance of interruption.

He had been at Scotland Yard for almost two hours before he was disturbed by the arrival of a clerk.

'Excuse me, Inspector,' said the man, putting his head around the door. 'There's a young lady to see you.'

'Miss Andrews?' asked Colbeck, hoping that it might be her.

'No, sir. She gave her name as Miss Woodhead.'

'Then you had better shown her in.'

When his visitor came into the room, Colbeck got to his feet for the introductions. Nobody could have been less like Madeleine Andrews than the shy, hesitant creature who stood before him in a state of such obvious distress. Bella Woodhead was a short, plump and decidedly plain young woman in nondescript clothing and a faded straw hat. Offered a chair, she sat on the very edge of it. Colbeck could see that her hands were trembling.

'You wished to see me, Miss Woodhead?' he inquired.

'Yes, Inspector. I have something to tell you.'

'May I know what it concerns?'

She swallowed hard. 'Mr Ings,' she murmured.

'William Ings?'

'We read the newspaper this morning and saw the report of his death.' She gave a shudder. 'We could not believe it at first. When we saw that William – Mr Ings, that is – might actually be connected with this train robbery, we were shocked. It was like a blow in the face.'

'How did you come to know Mr Ings?' asked Colbeck.

'I work at the Post Office.'

'I see.'

184

'Only in a minor capacity, of course,' she said with a self-effacing smile. 'I am merely a clerk there. He was far more senior. Mr Ings was well-respected. The Post Office held him in high regard.'

Colbeck could tell from the way that she said the man's name that she had enjoyed a closer relationship with Ings than any of his other colleagues. Bella Woodhead was too honest and unschooled to disguise her feelings. Stunned by the news of his murder, she had come to make a confession that was clearly causing her intense pain. Colbeck tried to make it easier for her by anticipating what she was going to say.

'I believe that you were very fond of Mr Ings,' he suggested.

'Oh, I was, I was.'

'And he, in turn, was drawn to you.'

'That's what he told me,' she said, proudly, 'and it changed my life. No man had taken the slightest interest in me before. For a time, it was like living in a dream.' Her face crumpled. 'Now I see that he did not mean a word of it.' She looked up at Colbeck. 'Is it true that he was found dead in the Devil's Acre?'

'Yes, Miss Woodhead.'

'In the company of a woman?'

Colbeck nodded and she promptly burst into tears. He came across to put a consoling arm around her shoulders but it was minutes before she was able to speak again.

'Mr Ings betrayed me,' she said, finally controlling her sobs and dabbing at her eyes with a handkerchief.

'He swore that he loved me. He told me that he would leave his wife and that we would be together. Yet all the time . . .'

She put both hands to her mouth to stifle another fit of crying. Colbeck could well understand how the relationship with William Ings had developed. His position at the Post Office would have impressed Bella Woodhead and made her vulnerable to any favour that was shown to her. Patently, Ings had exploited her but the detective could not understand why. Since the man's taste ran to women like Polly Roach and Kate Piercey, why had he turned to someone as virginal and inexperienced as Bella Woodhead?

'Did he offer to marry you?' he wondered, softly.

'Of course,' she replied with a touch of indignation. 'Do you think that I would have become involved with him on any other basis? Mr Ings was a decent man – or so I thought at the time. He told me that he would arrange a divorce somehow. All that happened between us, Inspector, was an exchange of vows. I must ask you to believe that.'

'I accept your word without reservation, Miss Woodhead.'

'Mr Ings wanted everything to be done properly.'

'Properly?'

'He wanted to make me his wife so that we could, in time, live together openly. That was why he insisted on meeting my parents.'

'Oh?'

'He knew how protective they were of me – especially my father. At first he was very unhappy about my friendship, but Mr Ings persuaded him in the end. Father and he got on well. In fact,' she said, 'when he came to the house, he spent more time talking to my father than he did to me.' She blew her nose into the handkerchief. 'Now I know why.'

'Do you?'

'Yes. Mr Ings only wanted to hear about Father's job.'

'Why?' asked Colbeck. 'Where does your father work?'

'At the Royal Mint.'

It was a warm day but there was nevertheless a fire in the grate. Sir Humphrey Gilzean tossed another bundle of envelopes on to it and, putting one hand on the marble mantelpiece to steady himself, stirred the blaze with a poker. Wisps of black paper went up the chimney.

'That's the last of them, Thomas,' he observed.

'Good,' said the other. 'Such a dreary business, reading through other people's correspondence.'

'Dreary but rewarding. How much did Lord Holcroft give us?'

'Five hundred pounds.'

'This mistress of his must be a remarkable lady if she is deemed to be worth five hundred pounds. Lord Holcroft would rather lose the money than surrender the charms of Miss Anna Grayle.'

'All that money for two pieces of stationery.'

'And not a blow given or a risk taken,' noted Gilzean. 'Blackmail is a much easier way to make a living than by robbing trains. Secrecy is a valuable commodity, Thomas. I wish that we had more of it to sell.'

'So do I, Humphrey.'

They were in the library at Gilzean's house, an extensive property that overlooked a formal garden of almost three acres. Thomas Sholto was the bearded individual who had accosted Lord Holcroft in Hyde Park with a copy of the compromising letter. Like his friend, he was a man of impressive demeanour and military bearing. Sholto was pleased at their record of success.

'Mr Blower was a more difficult target,' he recalled.

'Remind me who he was.'

'The financier who was fishing in murky waters.'

'Ah, yes,' said Gilzean. 'Mr Jeremiah Blower. His letter disclosed confidential information about a forthcoming merger. Had his company known how treacherous he was being, they would have dismissed him on the spot. What value did we set on his ill-judged letter?'

'Three hundred pounds.'

'Yet he refused to pay up.'

'Initially,' said Sholto. 'He made all kinds of wild threats and was even foolish enough to strike out at me. He soon regretted that. I knocked him flat. And because he had the gall to haggle with me, I put up the price. He ended up paying twice as much as we asked.'

'What with Lord Holcroft and the others, we've made

a tidy profit out of this little venture. I told you that we should steal the mail bags as well. Admittedly,' said Gilzean, watching the flames die down, 'we had to pick our way through a deal of worthless trivia, but the result more than justified the effort involved. And we learnt a valuable lesson in the process.'

'Be careful what you commit to paper.'

'Precisely, Thomas.'

Sholto rubbed his hands together. 'When do we strike again?'

'Soon,' said Gilzean. 'The important thing was to ensure that there were no loose ends hanging. Thanks to you, the only two people who could have led this Inspector Colbeck to us are now in no position to speak to anyone.'

'Daniel Slender's head cracked open at one blow,' recalled Sholto with a grin. 'It was all over in less than thirty seconds. Mr Ings had a much harder skull.'

'Of more use to us was the fact that both of them had soft brains. They foolishly believed that we'd let them live when they knew too much about us. How could they be so naïve?'

'It served our purpose, Humphrey.'

'Supremely well.'

'Killing the pair of them was child's play,' boasted Sholto.

'It should be for a trained soldier like you, Thomas. The beauty of the two murders is,' said Gilzean, smugly, 'that they help to confuse this gifted detective who is supposed to be on our trail. Inspector Robert Colbeck will never be able to connect the victims with us. We are free to make our next move.'

Superintendent Edward Tallis was in an even more irascible mood than usual. Apart from the criticism he was receiving in the press, he was troubled by toothache and smarting from the reproaches of the Police Commissioners. Two cigars did nothing to dispel his feeling that he was the victim of unjust persecution. Summoned to his office, Colbeck decided to take Victor Leeming with him, not because he thought there would be safety in numbers, but because he wanted his colleague to be given some credit for his intuition.

When Tallis had stopped fulminating, Colbeck said his piece.

'Valuable information has come into our hands, sir,' he explained. 'We have learnt that William Ings befriended a female colleague at the Post Office in order to win the confidence of her father, Albert Woodhead. It transpires that Mr Woodhead is employed at the Royal Mint.'

'So?'

'We now know where the other breach of security occurred. An unguarded remark by Mr Woodhead about the transfer of money was seized on by Mr Ings and passed on to the robbers. Victor's instinct told him that a leak had occurred at the Mint,' continued Colbeck, turning to his colleague. 'I believe that he deserves some praise.'

'Yes,' said Tallis, grudgingly. 'I suppose that he does.'

Leeming took his cue. 'I've just returned from my third visit to the Mint, sir,' he said, 'where I spoke to the manager, Charles Omber. He confirmed that Albert Woodhead had owned up to his folly. Even though it was not deliberate, he has been suspended from his job.'

'And is full of contrition,' said Colbeck. 'After his daughter came to see me this morning, I called on Mr Woodhead and found him in a sorry state. It is not only his humiliating suspension that is upsetting him. The murder of William Ings has brought to the light the cruel way in which he used Miss Woodhead. Her father feels that, to some extent, he may have condoned it.'

'This is all very interesting, Inspector,' said Tallis, brooding behind his desk, 'but where does it get us?'

'It explains exactly where the necessary information came from and it absolves the railway company of any blame.'

'Yes,' added Leeming. 'It also tells us why Mr Ings was paid such a large amount of money. He had vital intelligence to sell.'

'Who bought it from him?' asked Tallis.

'We have yet to determine that, sir.'

'And how much longer do I have to wait before you do?'

'That depends on what he does next,' said Colbeck.

'Next?' repeated Tallis. 'Are you telling me that we may expect another train robbery or additional murders?'

'No, Superintendent. I am simply saying that the man

who is behind these crimes will act in character – and that we now have a clear idea of what that character is.'

'So do I. He is cunning, merciless and able to outwit us with ease.'

'He has stayed one step ahead of us so far,' agreed Colbeck, 'but that will soon change. The aspect of his character that I would point to is his rooted dislike of railways. It amounts to abhorrence. I would not at all be surprised to learn that he is a landowner whose property has been encroached upon by a railway company. Robbing that train and wrecking that locomotive was his way of striking back.'

'And?'

'There will be more to come, sir.'

'Why do you think that?'

'This man wants blood.'

Since its mail train was ambushed, the London and Birmingham Railway Company had tightened its security. Two policemen now guarded each end of the various tunnels that punctuated the 112 miles of track between the two cities. No risks were taken. Running to almost a mile and a half, the Kilsby Tunnel in Northamptonshire was the longest on the line and by far the costliest to build, taking all of two years to complete. It was the work of Robert Stephenson and a model of its kind. Most people marvelled at its construction but the three men who crept towards it that evening did not share in the general admiration of an outstanding feat of engineering.

The seized their moment. One of the railway policemen on duty was relieving himself behind a bush and the other was stuffing tobacco into his pipe. Both men were overpowered and tied up without offering any real resistance. The newcomers could carry on with their business. After checking their watches to see how much time they had before the next train, they went into the mouth of the tunnel at the Northamptonshire end. A small barrel of gunpowder was rolled against the brickwork. Loose stones were packed around it to keep it firmly in place.

Having lit the long fuse, the three men scampered to a place of safety and thought about the rich reward that they would earn. It was only a matter of time before the explosion occurred.

Returning to his office, Colbeck was both astonished and delighted to see Madeleine Andrews waiting for him there. She gave him a tentative smile.

'I hope that I am not intruding, Inspector,' she said.

'Of course not.'

'I know how busy you must be.'

'That's a hazard of my profession, Miss Andrews,' he said, indicating the huge pile of papers on his desk. 'Crimes are committed in London every hour of the day. Being a detective means that one is kept constantly on one's toes.'

'Then I'll not hold you up for long.'

'At least, take a seat while you are here.'

'Thank you,' she said, lowering herself on to a chair and spreading her skirt out. 'I really called to see if any progress had been made.'

'A little, Miss Andrews. A little.'

'The report in today's newspaper was not very encouraging.'

'Do not pay too much attention to what you read,' he counselled. 'Newspapers do not always have the full facts at their fingertips and some of them appear to take pleasure in baiting us. I can assure you that we have made more headway than they would lead you to believe.'

'We were horrified to learn that there had been two murders. Is it true that they may possibly be related to the train robbery?'

'Undeniably so.'

'Why were they killed?'

'The murder victims were accomplices who had to be silenced.'

'How terrible!'

'Except for the young woman, that is. She was an innocent person who happened to be in the wrong company at the wrong time.'

'Yet they still cut her throat?'

'We are dealing with ruthless men, Miss Andrews.'

'Father discovered that.'

'How is he, by the way?'

'He gets better each day,' she said, brightening. 'Unfortunately, he also gets angrier and louder. I have difficulty in calming him down.'

'I refuse to believe that. You know exactly how to handle him.'

His fond smile was tinged with disappointment. Madeleine met his gaze and held it for some time, trying to read the message in his eyes while sending a covert signal in her own. Colbeck was strongly aware of the mutual interest between them but he did not feel able to explore it. His visitor eventually broke the long silence.

'I had a more personal reason for coming, Inspector,' she said.

'Indeed?'

'Yes, I feel that I owe you an apology.'

'Whatever for?'

'My behaviour when you called at our house.'

'I saw nothing that could warrant an apology, Miss Andrews.'

'My father spoke out of turn.'

'He does seem to have an impulsive streak.'

'It led him to say something that he had no right to say,' explained Madeleine, 'and I did not wish you to be misled by it. The person that he mentioned – Gideon Little, a fireman – is a family friend, but, as far as I am concerned, he can never be more than that. Father thinks otherwise.'

'Your private life is no business of mine,' he said, trying to ease her obvious discomfort. 'Please do not feel that you have to offer either an apology or an explanation.'

'I just wanted you to understand.'

'Then I am grateful that you came.'

'Really?'

'Really,' he confirmed.

Madeleine smiled with relief. 'Then so am I, Inspector Colbeck.' She got to her feet. 'But I must let you get on with your work. What am I to tell my father?'

'That he has a very beautiful daughter,' said Colbeck, letting his admiration show, 'though I daresay that he already knows that. As for the train robbery,' he went on, 'I can give him no hope of an early arrest. Indeed, I think you should warn him to brace himself.'

'Why?'

'Because the man behind the robbery will be back. In my view, he is conducting a feud against the railway system and he will not rest until he has inflicted more serious damage upon it.'

'What do you mean?' roared Sir Humphrey Gilzean, striking the side of his boot with his riding crop. 'The attempt *failed*?'

'It was only a partial success,' said Thomas Sholto.

'How partial? Was there no explosion?'

'Yes, Humphrey.'

'Then what went wrong?'

'The gunpowder, it seems, was not in the ideal position. All that it did was to dislodge the brickwork on one side of the tunnel.'

'It was intended to block the entrance completely.'

'That did not happen, alas.'

'Why ever not, Thomas? I gave orders.'

'They were disobeyed,' said Sholto. 'The men decided that they could achieve the same results with a smaller amount of gunpowder than you had decreed. They were proved wrong.'

'Damnation!'

'They've been upbraided, believe me.'

'I'll do more than upbraid them,' snarled Gilzean, slapping the back of a leather armchair with his crop. 'I gave them precise instructions. Had they followed them to the letter, the train that was coming from the opposite direction would have crashed into the debris and put the Kilsby Tunnel out of action for a considerable time.'

'That did not happen, Humphrey. Damage was limited.'

'I *knew* that we should have done the job ourselves.'

'Jukes and the others have never let us down before.'

'They'll not get the chance to do so again,' vowed Gilzean, prowling vengefully around the hall of his house. 'I know that. Instead of disrupting the railway, we simply gave them a salutary warning. The Kilsby Tunnel will be guarded by an army of policemen from now on.' He flung his crop onto the armchair. 'We lost our chance through sheer incompetence.'

'They did not realise how solid that brickwork was.'

'Almost as solid as their heads, by the sound of it. I don't like it, Thomas. This is a bad omen. Until now, everything has gone so smoothly.'

'Our luck had to change at some time.'

'Luck does not come into it, man,' retorted the other.

'It is merely a question of good preparation and perfect timing. That is what served us so well with the train robbery – discipline. Were I still in the regiment,' he said, waving a fist, 'I'd have the three of them flogged until they had no skin left on their backs. Just wait until I see them. Disobey orders, will they?' he cried. 'By God, the next time I try to blow up a tunnel, I'll make sure that each one of those blithering idiots is inside it!'

Madeleine Andrews made no objection this time when he suggested that she might return home in a cab. Shadows were lengthening and Camden began to seem a long way away. As they stood in Whitehall, however, she made no effort to hail a cab and neither did Colbeck. She wished to stay and he wanted her to linger. Their brief conversation in his office had redeemed his whole day. When a cab went past, they both ignored it.

'I read what the newspaper said about you, Inspector.'

'Did you?'

'Yes,' replied Madeleine. 'It listed some of the other cases in which you've been involved. You've had a very successful career.'

'I am only one of a team, Miss Andrews,' he said, modestly. 'Any success that I've enjoyed as a detective is due to the fact that I have people like Sergeant Leeming around me.'

'That face of his would frighten me.'

'Victor has many compensating virtues.'

'I'm sure that he has.' She looked up quizzically

at him. 'How did you come to know so much about locomotives?'

'They interest me.'

'Father could not believe that you could tell the difference between a Bury and a Crampton locomotive. That pleased him so much.'

'Good,' said Colbeck, studying her dimples. 'Driving a train has always seemed to be to be an exciting occupation.'

'Not to those who actually do it, Inspector. Father has to work long hours in all weathers. Standing on the footplate in heavy rain or driving snow is an ordeal. And think of the dirt. His clothing gets so filthy that I have to wash it in several waters to get it clean.'

'Has he ever wanted to change his job?'

'No,' she admitted. 'He loves it too much.'

'In spite of what happened to him this week?'

'In spite of it.'

Colbeck grinned. 'I rest my case.'

'Being in a railway family is hard for any woman,' she said. 'Talk to Rose Pike. Her husband was the fireman. Rose will tell you how often Frank has come home with burns on his hand from the firebox or a mark on his face where some flying cinders have hit him. When she heard about the train robbery, she was terrified.'

'Be fair, Miss Andrews. It was a unique event.'

'That made no difference to Rose.'

Colbeck began to fish. 'Coming back to what you were saying about a railway family,' he said, casually. 'Is it because you were brought up in one that you have no desire to marry a railwayman?'

'I've no desire to marry anyone at present,' she replied.

'Yet you have a suitor.'

'An unwanted suitor.'

'Because he works on the railway?'

'No, Inspector,' she said with a shrug. 'Because he is not the right husband for me. Gideon Little is a pleasant enough young man and I have always liked him, but that is the extent of my interest in him.'

'You do not have to account to me for your feelings.'

'I wanted you to appreciate the true position, Inspector.'

'Thank you.'

'Just as I now appreciate your situation.'

'Is it so transparent, Miss Andrews?'

'I think so,' she said, looking him full in the eye. 'You are married to your work, Inspector. It occupies you completely, does it not? Nothing else in your life matters.'

'You may be wrong about that,' said Colbeck with a slow smile. 'Though I suspect that it may take time to convince you of it.' The clatter of hooves made him look up. 'Ah, here's a cab at last!' he noted. 'Shall I stop it or do you reserve the right to hail it yourself?'

'I accept your kind offer, Inspector. Thank you.'

Colbeck raised an arm and the cab drew up alongside them. He had the momentary pleasure of holding her hand to help her into the cab. There was an exchange of farewells. Madeleine gave an address to the driver and he flicked his reins. The horse trotted off up Whitehall. Colbeck had a sudden desire to sit beside her in the cab and continue their conversation indefinitely but other priorities called. Forcing himself to forget Madeleine Andrews, he went swiftly back to his office.

The dark-eyed young man in the ill-fitting brown suit emerged from the doorway where he had been lurking. Gideon Little set off with long strides in pursuit of the cab.

CHAPTER NINE

Darkness had fallen by the time that news of the explosion in the Kilsby Tunnel finally reached Scotland Yard. Superintendent Tallis was not entirely convinced that it was the work of the same people who had robbed the mail train, but Inspector Colbeck had no doubts whatsoever on the subject. He decided to visit the scene of the crime in daylight. Accordingly, early next morning, he and Victor Leeming caught a train that would take them there with a minimum number of stops on the way. Knowing that his companion was a reluctant rail traveller, Colbeck tried to divert him with some facts about their destination.

'What do you know about the tunnel, Victor?' he asked.

'Nothing – beyond the fact that it goes under ground.'

'It's a work of art. On my visit to the Midlands, I went through it twice and was struck by the sheer size of it. The Kilsby Tunnel is cavernous. It's like being in a subterranean kingdom.'

'I'll take your word for it, Inspector.'

'When he undertook the project, Mr Stephenson thought it would be relatively straightforward because they would be cutting their way through a mixture of clay and sand. Unhappily,' said Colbeck, 'much of it turned out to be quicksand so the whole area had first to be drained. It was slow and laborious work.'

'Like being a detective,' noted the other, lugubriously.

Colbeck laughed. 'Only in the sense that we, too, come up against unforeseen hazards,' he said. 'But our job is far less dangerous than that of the miners who sunk those enormous ventilation shafts or the navvies who dug out all that soil. How many bricks would you say were needed to line the tunnel?'

'Hundreds of thousands, probably,' guessed Leeming, unable to share the Inspector's enthusiasm for the topic. 'I hope that you are not asking me to count them when we get there.'

'It would take you a lifetime, Victor.'

'Why, sir?'

'Because millions of bricks were used,' said Colbeck. 'A steam clay mill and kilns were built on site by Mr Stephenson so that he had a constant supply of 30,000 bricks per day. Imagine that, if you will.' Leeming stifled a yawn. 'The original estimate – would you believe – was for a total of 20 million bricks, some of them made from the clay that was excavated from the tunnel itself.'

'How do you know all this, Inspector?'

'I took the trouble to do some research on the subject.'

'In that library of yours, you mean?'

'Yes, Victor.'

'I wouldn't know where to look.'

'Start with a history of the London and Birmingham Railway,' said Colbeck. 'That was the name of the company that operated this line when the tunnel was built. It was only amalgamated into the London and North Western Railway Company five years ago.'

'Now that's something I *did* know,' said Leeming. 'Every person I spoke to at the company made a point of telling me.' He gave Colbeck a meaningful glance. 'But not one of them mentioned how many bricks there were in the Kilsby Tunnel.'

'Point taken,' said Colbeck, smiling. 'You are not in the mood for a lecture about the railway. Given the choice, I suspect, you would rather be making this journey on horseback.'

'Or in the comfort of a stage coach, sir.'

'Either way, you would have been much slower.'

'Would I?'

'By the time you got to Northamptonshire, I would have been back at my desk in London. Railways are helping to defeat time.'

When the train passed through Leighton Buzzard Station, they were pleased to see that the wrecked locomotive near the Linslade Tunnel had been removed, leaving deep indentations in the grass where it had come to rest. Though the robbery had been a serious crime with murderous consequences, Colbeck was very conscious of the fact that it had introduced him to Madeleine Andrews. He regarded that as an incidental bonus. His mind was filled with pleasant thoughts of her as they crossed the county border.

Stations flashed pass them at regular intervals then – to Leeming's obvious relief – the train began to slow down. The detectives alighted at Crick to be greeted by a familiar sight. The hulking figure of Inspector Rory McTurk came along the station platform to give them a blunt reception.

'What are *you* doing here, Inspector Colbeck?' he asked.

'We wanted the pleasure of renewing your acquaintance,' replied Colbeck, touching the brim of his hat with courtesy. 'I'm sure that you remember Sergeant Leeming.'

'I do,' grunted the Scotsman.

'Good morning, Inspector,' said Leeming.

'Neither of you is needed here. This is railway business.'

'Not when it's related to the train robbery,' asserted Colbeck.

'What makes you think that?'

'I'll tell you when we have examined the scene.' The locomotive was starting up again. 'I see that the line has been reopened.'

'In both directions,' said McTurk. 'A team of men

worked through the night to clear the obstruction. Everything is as it should be now.'

'Were there no policemen on duty at the tunnel?'

'Two of them, Inspector. They were both overpowered.'

'What game of cards were they playing *this* time?' asked Leeming.

McTurk scowled. 'Follow me,' he said.

When the train had departed, they went down onto the track and strolled in the direction of the Kilsby Tunnel. McTurk walked with a proprietary strut. Since he was landed with him, Colbeck tried to make use of the combative Scotsman.

'The news reached us by telegraph,' he said. 'Details were scarce.'

'Then how can you link this outrage with the train robbery?'

'I was expecting it.'

'You expected it?' said McTurk. 'Why did you not forewarn us?'

'Because I had no idea *where* they would strike, Inspector, only that an attack of some sort was imminent. From what I gather,' Colbeck went on, 'you had something of a lucky escape.'

McTurk frowned. 'Two railway policemen injured and an explosion in the longest tunnel on the line – I fail to see how you can talk about luck. It could have been worse,' he admitted, 'much worse, but it is still bad enough.'

He grumbled all the way to the mouth of the tunnel itself. Colbeck and Leeming said nothing to interrupt

206

him. The first thing they noticed was the large pile of rubble to the side of the track that carried up trains to London. Working from ladders and trestles, bricklayers were already trying to repair the damage. Leeming saw an opportunity to air his limited knowledge of tunnel construction.

'Tell me, Inspector McTurk,' he said. 'Do you happen to know how many bricks were used in the Kilsby Tunnel?'

'Too bloody many!' came the tart reply.

Leeming chose not to pursue the conversation.

Colbeck went into the tunnel to examine the full extent of the damage. He tried to work out where the gunpowder must have been when it exploded. McTurk came to stand at his shoulder.

'By the end of the day,' he said, 'it will be as good as new.'

'What about the two men who were attacked?' asked Colbeck. 'Are they as good as new, Inspector?'

'They're still a bit shaken, but they'll be back at work soon.'

'Were they able to give a description of their assailants?'

'No,' said McTurk. 'They were grabbed from behind, knocked unconscious and tied up. They didn't even hear the explosion go off. There's no point in talking to them.'

'Perhaps not.' He felt inside a hole where the brickwork had been blasted away. 'What was the intention behind it all?'

McTurk was contemptuous. 'I'm surprised that a man

of your experience has to ask that, Inspector Colbeck,' he said. 'The intention is plain. They tried to close the tunnel in order to disrupt the railway.'

'I think that there is more to it than that.'

'What do you mean?'

'These people do nothing at random, believe me. The explosion would have gone off at a specific time and for a specific purpose. When was the next up train due to enter the tunnel at the other end?'

'Not long before the explosion. Fortunately, it was late.'

'There's your answer, Inspector McTurk.'

'Is it?'

'The tunnel was supposed to collapse just before the train reached it. The driver would have been going too fast to stop. The locomotive would have ploughed into the rubble and the whole train would have been derailed. *That* was their intention,' declared Colbeck. 'To block the tunnel, destroy a train and kill passengers in the process.'

'But there were no passengers on board the train.'

'Then what was it carrying?'

'Goods.'

'Any particular kinds of goods?'

'Why do you ask?'

'Because it may be significant.'

'I don't see how,' said McTurk, irritably. 'My information is that the wagons were simply carrying huge pieces of glass from the Chance Brothers' Factory.'

'Of course!' cried Colbeck. 'That explains it.'

McTurk looked blank. 'Does it?'

'I'm as mystified as Inspector McTurk,' confessed Leeming as he joined them. 'How can some sheets of glass provide the explanation?'

'Think of where they would be going, Victor,' advised Colbeck.

'To the customer who bought them, I suppose.'

'What's so remarkable about that?' said McTurk.

'The customer in question happens to be Joseph Paxton,' replied Colbeck, 'the man who designed the Crystal Palace. And who had the contract for supplying all that glass? Chance Brothers.'

McTurk lifted his hat to scratch his head. 'I'm still lost.'

'So am I,' said Leeming.

'Then you have obviously not been reading all the advertisements for the Great Exhibition. What is it,' said Colbeck, 'but a celebration of British industry? One of the main elements in that is the primacy of our railway system. A number of locomotives will be on display – but only if the structure is finished, and that depends on the supply of the glass panels that were commissioned from Chance Brothers.'

Leeming blinked. 'They were trying to *stop* the Great Exhibition?'

'At the very least, they were doing their best to hamper the completion of the Crystal Palace,' argued Colbeck. 'The explosion was contrived by someone who not only wanted to put the tunnel out of action, he also hoped to delay an exhibition in which the steam locomotive will have pride of place.'

'All I see is wanton damage,' said McTurk, looking around.

'Look for the deeper meaning, Inspector.'

'I've tried. But I'm damned if I can spot it.'

'What happened to the train carrying the glass?' said Leeming.

'I told you, Sergeant. It was late. The driver was a mile or so short of the tunnel when the explosion went off. Must have sounded like an earthquake to him.'

'The noise would have echoed along the whole tunnel.'

'And well beyond,' said McTurk. 'When the driver heard it, he slowed the train immediately. The signalmen at the other end of the tunnel were, in any case, flagging him down.'

'So the sheets of glass were undamaged?'

'They were taken on to London as soon as the line was cleared.'

'Thank you, Inspector McTurk,' said Colbeck, shaking his hand. 'You have been a great help. Forgive us if we rush off. We need to catch the next train back to Euston.'

'Do we?' asked Leeming. 'But we have not seen everything yet.'

'We've seen all that we need to, Victor. The man we are after has just given himself away. I know what he will do next.'

Leaving a bewildered Inspector McTurk in his wake,

Colbeck led his companion back towards Crick Station. There was a spring in the Inspector's step. For the first time since the investigation had begun, he felt that he might have the advantage.

It was Gideon Little who told them about the incident. His ostensible reason for calling at the house was to see how Caleb Andrews was faring and to pass on details of the attack on the Kilsby Tunnel. A train on which Little had been the fireman that morning had been as far as Northampton and back. He had picked up all the news. In telling it to Andrews, he was also able to get close to Madeleine once more. She was as alarmed as her father by what she heard.

'Was anyone hurt, Gideon?'

'Only the railway policemen on duty,' said Little, enjoying her proximity. 'They were ambushed and knocked on the head.'

Andrews was rueful. 'I know how *that* feels!'

'Why would anyone damage the tunnel?' asked Madeleine.

'I wish I knew,' said Little. 'It's very worrying. If a train had been coming through at that time, there would have been a terrible crash.'

'Thank heaven that never happened!'

'Railways still have lots of enemies,' said Andrews. 'I'm old enough to remember a time when landowners would do anything to stop us if we tried to go across their property. Boulders on the line, track pulled up, warning

211

fires lit – I saw it all. And it was not just landowners.'

'No,' added Little, mournfully. 'People who ran stage coaches feared that railways might put them out of business. So did canal owners. Then there are those who say we destroy the countryside.'

'We are not destroying it, Gideon. Railways make it possible for people to *see* our beautiful countryside. The many who are stuck in ugly towns all week can take an excursion train on a Sunday and share in the pleasures that the few enjoy. We offer a public service,' Andrews went on with conviction. 'We open up this great country of ours.'

They were in the main bedroom and the driver was resting against some pillows. His arm was still in a sling and his broken leg held fast in a splint. An occasional wince showed that he was still in pain. Pressed for details, Little told him everything that he could about the explosion but his eyes kept straying to Madeleine, hoping to see a sign of affection that never materialised. When it was time for him to go, she showed the visitor to the door but did not linger.

'Goodbye, Madeleine,' said Little.

'Thank you for coming to see Father.'

'It was you that I came to see.'

She forced a smile. 'Goodbye.'

Madeleine closed the door after him then went back upstairs.

'Is there anything I can get you, Father?' she said.

'A pair of crutches.'

'The doctor told you to stay in bed.'

'I'll die of boredom if I'm trapped in here much longer.'

'You've had plenty of visitors,' Madeleine reminded him. 'Frank Pike came yesterday, so did Rose. Today, it was Gideon's turn.'

'He'd be here every day if he had some encouragement.'

She inhaled deeply. 'You know how I feel on that score.'

'Give the lad a chance, Maddy. He dotes on you.'

'Yes,' she said, sadly, 'but I do not dote on Gideon.'

'Your mother didn't exactly dote on me at first,' he confided with a nostalgic sigh, 'but she took me on and – God bless her – she learnt to love me in time. I think I made her happy.'

'You did, Father. She always said that.'

'I miss her terribly but I'm glad that she's not here to see me like this. I feel so *helpless*.' He peered up at her. 'Gideon will be a driver one day, Maddy – just like me. You could do a lot worse.'

'I know that.'

'So why do you give the poor man a cold shoulder?'

'I try to be polite to him.'

'He wants more than politeness.'

'Then he wants more than I am able to offer,' she said.

His voice hardened. 'Gideon is not good enough for you, is that it?'

'No, Father.'

'You think that you are above marrying a railwayman.'

'That's not true at all.'

'I brought you up to respect the railway,' he said with a glint in his eye. 'It served me well enough all these years, Maddy. Your mother was proud of what I did for a living.'

'So am I.'

'Then why are you giving yourself these airs and graces?'

'Father,' she said, trying to remain calm, 'the situation is simple. I do not – and never could – love Gideon Little.'

'You've set your sights higher, have you?'

'Of course not.'

'I'm not blind, Maddy,' he told her. 'Something has happened to you over the past few days and we both know what it is. Run with your own kind, girl,' he urged. 'That's where your future lies. Why look at a man who will always be out of your reach?'

'Please!' she said. 'I don't wish to discuss this any more.'

'I only want to stop you from getting hurt, Maddy.'

'You need rest. I'll leave you alone.'

'Stick to Gideon. He's one of our own. Be honest with yourself,' he said. 'No man in a silk top hat is going to look at you.'

Madeleine could take no more. Her feelings had been hurt and her mind was racing. Holding back tears, she opened the door and went out.

Superintendent Tallis did not even bother to knock. He burst into Colbeck's office in time to find the Inspector poring intently over a copy of the *Illustrated London News*. Colbeck looked up with a dutiful smile.

'Good afternoon, sir,' he said.

'Where have you been, Inspector?'

'To the Kilsby Tunnel and back.'

'I know that,' said Tallis, leaning over the desk at him. 'Why did you not report to me the moment that you got back?'

'I did, Superintendent. You were not in your office.'

'I was in a meeting with the Commissioners.'

'That's why I came back here to do some work.'

'Since when has reading a newspaper been construed as work?'

'Actually,' said Colbeck, turning the paper round so that Tallis could see it, 'I was studying this illustration on the front page. I suggest that you do the same, sir.'

'I do not have time to look at illustrations, Inspector,' rasped the other, ignoring the paper, 'and neither do you. Now what did you learn of value in Northamptonshire?'

'That it really is a charming county. Even Victor was impressed.'

'Did you establish how the tunnel was damaged?'

'I did much more than that.'

'Indeed?'

'I discovered why they chose that particular target. More to the point,' Colbeck announced, 'I believe that I know where they will direct their malign energies next.'

'And where is that, Inspector?'

'At this.' Colbeck tapped the illustration that lay before

him. '*The Lord of the Isles*. It's a steam locomotive, sir.'

'I can see that, man.'

'The pride of the Great Western Railway. What more dramatic way to make his point than by destroying this symbol of excellence?'

'Who are you talking about?'

'The man who organised the train robbery and who instigated the attack on the Kilsby Tunnel. If you take a seat, Superintendent,' he said, indicating a chair, 'I will be happy to explain.'

'I wish that somebody would.'

As soon as Tallis sat down, Colbeck told him about the visit to the scene of the latest crime and how he had become convinced of where the next attack would be. Tallis had grave doubts.

'It's a wild guess, Inspector,' he said.

'No, sir. It's a considered judgement, based on what I know of the man and his methods. He is conducting a vendetta against railways.'

'Then why not blow up another tunnel or destroy a bridge?'

'Because he can secure infinitely more publicity at the Crystal Palace. Every newspaper in Britain and several from aboard would report the event. After all, the Exhibition has an international flavour,' said Colbeck. 'The whole civilised world will be looking at it. That is what this man craves most of all, Superintendent – an audience.'

'Why should he pick on the *Lord of the Isles*?'

'Because that will set the standard of locomotive construction for years to come, sir. It repeats the design of Daniel Gooch's *Iron Duke*, built for the Great Western Railway at Swindon. Other locomotives will be on display,' he continued, 'including the famous *Puffing Billy* and the *Liverpool*, designed by Thomas Crampton. Our man may choose one of them instead or create an explosion big enough to destroy all the railway exhibits. Inside a structure like the Crystal Palace, of course, any explosion will have a devastating effect.'

'Only if it were allowed to happen.'

'That is why we must take preventative measures.'

'They are already in hand,' Tallis informed him. 'I attended a first meeting with the Commissioners about security at the Exhibition in November of last year. We recommended that an extra 1,000 police officers were needed.'

'Yes, but only to control the massive crowds that are expected.'

'A moment ago, you mentioned the *Iron Duke*. It may interest you to know that the real Iron Duke, the Duke of Wellington, advocated a force of 15,000 men. I put forward the notion of swearing in sappers as special constables but it was felt – wrongly, in my opinion – that they would be seen as too militaristic.' He stroked his moustache. 'As an army man, I believe in the power of the uniform.'

'The problem is,' said Colbeck, 'that a uniform gives the game away. It sends out a warning. Besides,

Superintendent, you are talking about security arrangements *during* the Exhibition. I think that the attack will be made before it.'

'How have you arrived at that conclusion?'

'By putting myself in the mind of the man we are after.'

'But you do not even know his name.'

'I know his type, sir,' said Colbeck. 'Like you, he was a military man. He understands that he must use surprise to maximum effect and strike at the weakest point. Look at the train robbery,' he suggested. 'The weak points were William Ings and Daniel Slender. Once their loyalty had been breached, the ambush could be laid.'

Superintendent Tallis ruminated. Crossing to the desk, he picked up the paper and looked at the illustration of the *Lord of the Isles*. After a moment, he tossed it down again.

'No,' he decided. 'Simply because there was an explosion in the Kilsby Tunnel, I do not foresee an outrage at the Crystal Palace.'

'What if you are mistaken, sir?'

'That is highly unlikely.'

'But not impossible,' reasoned Colbeck. 'If there *is* some sort of attack on those locomotives, you will be blamed for not taking special precautions when you had been advised to do so. All that I am asking for is a small number of men.'

'To do what?'

'Mount a guard throughout the night. Nobody would

be reckless enough to attempt anything in daylight – there would be far too many people about, helping to set up the exhibits.'

'Are you volunteering to lead this guard detail?'

'Provided that I have a free hand to choose my team.'

'It could be a complete waste of time, Inspector.'

'Then I will be the first to admit that I was wrong,' said Colbeck, firmly. 'If, on the other hand, we do foil an attempt to damage the locomotives, you will be given the credit for anticipating it.'

Tallis needed a few minutes to think it over. Inclined to dismiss the idea as fanciful, he feared the consequences if the Inspector were proved right. Robert Colbeck had a habit of coming up with strange proposals that somehow, against all the odds, bore fruit. A man who was ready to endure sleepless nights at the Crystal Palace had to be driven by a deep inner conviction. After meditation, Tallis elected to trust in it.

'Very well, Inspector,' he said. 'Take the necessary steps.'

Thomas Sholto had known him for several years. Educated at the same school, they had been commissioned in the same regiment and served together in India. For all that, he could still be amazed at the dedication that Sir Humphrey Gilzean brought to any project. It was in evidence again when they met that morning to discuss their latest scheme. A large round mahogany table stood in the library at Gilzean's house. Sholto was astounded to see what was lying on it. As well as a detailed floor plan of the Crystal Palace, there was a copy of the *Official Catalogue* for the Great Exhibition.

'How on earth did you get hold of these?' asked Sholto.

'By a combination of money and persuasion,' replied Gilzean, picking up the catalogue. 'This is the first of five parts but the printers only have this one ready for the opening ceremony on May Day. Did you know that there are over 100,000 separate items on show, sent in from all over the world by individual and corporate exhibitors?'

'Prince Albert wants it to be a truly unforgettable event.'

'We will make sure that it is, Thomas.' He put the catalogue down and scrutinised the plan. 'Everything on show is divided into four different classes – Raw Materials, Machinery, Manufactures and Fine Arts.'

'Any mention of the British Army? That's what made the Empire.'

'Only a display of Military Engineering and Ordnance.'

'No bands, no parades, no demonstrations of military skills?'

'No, Thomas. The emphasis is on industry in all its forms.' He drew back his lips in a sneer. 'Including the railways.'

'Where are the locomotives housed, Humphrey?'

'Here,' said Gilzean, indicating a section of the ground floor plan. 'What we are after is in an area devoted to Machinery for Direct Use.'

'On the north side,' observed Sholto. 'It should not be difficult to gain access there. I took the trouble to have a preliminary look at the Crystal Palace when I accosted Lord Holcroft in Hyde Park. It is a vast cathedral of glass that looks like nothing so much as a giant conservatory. But, then, what else should one expect of a man like Joseph Paxton who is a landscape gardener?'

'As far as I am concerned, Thomas, his notoriety lies elsewhere.'

'Yes, Humphrey. He is a director of the Midland Railway.'

'Had he not been,' said Gilzean scornfully, 'he might never have been employed to design that monstrous edifice. I am told, on good authority, that Joseph Paxton came down to the House of Commons last year for a meeting with Mr John Ellis, Member of Parliament and chairman of the Midland Railway, a ghastly individual with whom I've crossed swords more than once in the Chamber.'

'Yes, Humphrey. I recall how you opposed his Railway Bill.'

'It was a matter of honour. To return to Paxton,' he said. 'When our landscape gardener discovered how poor the acoustics were in the House of Commons, he decried the architect, Mr Barry. He then went on to say that those designing the hall for the Great Exhibition would also botch the job – even though he had not seen their plans.'

'Mr Paxton is an arrogant man, by the sound of it.'

'Arrogant?' said Gilzean, scornfully. 'The fellow has a conceit to rival Narcissus. At a meeting of the board of his railway company, he had the gall to sketch his idea for the building on a piece of blotting paper. That, Thomas, is how this Crystal Palace came into being.'

'On a piece of blotting paper?'

'The design was shown to Ellis, who passed it on to someone in authority and, the next thing you know, Paxton is invited to submit a plan and an estimate of its cost. To cap it all,' said Gilzean through gritted teeth, 'he is given an audience with Prince Albert himself. His Royal Highness was not the only one to approve of the design. Paxton managed to win the support of no less a personage than Robert Stephenson.' He arched an imperious eyebrow. 'The two of them met – appropriately enough – during a train journey to London.'

'The railway has a lot to answer for, Humphrey.'

'More than you know,' returned the other. 'In the early days, when we were doing our best to oppose the scheme, it looked as if the Great Exhibition might not even take place. It was dogged by all sorts of financial problems. Then in steps Mr Peto, the railway contractor, and offers to act as guarantor for the building by putting down £50,000. Once he had led the way,' said Gilzean, 'others quickly followed. Mr Peto also put his weight behind the choice of Paxton as the architect.'

'At every stage,' noted Sholto, 'crucial decisions have been made by those connected with the railways. You can see how they stand to reap the benefit. When the Exhibition opens, excursion trains will run from all over the country. Railway companies will make immense profits.'

'Not if I can help it, Thomas.'

'The men are in readiness.'

'They had better not repeat their failure at the Kilsby Tunnel.'

'After what you said to them, Humphrey, they would not dare. They are still shaking. You put the fear of God into them.'

'They deserved it.'

'I agree,' said Sholto. 'Have you chosen the day yet?'

'Thursday next.'

'I'll give them their orders.'

'No, Thomas,' said Gilzean, folding up the floor plan, 'I'll do that myself. I intend to be at my town house in London this week. I want to hear those locomotives being blown apart.'

'They'll take a large part of the Crystal Palace with them. That glass is very fragile. It will shatter into millions of shards.' Sholto laughed harshly. 'A pity that it will happen in darkness – it should be a wondrous sight. Farewell to the Great Exhibition!'

'Farewell to the *Lord of the Isles* and all those other locomotives,' said Gilzean, bitterly. 'I'll never forgive the railways for what they did to me. My ambition is to act as a scourge to the whole damnable industry.'

* * *

The meeting was not accidental. As she came out of the shop, Madeleine Andrews was confronted by Gideon Little, who pretended that he was about to go in. Since he lived half a mile away, and had several shops in the vicinity of his house, there was no need for him to be in Camden at all. After greeting Madeleine, he invented an excuse.

'I thought of calling on your father again,' he said, diffidently.

'He is asleep, Gideon. It is not a good time to visit.'

'Then I'll come another time.'

'Father is always pleased to see you.'

'What about you, Madeleine?'

'I, too, am pleased,' she said, briskly. 'I believe that any friend of Father's is welcome at our house, especially if he is a railwayman.'

'I am not talking about Caleb,' he said, quietly.

'I know.'

'Then why do you not answer my question?'

There was a long and uncomfortable pause. When she walked to the end of the street to buy some provisions, Madeleine had not expected to be cornered by a man whose devotion to her had reached almost embarrassing proportions. She had tried, in the past, to discourage him as gently as she could, but Gideon Little had a keen ally in her father and a quiet tenacity that drove him on past all her of rebuffs. Madeleine had the uneasy feeling that he had been lurking outside the house in case she came out.

'Why are you not at work?' she asked.

'I was on the early shift today.'

'Then you must be very tired.'

'Not when I have a chance to see you, Madeleine.' He offered a hand. 'Let me carry your bag for you.'

'No, thank you. I can manage.'

He was hurt. 'Will you not even let me do that?'

'I have to go, Gideon.'

'No,' he said, stepping sideways to block her path, 'you have walked away from me once too often, Madeleine, and it has to stop. I think it's time you gave me an answer.'

'You *know* the answer,' she said, seeing the mingled hope and determination in his eyes. 'Do I really have to put it in words?'

'Yes.'

'Gideon—'

'At the very least, I deserve that. It's been two years now,' he told her. 'Two years of waiting, wanting, making plans for the two of us.'

'They were *your* plans – not ours.'

'Will you not even listen to what they are?'

'No,' she said with polite firmness. 'There would be no point.'

'Why are you so unkind to me? Do you hate me that much?'

'Of course not, Gideon. I like you. I always have. But the plain truth is – and you must surely realise this by now – that I can never see you as anything more than a friend.'

'*Never?*' he pleaded.

'Never, Gideon.'

Madeleine did not want to be so blunt with him but she had been left with no choice. Her father's condition gave Gideon Little an opportunity to call at the house on a regular basis, and he would try to urge his suit each time. The prospect dismayed Madeleine. It was better to risk offending him now than to let him harry her and build up his expectations. Wounded by her rejection, Little stared at her in disbelief, as if she had just thrust a dagger into him. His pain slowly gave way to a deep resentment.

'You were not always so cruel to me, Madeleine,' he said.

'You asked for the truth.'

'We were real friends once.'

'We still are, Gideon.'

'No,' he said, glaring at her. 'Since Caleb was injured, something has changed. You no longer have any interest in me. A fireman on the railway is beneath you now.'

'Let me go past, please.'

'Not until we settle this. You've met someone else, Madeleine.'

'I have to get back.'

'Someone you think is better than me. Don't lie,' he said, holding up a hand before she could issue a denial. 'Your father has noticed it and so have I. When you went to see Inspector Colbeck for the second time, I followed you. I saw the way you looked at him.'

Madeleine was furious. 'You *followed* me?'

'I knew that you wanted to see him again.'

'You had no right to do that.'

'Caleb told me how you behaved when the Inspector came to the house. He said that you put your best dress on for him. You never did that for me, Madeleine.'

'This has gone far enough, Gideon,' she asserted. 'Following me? That's dreadful. How could you do such a thing?'

'I wanted to see where you were going.'

'What I do and where I go is my business. The only reason I spoke to Inspector Colbeck again is that he is investigating the train robbery in which Father was injured.'

'Yet you never even mentioned it to Caleb,' said Gideon, hands on his hips. 'When I asked him if you had been back to Whitehall, he shook his head. Why did you mislead him, Madeleine?'

'Never you mind,' she said, flustered.

'But I do mind. This means a lot to me.'

Madeleine tried to move. 'Father will be expecting me.'

'You told me that he was asleep.'

'I want to be there when he wakes up.'

'Why?' he challenged, obstructing her path. 'Are you going to admit that you went out of your way to see Inspector Colbeck again because you like him so much?'

'No,' she retorted. 'I am going to tell him that I do not want you in the house again. I'm ashamed of you for what you did, Gideon.' She brushed past him. 'I will not be spied on by anyone.'

'Madeleine!' he cried, suddenly penitent.

'Leave me be.'

'I did not mean to upset you like that.'

But she was deaf to his entreaties. Hurrying along the pavement, she reached her house, let herself in and closed the door firmly behind her. Gideon Little had no doubt what she felt about him now.

On the third night, Victor Leeming's faith in the Inspector began to weaken slightly. It was well past midnight at the Crystal Palace and there had been neither sight nor sound of any intruders. Leeming feared that they were about to have another long and uneventful vigil.

'Are you sure that they will come, sir?' he whispered.

'Sooner or later,' replied Colbeck.

'Let someone else take over from us.'

'Do you want to miss all the excitement, Victor?'

'There's been precious little of that so far, Inspector. We've had two nights of tedium and, since the place is in darkness, we cannot even divert ourselves by looking at the exhibits. Also,' he complained, shifting his position, 'it is so uncomfortable here.'

Colbeck grinned. 'I did not have time to instal four-poster beds.'

The detectives were in one of the massive exhibition halls, concealed behind *Liverpool*, a standard gauge locomotive designed for the London and North Western

Railway by Thomas Crampton. Built for high speed, it had eight foot driving wheels and an unprecedentedly large heating surface. Having learnt its specifications, Colbeck had passed them to Leeming in the course of the first night, trying in vain to interest his Sergeant in the facts that the boiler pressure was 120 per square inch and that the cylinders were 18 by 24 inches. All that Leeming wanted was to be at home in bed with his wife, whose total ignorance of locomotives he now saw as a marital blessing.

'I think that *Liverpool* has a chance of winning a gold medal,' said Colbeck, giving the engine a friendly pat. 'That would really annoy Daniel Gooch at the Great Western.'

'I think that *we* deserve a gold medal for keeping watch like this,' said Leeming, yawning involuntarily. 'Mr Tallis had a feeling that we'd be chasing shadows.'

'Try to get some sleep, Victor.'

'On a floor as hard as this?'

'In any surveillance operation, you have to make the best of the conditions that you are given. We are, after all, indoors,' said Colbeck. 'Would you rather be outside in all that drizzle?'

'No, Inspector.'

'Then cheer up a little. We could be on the brink of an arrest.'

'Then again,' said Leeming under his breath, 'we could not.'

'Go on, Victor. Put your head down.'

'There's no point.'

'Yes, there is. You need some sleep.'

'What about you, Inspector?'

'I prefer to stay on duty. If anything happens, I'll wake you.'

'And if nothing happens?'

'In that case,' said Colbeck, beaming, 'you'll be able to tell your grandchildren that you once slept beneath one of the finest locomotives of its day. Good night, Victor. Remember not to snore.'

There were three of them. Having studied the plan that had been obtained for them by Sir Humphrey Gilzean, they were familiar with the layout of the Great Exhibition. Their leader, Arthur Jukes, a big bulky man in his thirties with ginger whiskers, had taken the precaution of visiting the site on the previous night to reconnoitre the area and to look for potential hazards. They were few in number. Security was light and the guards who patrolled the exterior of the Crystal Palace could be easily evaded. As he and his companions crouched in their hiding place, Jukes had no qualms about the success of the operation.

'We should've done it last night,' said Harry Seymour, the youngest of the three. 'When it wasn't so bleeding wet.'

'This drizzle will help us, Harry. It will put the guards off. They'll want to stay in the dry with a pipe of baccy.'

'So would I, Arthur.'

'You ready to tell that to Sir Humphrey?'

Seymour trembled. 'Not me!'

'Nor me,' said his brother, Vernon, the third of the men. 'It was bad enough facing Tom Sholto after that mishap at the Kilsby Tunnel. But Sir Humphrey was far worse,' he recalled with a grimace. 'I thought he was going to horsewhip us.'

'He'll do more than that if we fail,' said Harry Seymour.

Jukes was confident. 'No chance of that,' he boasted, looking to see of the coast was clear. 'Are you ready, lads?'

'Ready,' said the brothers in unison.

'Then let's go.'

Keeping low and moving swiftly, Jukes headed for the entrance to the north transept. Harry and Vernon Seymour followed him, carrying a barrel of gunpowder between them in a large canvas bag with rope handles. The three of them reached the door without being seen. Jukes had brought a lamp with him and he used it to illumine the lock so that he could work away at it with his tools. In less than a minute, it clicked open and he eased the door back on its hinges. The three of them went quickly inside. Jukes immediately closed the metal cover on the lamp so that the flame would not be reflected in the vast acreage of glass that surrounded them. Having memorised the floor plan, he knew exactly where to go.

Shutting the door behind them, they paused to take their bearings. In the gloom of the transept, everything was seen in ghostly outline. High above them, under a film of drizzle, was the magnificent arched roof of the transept, so tall that it allowed trees to continue growing beneath it, thereby providing an outdoor element in an essentially indoor space. Ahead of them, they knew, was the refreshment court, and beyond that, heard but not seen, was the first of the fountains that had been built. Harry Seymour remembered something else he had seen on the plan.

'We go past the exhibits from India,' he noted.

'So what?' said his brother.

'We could look at that stuffed elephant they got.'

'I saw enough real ones when we was over there, Harry.'

'So did I,' added Jukes, 'and we're not here to admire the place. We got orders. Let's obey them and be quick about it.'

Followed by the two brothers, he swung to the right and took a pathway that led between statues, exhibits and the forest of iron pillars that supported the structure. They did not even pause beside the stuffed elephant with its opulent howdah. Their interest was in the section devoted to Railways and Steam. It was in between an area set aside for Machinery in Motion and one shared by Printing and French Machinery, and Models and Naval Architecture. By the time that the shape of the first locomotive emerged from the darkness, all three of them were feeling a rush of exhilaration. They were about to earn a lot of money.

After peering at the various exhibits, Jukes stood

beside one of the biggest on display and ran a hand over it. He was satisfied.

'This is the one,' he declared.

'How do you know?' asked Harry Seymour.

'Because I can feel the name with my fingers. This is the *Lord of the Isles*. Put that gunpowder underneath her, lads, then we'll blow her to smithereens.'

'Let *me* light the fuse this time, Arthur.'

'Nobody is lighting any fuse,' shouted Colbeck.

'Not when I'm in here, at any rate,' said Brendan Mulryne, popping up in the tender and vaulting to the ground. 'Now which one of you bastards was ready to send me to my Maker?'

Colbeck marched towards them. 'All three of you are under arrest,' he said with Victor Leeming at his side. 'Handcuff them, Sergeant.'

'Yes, Inspector.'

But the three men were not going to surrender easily. Swinging the barrel between them, the Seymour Brothers hurled it at Mulryne but he caught it as if it were as light as a feather. He was thrilled that the men were ready to fight. With a roar of delight, he put the barrel down, jumped forward, grabbed them both by their throats and flung them hard against the side of the locomotive. When they tried to strike back, Mulryne hit them in turn with heavy punches that sent them to their knees. Leeming stepped in quickly to handcuff the two captives.

Jukes, meanwhile, had opted to run for it, blundering his way into an area where visitors to the exhibition would be able to see machines in action as they spun flax and silk or made lace. Colbeck went after him. Although he was armed with a pistol, he did not wish to risk firing it inside the glass structure in case it caused damage. Jukes was fast but he was in unknown territory. Colbeck, on the other hand, had visited the Crystal Palace in daylight and had some idea of where the exhibits were placed. While one man collided with heavy items, the other was able to avoid them.

He overhauled Jukes by the rope-making machine, tackling him around the legs to bring him crashing to the ground. Swearing volubly, Jukes kicked him away and tried to get to his feet, but Colbeck tripped him up again before flinging himself on top of the man. They grappled fiercely for a couple of minutes, each inflicting injuries on the other. With an upsurge of energy, Colbeck was eventually able to get in some telling punches to subdue his man. Bloodied and dazed, Jukes put up both hands to protect his face from further punishment.

Colbeck snapped a pair of handcuffs on his wrists before getting up. Mulryne came lumbering out of the darkness to join them. When he saw Jukes on the floor, he was disappointed.

'Why didn't you leave a piece of him for *me*, Inspector?' he said.

CHAPTER TEN

Within the ranks of the Metropolitan Police Force, Richard Mayne had acquired an almost legendary status. A surprise appointment as Joint Commissioner when the force was founded in 1829, he had worked tirelessly to develop effective policing of the capital, and with his colleague, Colonel Charles Rowan, had tried to make London a safer place for its citizens. Since the retirement of Colonel Rowan in the previous year, Mayne had become Senior Commissioner and, as such, made all the important executive decisions.

In the normal course of events, Robert Colbeck had little direct contact with him but, in the wake of the Inspector's success at the Crystal Palace, Mayne insisted on congratulating him in person. First thing that morning, therefore, Colbeck was summoned to his office along with Superintendent Edward Tallis who, in spite of a tinge of envy, emphasised that the idea of setting a trap at the Great Exhibition had come originally from Colbeck.

'Well done, Inspector,' said Mayne, shaking Colbeck's hand.

'Thank you, sir.'

'Both you and your men performed a splendid service.'

'We could not have done so without the active support of the Superintendent,' said Colbeck, indicating Tallis. 'He should have some share of the glory.'

'Indeed, he should.'

He gave Tallis a nod of gratitude and the latter responded with a half-smile. Turning back to Colbeck, the Commissioner appraised the elegant Inspector.

'I trust that you did not dress like that last night,' he said.

'No, sir,' replied Colbeck. 'I would never risk creasing my frock coat or scuffing my trousers in a situation of that kind. More practical clothing was needed. I had a feeling that some violence might occur.'

'Yet only three of you were on duty.'

'I reasoned that we would only have to deal with a few men. That is all it would have taken to set up the explosion. Besides, the less of us, the easier it was to conceal ourselves.'

'I have read your report of the incident,' said Mayne, 'and found it admirably thorough, if unduly modest. Why not tell us what *really* happened, Inspector?'

Clearing his throat, Colbeck gave him a full account of how the arrests were made, praising the work of his two

236

assistants while saying little about his own involvement. The bruising on his face and the bandaging around the knuckles of one hand told a different story. Mayne was enthralled. Irish by extraction, he was a handsome man in his mid-fifties with long wavy hair, all but encircling his face, and searching eyes. As the person in charge of the special police division, raised to take care of security at the Crystal Palace, he had a particular interest in the events of the previous night. Thanks to Colbeck and his men, the reputation of the Metropolitan Police Force had been saved.

'Had they succeeded,' observed Mayne, drily, 'the results would have been quite horrific. You saved the Great Exhibition from utter destruction, Inspector Colbeck. The very least that you may expect is a letter from Prince Albert.'

'With respect, sir,' said Colbeck, 'I would rather His Royal Highness stayed his hand until this investigation is over. All that we have in custody are three members of a much larger gang. Its leader remains at large and, until he is caught, we must stay on the alert.'

'Have these villains not disclosed his identity?'

'No, sir. They are very loyal to him.'

'Army men, all three of them,' said Tallis, eyebrows twitching in disapproval. 'It shocked me that anyone who had borne arms for this country should lower himself to such an unpatriotic action as this.'

'It is disturbing,' agreed Mayne.

'The Exhibition has the stamp of royalty upon it. To

237

threaten it in this way is, in my book, tantamount to an act of treason. Left to me, they would be prosecuted accordingly.'

'The court will decide their fate, Superintendent.'

'The gravity of this crime must not be underestimated.'

'It will not be, I can assure you of that.'

'If you want my opinion—'

'Another time,' said Mayne, interrupting him with a raised hand. 'Would you mind leaving us alone for a few moments, please?' he asked. 'I'd value a few words in private with Inspector Colbeck.'

'Oh, I see,' said Tallis, discomfited by the request.

'Thank you, Superintendent.'

Tallis paused at the door. 'I'll want to see you in my office later on, Inspector,' he warned.

'Yes, sir,' said Colbeck.

Tallis went out and closed the door behind him. Mayne sat down behind his desk and waved Colbeck to a chair opposite him. Now that the two men were alone, the mood became less formal.

'The Superintendent is a typical army man,' observed Mayne, 'and I say that in no spirit of criticism. Colonel Rowan was another fine example of the breed. He had a wonderful capacity for organisation.'

'So does the Superintendent, sir,' said Colbeck, giving credit where it was due. 'And unlike Colonel Rowan, he does not insist on retaining his army rank. He chooses to be plain Mister instead of Major Tallis.'

Mayne smiled. 'He will always be Major Tallis to me,'

he said, wryly. 'But enough of him, Inspector – tell me a little about yourself.'

'You have my police record in front of you, sir.'

'I am more interested in your life before you joined us. Like me, I believe, you trained as a lawyer. Were you called to the bar?'

'Yes, sir.'

'Why did you not pursue that career? I should imagine that you cut quite a figure in a courtroom.'

'Personal circumstances had a bearing on my decision to turn my talents elsewhere,' explained Colbeck, not wishing to provide any details. 'In any case, I found the life of a barrister far less fulfilling than I imagined it would be.'

'I had the same experience, Inspector. Unless one is successful, it can be an impecunious profession.'

'Money was not that issue in my case, sir. I was disillusioned because I was always dealing with crime after the event, and it seemed to me that, with sensible policing, so much of it could have been prevented from happening in the first place.'

'Prevention is ever our watchword.'

'It's the main reason that I joined the Metropolitan Police Force.'

'You were far more educated than our average recruit.'

'Educated in criminal law, perhaps,' said Colbeck, 'but I had a lot to learn about the criminal mind. One can only do that by pitting oneself against it on a daily basis.'

'Judging by your record, you were an apt pupil.'

'I was fortunate enough to secure an early promotion.'

'It is we who are fortunate to have you,' said Mayne, glancing down at the open file on his desk. 'Though your service record has not been without its minor setbacks.'

'I prefer to see them as my idiosyncrasies, sir.'

'That's not what Superintendent Tallis calls them. He has had to reprimand you more than once. This time, of course,' he went on, closing the file, 'he will have nothing but praise for you.'

'I am not sure about that.'

'You are the hero of the hour, Inspector Colbeck.'

'There were three of us involved in that surveillance, sir.'

'I am well aware of that.'

'What you may not be aware of is the means by which Brendan Mulryne came to be on the scene. Sergeant Leeming had a perfect right to be there,' said Colbeck, 'but there is a slight problem where Mulryne is concerned. To that end, I wonder if I might ask you a favour?'

'Please do,' said Mayne, expansively. 'After your achievements last night, you are in a position to ask anything.'

'Thank you, sir. The truth is that I need your help.'

After making discreet inquiries, Thomas Sholto repaired immediately to Sir Humphrey Gilzean's house. He steeled himself to break the bad news. Ashen with cold fury, Gilzean had already anticipated it.

'They failed,' he said.

'Yes, Humphrey.'

'They let me down again.'

'Not for want of trying.'

'With all that gunpowder, they could not even contrive a small explosion. I lay awake in bed, listening – and nothing happened.'

'That's not quite true.'

Gilzean stamped a foot. 'They'll wish they'd never been born!'

'You would never get close enough to chastise them,' said Sholto. 'The tidings are worse than you feared. Jukes and the Seymour brothers walked into an ambush at the Crystal Palace.'

'An ambush?'

'All three are taken, Humphrey.'

'What!' exclaimed Gilzean.

'They are in police custody. From what I can gather, this Inspector Colbeck laid a trap for them and they walked into it.'

'But how could he possibly know that they would be there?'

'I think that he is much cleverer than we imagined.'

Gilzean's fury changed to concern. Dropping into a high-backed leather armchair, he became pensive. The house was in Upper Brook Street, close enough to Hyde Park for him to hear any explosion that occurred in the Crystal Palace. Long before dawn had broken, he realised that the mission had been unsuccessful but it had never crossed his mind that his men had been arrested.

'We have one comfort,' said Sholto. 'They will not betray us.'

'They have already done so, Thomas.'

'How?'

'By getting themselves caught,' said Gilzean. 'If this Inspector is clever enough to apprehend them, it will not take him long to find out that all three served in our regiment. That will set him on a trail that leads directly to us.'

'Perhaps we should quit London and go into hiding.'

'No, Thomas. There is no danger yet.'

'But there soon will be.'

'Only if we let things take their natural course.'

'What else can we do, Humphrey?'

'Divert them,' said Gilzean, getting to his feet. 'At every stage, we have relied on the slowness and inefficiency of the police. We have out-manoeuvred them with comparative ease. Until now, that is. It seems that we underestimated them, Thomas. They have one man within their ranks who has a keen intelligence.'

'Inspector Robert Colbeck.'

'What do we know about him?'

'Only what we have read in the newspaper.'

'Find out more,' said Gilzean. 'We need to identify his weakness. Is he married? Does he have children? Who are the loved ones in his life? If we have that information in our hands, we can distract him from his investigation and buy ourselves some valuable time.'

'Supposing that he is a bachelor with no family ties?'

'Every man has someone he cares about,' insisted Gilzean, dark eyes gleaming. 'All you have to do is to find out who it is.'

Madeleine Andrews was pleased when the visitor arrived. Still in his working clothes, Frank Pike had called on his way home from Euston Station and he had brought plenty of gossip to share with his friend. After all this time, the fireman was still blaming himself for the injury to Caleb Andrews and he began with another battery of apologies. Madeleine hoped to leave the two men alone in the bedroom, but her father decided to use Pike as a court of appeal.

'What do *you* think, Frank?' he asked.

'About what?'

'Gideon Little.'

'I think he'll be a driver before I am,' said Pike, honestly. 'Gideon may be younger than me but he learns faster. I think that he's one of the best fireman in the company.'

'There you are, Maddy,' said Andrews, pointedly.

'I never doubted his abilities,' she replied.

'Gideon has a bright future ahead of him. All that he needs is a loving wife to support and cherish him.'

Pike grinned. 'Is there an engagement in the wind?' he asked.

'No,' said Madeleine.

'Not yet, anyway,' said Andrews.

'Father!'

243

'You may come to your senses in the end, Maddy.'

'It would make Gideon the happiest man on the railway,' said Pike, 'I know that. He never stops talking about you, Madeleine. Some of the others tease him about it.'

She was roused. 'So my name is taken in vain, is it?'

'No, no.'

'You and the others are having a laugh at my expense.'

'I'd never do that, Madeleine,' said Pike, overcome with remorse, 'and I'm sorry if I gave you that idea. No,' he went on, 'I promise you that nobody would dare to mock you.'

'They'd have me to answer to, if they did,' said Andrews.

'Gideon is the only one they tease.'

'Yes,' she said. 'About me.'

'About . . . being the way that he is.'

'Besotted with my daughter,' observed Andrews. 'You cannot stay single for ever, Maddy. Choose the right person and marriage is the most wonderful institution ever invented. Am I right, Frank?'

'Yes, Caleb.'

'Do you wish that you were still a bachelor?'

'Not for a moment,' said Pike, chuckling merrily. 'Rose has made me very happy and she seems to be content with me.'

Andrews cackled. 'Heaven knows why!'

'Getting married changed my life for the better.'

'You hear that, Maddy?'

'I can recommend it,' said Pike.

'So can I,' said Andrews. 'How much longer do we have to wait?'

Madeleine did not trust herself to reply. She was fond of Frank Pike and did not wish to have a quarrel with her father in front of him. More to the point, she did not want to deal with an issue that, as far as she was concerned, had finally been settled. Hounded for a decision, Madeleine had told Gideon Little the painful truth. What she had not admitted was that her affections had been placed elsewhere. For a woman like her, Robert Colbeck might be unobtainable but that only served to increase his attraction.

'I'll make some tea,' she said, and went out abruptly.

Since a window had been opened to admit fresh air, the office was free from the stink of cigar smoke for once yet the atmosphere remained unpleasant. Superintendent Edward Tallis was spoiling for a fight. He stood inches away from Inspector Colbeck.

'Whatever did you think you were *doing*?' he yelled.

'Taking the necessary steps to achieve an objective, sir.'

'Brendan Mulryne was supposed to be in custody.'

'Arrangements were made,' said Colbeck.

'What sort of arrangements?'

'I looked more closely at the charges against him, Superintendent. There are several witnesses at The Black Dog in the Devil's Acre, who will swear that Mulryne did not start the affray. He was not even there when it flared up. Mulryne is paid to quell such outbursts. Those he knocked out during the brawl certainly have no complaint against him. They made the mistake of taking on a stronger man. As for the damage he caused to a window,' he revealed, 'nobody is prepared to bring a charge against him on that account.'

'That Irish gorilla assaulted four policemen,' said Tallis.

'Only because they provoked him, sir,' replied Colbeck, 'and they now admit that. I spoke to the custody sergeant. Since he's been behind bars, Mulryne has been a model prisoner. He's even made his peace with the four men who tried to arrest him.'

'Turning on that blarney of his no doubt!'

'Mulryne was one of them, remember. In his heart, I suspect, he would still like to be.'

'Not as long as I have anything to say about it!'

'I raised the matter with Mr Mayne earlier on.'

Tallis was horrified. 'You tried to get Mulryne reinstated?'

'No,' said Colbeck, 'that would have been asking too much, and in any case, it's too late for that. No, Superintendent, I wanted to discuss a point of law with him.'

'When it comes to law, you only need to know one thing with regard to Brendan Mulryne. He's on the wrong side of it.'

'Technically, he's not.'

'He resisted arrest.'

'The four officers involved see it rather differently now.'

'They cannot change their minds about a thing like that.'

'According to Mr Mayne,' said Colbeck, levelly, 'they can. If, on mature reflection, they feel that their report of the incident was slightly inaccurate, they can amend it when they give their statements in court. Like me, Mr Mayne agreed that Mulryne should get off with a small fine.'

'A small fine!' roared Tallis.

'I will be happy to pay it on his behalf.'

'Inspector, he attacked four policemen.'

'I prefer to remember the two villains whom he took on last night, sir. Both were armed but Mulryne squared up to them nevertheless. All that Sergeant Leeming had to do was to snap on the handcuffs.'

'Mulryne had no right to be there in the first place.'

'You said that I had a free hand to choose my men.'

'I assumed they would be from inside the police force.'

'Nobody else could have done what Mulryne did last night.'

'That does not exonerate him, Inspector,' said Tallis, sourly. 'Or you, for that matter.'

Colbeck met his glare. 'Mr Mayne felt that it did, sir,' he pointed out, calmly. 'Since you feel so strongly about it, perhaps you should take it up with him.'

Tallis was halted in his tracks. Whatever else he did, he could not countermand the orders of his superior. Colbeck not only had the Police Commissioner on his side, he had, by effecting the three arrests at the Crystal Palace, earned the admiration of the whole department. A vital breakthrough had at last been made in the investigation. To harry him after such a triumph would be seen as sheer vindictiveness. Tallis retreated to the safety of his desk and took out a cigar from its case. Inhaling deeply as he ignited it, he watched Colbeck through the smoke.

'I will remember this, Inspector,' he said, sternly.

'It is all a matter of record, Superintendent.'

'What do you intend to do now?'

'Question the three men in custody,' said Colbeck. 'They may not give us the name that we want but we can still squeeze some information out of them. Arthur Jukes is their leader. I'll start with him. To be frank, I hoped that you might join me, sir.'

'Me?'

'You know how to speak to an army man.'

'That's true,' said Tallis, slightly mollified, 'though all three of them are a disgrace to their regiment. If they were still in uniform, they'd be court-martialled.'

'Make that point to them,' advised Colbeck. 'If I introduce you as Major Tallis, it will increase your authority. Do you agree, sir?'

Tallis straightened his back. 'Yes, Inspector. I think that I do.'

'And we will need the services of an artist.'

'An artist?'

'To draw sketches of the three men,' explained

Colbeck. 'I want to see if Caleb Andrews recognises any of them. Since he is unable to come here to identify the prisoners, we will have to take a likeness of them to him. He might pick out the man who assaulted him.'

'The fireman can do that – what was his name?'

'Frank Pike.'

'Arrange for him to call here.'

'I will, sir,' said Colbeck, smoothly, 'but I think that Mr Andrews is entitled to have a first look at these three men. After all, he was the real victim.'

'True enough.'

'He also deserves to know that we have taken such an important step forward in the investigation. When we finish questioning the prisoners, I'll go across to Camden to apprise him of the situation. I have more than one reason for wishing to see him,' he added, thinking of Madeleine. 'Please put an artist to work as soon as you can.'

Thomas Sholto moved swiftly. In the space of a few hours, he had gathered sufficient information about Robert Colbeck to take back to the house in Upper Brook Street. Sir Humphrey Gilzean was waiting for him. When his manservant showed the visitor into the drawing room, Gilzean got to his feet with urgency.

'Well?' he said.

'I arrived just in time, Humphrey.'

'In what way?'

'When I got to Scotland Yard, there was a crowd of

reporters waiting to hear details of the arrests. I mingled with them.'

'Did you get inside?'

'Yes,' said Sholto, 'I pretended that I worked for a provincial newspaper. Nobody paid any attention to me, tucked away at the back.'

'Who gave the statement? Inspector Colbeck?'

'No, it was Superintendent Tallis. A military man, by the look of him. He introduced us to the Inspector but would not let him answer any questions. Tallis has taken some severe criticism in the press,' explained Sholto. 'He wanted to make sure that he was seen in a better light this time. That's why he stole all the attention.'

'So what exactly *did* take place at the Crystal Palace last night?'

'Three men lay in wait near the locomotives. When Jukes and the others gained entry, they were promptly arrested.'

'Three against three? Why did they not fight their way out?'

'They tried, Humphrey, but they were soon overpowered.'

'Inspector Colbeck is a brave man,' said Gilzean, 'but he took a foolish risk when he fought on equal terms. He is obviously no soldier or he would have had a dozen policemen at his back.'

'Nevertheless, he got the better of Jukes and the Seymours.'

'How on earth did he come to be there in the first

place? Was it a complete coincidence or a case of inspired guesswork?'

'Neither,' replied Sholto. 'According to the Superintendent, they realised that the shipment of glass for the Great Exhibition was the intended target of the Kilsby Tunnel explosion. That led them on – at least, it led Inspector Colbeck on – to the conviction that the locomotives on display at the Crystal Palace were in potential danger. Last night was the third during which he kept vigil.'

'A patient man, clearly.'

'And a powerful one. It seems that he tackled Arthur Jukes on his own and beat him into submission – even though he had to take a few blows himself.'

'Jukes is a tough character. He would have fought like a tiger.'

'The tiger has now been caged.'

Gilzean nodded soulfully. It had given him pleasure to organise the train robbery, to inflict damage on a railway company and to outwit the detectives who were put in charge of the case. The murders of William Ings and Daniel Slender had been necessities rather than sources of enjoyment, though they had also been carried out in order to muddy the waters of the investigation. Someone, it now transpired, was able to see clearly through muddy waters and it was troubling.

'What manner of man is this Robert Colbeck?' he asked.

'A positive dandy.'

'Yet able to acquit himself well in a fight.'

'I'd not like to take him on, Humphrey.'

Sholto went on to give of description of Colbeck's appearance and behaviour. Since the Inspector was clearly known to the other reporters, Sholto had taken the trouble to talk to as many of them as possible, picking up all kinds of anecdotes about Colbeck. He retailed them to Gilzean, who assimilated all the facts he had been given.

'Tall, handsome, single,' he noted. 'He must be a ladies' man.'

'Apparently not.'

Gilzean was curious. 'Are you telling me that he seeks exclusively *male* company?'

'No,' said Sholto. 'I would never accuse him of that.'

'Then he must have a social life of some kind.'

'One of the reporters told me that Colbeck is something of a mystery. He trained as a lawyer, went to the bar, then, for some inexplicable reason, chose to become a policeman.'

'There's no such thing as an inexplicable reason, Thomas. A man would only make such a radical change of direction if he were prompted by just cause. It would help us if we knew what it was.'

'There was one rumour.'

'Go on.'

'Someone told me that there had been an incident in his past,' said Sholto, 'involving a broken engagement.'

'Now we are getting somewhere!'

'It was some years ago, apparently.'

'Who was the lady in question?'

'I did not get a name.'

'See if you can discover what it is, Thomas,' said Gilzean. 'We may be able to use it as a lever. Inspector Robert Colbeck must have some human contact, surely. No parents still alive, no brothers or sisters, no close friends – I do not believe it. There has to be *someone*.'

'How can we find out?'

'By having him followed.'

'That will not be easy.'

'He does not spend twenty-four hours a day at Scotland Yard. And when he leaves, I doubt if he always goes home to an empty house. Have him followed, Thomas,' he instructed. 'We'll soon unravel the mystery of Robert Colbeck.'

When she finally had some time to herself, Madeleine Andrews chose to read the newspaper cuttings that she had kept since the train robbery. Her father's injuries were mentioned but the name that she paid most attention to was that of Robert Colbeck, wondering how she could manage to meet him again without seeming forward. Madeleine recalled their last conversation and smiled. She was still annoyed that she had been followed to Scotland Yard by Gideon Little but that did not prevent her feeling a pang of sympathy for him. If he were so obsessed with Madeleine that he would shadow her across London, he had to be pitied. She hoped that he would find someone else to whom he could transfer his stifling affections.

There was a loud knock at the door. Fearing that it might be Gideon Little, she was minded to ignore the caller at first but her father's yell from upstairs made that impossible. It might well be another visitor for him and she was grateful for anyone who could offer him some distraction. Putting the cuttings away in a drawer, therefore, she went to open the front door.

'Oh, my goodness!' she cried.

Her exclamation blended pleasure with sheer fright. While she was overjoyed to see Colbeck standing there, she was shocked at the sight of the bruising on his face.

'Hello, Miss Andrews,' he said, raising his hat.

'What happened to you?' she asked with concern.

'That is what I came to tell you.'

She noticed the bandage. 'And your hand is injured as well.'

'A minor problem. Is it convenient for me to come in?'

'Yes, yes,' said Madeleine, backing away and wishing that she had known that he was about to call. 'Forgive my appearance.'

'I see nothing whatsoever wrong with it.'

'This is my working dress, Inspector.'

'And very charming you look in it, Miss Andrews.'

'Thank you,' she said. 'Do you wish to see Father?'

'Yes, please. I have some good news for both of you.'

She led him up the staircase and he watched her hips swaying entrancingly to and fro in front of him. Stepping into the bedroom, he was greeted by a look of surprise from Caleb Andrews.

'Have you been fighting, Inspector?' he said, staring at his face.

'A light scuffle, Mr Andrews,' replied Colbeck. 'Nothing more. My injuries pale beside yours even though we may possibly have come up against the same man.'

'What do you mean?'

'Three arrests were made last night. The men were all members of the gang involved in the train robbery.'

'At last!' said Madeleine.

'We still have to round up the others, of course, but we feel that we are definitely closing in on them now. Last night was a turning point.'

'Tell us why, Inspector,' urged Andrews. 'We want the details.'

Without even saying that they had been acting on his initiative, Colbeck told them about the successful ambush at the Crystal Palace and gave them the names of the three men in custody. Madeleine clapped her hands together in delight but her father shook his head.

'Those names mean nothing to me,' he said.

'Perhaps their faces will, Mr Andrews.'

'You're going to bring the rogues here for me to see them?'

'I already have,' said Colbeck, taking some sheets of paper from inside his coat and opening them out. 'These are only sketches, mark you, but I think that the artist caught the salient features of each man. Here,' he went on, passing the first sketch to Andrews, 'this is Harry Seymour. Do you recognise him?'

'No,' said Andrews, squinting at the paper. 'No, I don't think so.'

'What about his brother, Vernon?'

'Let me see.' He took the second sketch then shook his head. 'No, this is not the man either. He was bigger and with an uglier face.'

'Perhaps it was Arthur Jukes, then,' said Colbeck, showing him the last drawing. 'Ignore the black eye,' he advised. 'That's what I gave him when he had the temerity to fight back. Those whiskers of his are ginger, by the way.'

'It's him!' asserted Andrews, waving the paper. 'This is him!'

'Are you certain?'

'As certain as I am of anything. This is the devil who hit me.'

'Then that's one more charge for him to answer.'

'Frank Pike was there as well,' recalled Madeleine. 'He probably got a closer look at this man than Father.'

'I intend to call on Mr Pike to show him these sketches,' said Colbeck. 'If he agrees with your father that Jukes is the man, he can come and see him in person, just to make sure.'

'Take me along as well, Inspector,' said Andrews.

'No, Father,' said Madeleine. 'You must stay here.'

'I want to tell that villain what I think of him, Maddy.'

'Mr Pike will surely do that on your behalf,' said

Colbeck, taking the sketches back and slipping them into his pocket. 'Well, I'm delighted that we have such a positive identification.'

'How many other men are involved?' wondered Madeleine.

'That has yet to be determined, Miss Andrews, but we intend to hunt down each and every one. Apart from the robbery, there are two murders and an explosion at Kilsby Tunnel to be laid at their door.'

'And an attempted outrage at the Crystal Palace.'

'Blowing up those wonderful locomotives?' said Andrews, still appalled at the idea. 'That's worse than a crime – it's downright evil.'

'They were all saved for the visitors to enjoy them,' said Colbeck. 'And what amazing machines they are! After spending three nights lying beneath *Liverpool*, I got to know her extremely well. Mr Crampton is a brilliant man.'

'A genius, Inspector.'

'I only wish that I could persuade Sergeant Leeming of that. He hates trains, I fear, and being forced to sleep under a locomotive did not endear him to the notion of rail travel.'

'Who is Sergeant Leeming?' said Andrews.

'Your daughter will explain – she's met him. Well,' said Colbeck, 'now that I've passed on the glad tidings, I'll be on my way.' He smiled at the invalid. 'I'm pleased to see that you're looking somewhat better, Mr Andrews.'

'I can't say the same about you, Inspector.'

'That's not very tactful, Father,' said Madeleine.

'It's an honest comment, Maddy.'

'It is,' agreed Colbeck. 'When I saw myself in the shaving mirror this morning, I had quite a shock. It looks far worse than it feels.'

After trading farewells, he went downstairs and made for the front door. Madeleine was at his heels, determined to have a word with him alone. When he let himself out, she stood on the doorstep. Colbeck kept his top hat in his hand while he talked.

'I hope that the news will act as a tonic for your father,' he said.

'It will, Inspector. It has certainly cheered me.'

'I have the feeling that he can be a difficult patient.'

'Quite impossible at times.'

'Fretful and demanding?'

'Only on good days, Inspector.'

They shared a laugh and he watched her cheeks dimple again. She had a way of putting her head slightly to one side that intrigued him. For her part, she noticed the sparkle of interest in his eyes. It implanted a distant hope in her breast.

'Where are you going now?' she asked.

'To call on Frank Pike,' he replied. 'After that, I have to go straight back to Scotland Yard.'

'Do you never rest, Inspector?'

'Not when I am in the middle of an investigation.'

'Your family must miss you terribly.'

'I live alone, Miss Andrews,' he said, glad of the

258

opportunity to reveal his circumstances. 'My parents died some years ago and I have never felt it entirely fair to invite anyone to share the life of a detective.' He pointed to his face. 'What wife wishes to see her husband coming home like this, especially after he has been absent from the marital couch for three nights?'

'Some wives have to put up with a lot more than that, Inspector.'

'By choice?'

'Of course,' she said, earnestly. 'If a woman really loves her husband, then she will happily endure all the disadvantages that his job might bring. I know that that was my mother's attitude. Being the wife of a railwayman has many drawbacks, believe me.'

'Is that why you spurned the opportunity yourself?'

'Not at all.'

'But I understood you to say that you had rejected your suitor.'

'Only because he was not the right man for me,' she explained. 'It was nothing to do with his occupation. If Gideon had been the husband of my choice, it would not have mattered whether he were a railwayman or a road sweeper.'

'I see that you are a romantic, Miss Andrews.'

'I have always thought of myself as a practical woman.'

'Even a practical woman can have romantic inclinations,' he said, holding her gaze for a long time. 'However,' he added, putting his hat on, 'I must not keep you talking out here in the street. You have things to do and I have somewhere to go. Goodbye, Miss Andrews.'

'Goodbye, Inspector.'

She offered her hand in the expectation that he would shake it but Colbeck instead brought it to his lips and planted a gentle kiss on it. Madeleine was thrilled and he was pleased with her reaction. The tender moment between them did not go unobserved. Seated in a cab a little way down the street was a man who had followed Colbeck all the way from Scotland Yard. Watching the two of them in conversation, he felt that he would have something of great interest to report.

Superintendent Tallis could not believe his eyes. As he stepped into the corridor, he saw Brendan Mulryne walking jauntily towards him, a broad smile covering his battered face. The Irishman offered his hand.

'Good day to you, Superintendent,' he said, cordially.

'What, in the name of Christ, are you doing here?' demanded Tallis, declining the handshake. 'You should be locked up.'

'I've been released on bail.'

'On whose authority?'

'Mr Mayne himself,' said the Irishman. 'I've just spoken to him. He wanted to congratulate me on the help that I gave at the Crystal Palace. I'm moving up in the world,' he went on, chuckling. 'I never thought that I'd get to meet a Police Commissioner face to face.'

'You should not have been at the Crystal Palace in the first place.'

'Inspector Colbeck wanted me there.'

'He was exceeding his authority.'

'What does it matter, sir?'

'It matters a great deal, Mulryne,' said Tallis, acidly, 'as you should know. A police force is run on discipline. It was a lesson that you never learnt when you were in uniform.'

'There were too many rules and regulations.'

'You managed to break each and every one of them.'

Mulryne beamed. 'I never was a man for half-measures.'

'You were an embarrassment to all of us.'

'Inspector Colbeck doesn't think so. Neither does Mr Mayne. By the way, Superintendent, did you know that we had something in common – me and the Police Commissioner, that is?'

'Beyond the fact that you both happen to be Irish,' said Tallis, superciliously, 'I can't see the slightest affinity.'

'That's because you don't know my background, see. It turns out that Mr Mayne's father was one of the judges of the Court of King's Bench in Dublin. In short,' said Mulryne, cheerily, 'he must have been the same Judge Mayne that sent my father to prison for three years for a crime that he didn't commit.'

'I should have guessed that you're the son of a convicted criminal.'

'It was the reason I wanted to be a policeman.'

'Old habits die hard, Mulryne.'

'Yes,' said the other, 'so I notice, Superintendent. You still have a habit of smoking those foul cigars.' He sniffed Tallis's lapel. 'Sure, I can smell the stink of them in your clothes.'

Tallis pushed him away. 'Get off, man – and get out of here!'

'Is there any chance of a word with Inspector Colbeck first?'

'No, the Inspector is busy.'

'I don't mind waiting.'

'I'll not have you on the premises. Besides,' he said, 'Inspector Colbeck may be some time. He is about to question one of the men who was arrested last night.'

'Have they given you the names of their accomplices yet?'

'Unfortunately, they have not.'

'Then you should let me talk to them,' offered Mulryne, pounding a fist into the palm of the other hand. 'Put me in a cell with one of them and I'd have him talking his head off inside two minutes.'

'We do not resort to violence.'

'A crying shame!'

'In any case, even you would not be able to beat a confession out of them. I have been interrogating criminals for several years but I could not break down their resistance.'

'Maybe you asked the wrong questions.'

'Inspector Colbeck is seeing one of the men for the second time,' explained Tallis. 'He feels that he now has a means of opening the man's mouth a little.'

Frank Pike had no hesitation in identifying the man. When he saw Arthur Jukes through the bars of his cell, he picked him out immediately as the person who had clubbed Caleb Andrews to the ground and forced the fireman to drive the locomotive off the track. Pike also recognised the Seymour brothers as having been involved in the robbery. Robert Colbeck's problem was to get the fireman out of there. Confronted with the man who had held a pistol on him, Pike wanted retribution and, denied the opportunity to attack the man, he yelled abuse at Jukes through the bars. Jukes replied in kind and the air was blue with ripe language. Colbeck needed the help of Victor Leeming to hustle the visitor out of the area.

When Pike had left, the detectives questioned Jukes in a room that contained nothing beyond a table and three chairs. Still handcuffed, Jukes was surly and withdrawn.

'You have been formally identified as the man who assaulted the driver of that train,' said Colbeck. 'Do you admit the crime?'

'No,' replied Jukes.

'Mr Andrews himself identified the artist's sketch of you.'

'So?'

'We have two eyewitnesses, Mr Jukes.'

'Had Mr Andrews died from his injuries,' said

263

Leeming, 'you might now be facing a charge of murder. That's a hanging offence.'

'Mr Jukes might still have the opportunity to mount the gallows,' Colbeck reminded him. 'The murders of William Ings and Daniel Slender have yet to be accounted for. Were you responsible for those, Mr Jukes?'

'No,' asserted the other.

'Are you sure?'

'I'm no killer, Inspector Colbeck.'

'Yet the army taught you how to take a man's life.'

'That was different.'

'Did you kill anyone when you were in uniform?'

'Only in combat.'

'You have admitted something at last,' said Colbeck, watching the prisoner's eyes. 'We are starting to make progress.'

'What about the explosion at the Kilsby Tunnel?' asked Leeming. 'I suppose that you were not party to that either.'

'No,' said Jukes. 'This is the first I've heard about it.'

'I think that you are lying.'

'You may think what you wish, Sergeant.'

'Since we caught you with a barrel of gunpowder at the Crystal Palace, it's logical to assume that you caused the earlier explosion. You and your accomplices are obviously experienced in such work.'

Jukes was stony-faced. 'Are we?'

'Let me ask you another question,' said Colbeck, changing his tack. 'Why did you leave the army?'

'Because I only enlisted for a certain number of years.'

'What occupation did you take up?'

'That's my business.'

'Discharged soldiers often find it difficult to get employment.'

'I managed,' said Jukes, uneasily.

'Even though you had no trade to follow?'

'One of the Seymour brothers told us that he worked as a slaughterman in an abattoir,' said Leeming. 'Is that the sort of job you were forced to take, Mr Jukes?'

'Of course not,' snarled the prisoner.

'You must have done something,' argued Colbeck. 'When you were arrested, you were wearing a wedding ring. I remember feeling it when you punched me,' he said, rubbing his chin. 'That means you have a wife to support, Mr Jukes. How did you do it?'

'Leave my wife out of this!'

'Do you have children, by any chance?'

'My family do not go short.'

'But they will suffer now, won't they?' Jukes scowled at him before turning his head away. 'What I am trying to suggest to you,' said Colbeck, gently, 'is that you may have been earning a paltry wage – or, perhaps, were actually out of work – when you received the invitation to take part in a train robbery. You are not, by instinct, a criminal, Mr Jukes. What drove you to break the law was the desire to do better for your family.'

'Is that true?' pressed Leeming.

'Does your wife *know* where all that money came from?'

'Did you tell her what you were going to do at the Crystal Palace?'

Jukes said nothing, but his silence was eloquent. As he stared unseeingly in front of him, there was a deep sadness in his eyes. The detectives noted how tense the prisoner's whole body had become.

'There is only one way to help yourself,' advised Colbeck, 'and that is by cooperating with us. Any assistance you give will be looked upon favourably by the judge.'

'It could well lead to a reduction in your sentence,' said Leeming.

'So tell us, Mr Jukes. Who organised the train robbery?'

'Was it someone you met in the army?'

'Or someone you were introduced to by the Seymour brothers? We will catch the man before long, Mr Jukes,' said Colbeck, 'make no mistake about that. But you are in a position to save us time and trouble. Now, then,' he went on, leaning forward across the table, 'why not think of your own plight and seek to ease it? Give us his name.'

'Never,' retorted Jukes.

'Your loyalty is mistaken.'

'You're the one who's mistaken, Inspector. You may have had the luck to catch us but that's as far as you'll get. Harry and Vernon are like me. We'd sooner hang than tell you the name you want. As for catching him before long,' he added with a mocking laugh, 'you are in for a big surprise. He can run rings around the Metropolitan Police Force. You'll never catch him in a month of Sundays.'

It happened in broad daylight. Madeleine Andrews had just made her father comfortable in bed next morning when she heard a knock at the front door. She glanced through the bedroom window and saw a uniformed policeman below. Thinking that he might have brought more news, she hurried downstairs to open the door. The policeman, a bearded man with a polite manner, touched the brim of his hat.

'Miss Madeleine Andrews?' he inquired.

'Yes.'

'I have come with a request from Inspector Colbeck. He wonders if you could spare an hour to call on him at Scotland Yard.'

Madeleine was taken aback. '*Now*?'

'I have a cab to take you there,' said the other, 'and it will bring you back to your house.'

'Did the Inspector say why he wished to see me?'

'No, Miss Andrews, but it must be a matter of some importance or he would not be summoning you like this.' He made to leave. 'I can see that it is not convenient. I'll tell Inspector Colbeck that he will have to meet you another time.'

'Wait,' she said. 'I can come with you. I just need to tell my father where I am going first. Please excuse me.'

'Of course.'

Madeleine went back upstairs, explained the situation

to her father and promised that she would not be long. She went quickly into her own bedroom to look at herself in the mirror and to adjust her clothing and hair. When she reappeared at the door, she was wearing a hat.

'This way, Miss Andrews,' said the policeman.

He escorted her to the waiting cab and helped her up into it. As soon as he sat beside her, however, his manner changed abruptly. One arm around Madeleine to restrain her, he used the other hand to cover her mouth with a handkerchief.

'Do as you're told,' ordered Thomas Sholto, 'or you'll never see your precious Inspector Colbeck again.'

The cab was driven away at speed.

CHAPTER ELEVEN

Arthur Jukes gave nothing away. No matter how much pressure they applied, the detectives could not get the answers that they required. They interrogated the other prisoners separately but with the same negative result. Vernon Seymour was openly defiant and his younger brother, Harry, boasted that they would not stay under lock and key for long. He seemed to have a naïve faith that someone would come to his rescue and confound the forces of law and order. When all three men were back in their cells, Robert Colbeck adjourned to his office with Victor Leeming. The Sergeant was not optimistic.

'It's like trying to get blood out of a stone,' he moaned.

'We need to be patient, Victor.'

'We failed. I thought it was a brilliant idea of yours to let Mr Tallis loose on them but even he, with his military background, could not frighten them into revealing the name of their paymaster. Why are they so loyal to this man?'

'I think it's a combination of loyalty and fear,' said Colbeck. 'They know just how ruthless he can be. Even if they were not directly involved in the murders of William Ings and Daniel Slender, they would surely be aware of them. If they betray their leader, they are afraid that they will be signing their own death warrants.'

'But they are in police custody.'

'I regret to admit it, Victor, but there are ways of getting to people even when they are in the most secure prisons. No,' said Colbeck, 'there's little chance that any of them will volunteer the name that we seek. All that we can do is to remain calm, question them at intervals and hope that one of them makes a slip.'

'Which one?'

'Harry Seymour would be my choice. He's the youngest.'

'He's convinced that he is about to be rescued.'

'That proves my point. Whoever has been employing the three men has persuaded them that he is invincible, and that he has the power to get them out of any situation. In other words, he must be a man of considerable influence.'

'Nobody is above the law,' said Leeming.

'This man obviously believes that he is.'

'Where do we go from here, Inspector?'

Colbeck rested against the edge of his desk and

pondered. Having caught the three men in the act of committing a heinous crime, he had hoped that they had taken a giant stride forward in the investigation but they had suddenly come to a halt. Evidently, Arthur Jukes and the Seymour brothers had been taught how to behave in the event of arrest. In taking them out of action, Colbeck and his men had performed a valuable service but the rest of the gang was at liberty and there was no simple way of identifying them. What was certain was that the failure of his plot to blow up the locomotives at the Crystal Palace would enrage the man who had set it in motion. Colbeck feared reprisals.

'First, we must find out which regiment they served in,' he said.

'They refused to tell us.'

'We have their names, Victor. It is only a question of checking the records. I leave that to you.'

'Where do I start?' asked Leeming, over-awed by the task.

'With regiments that have served in India.'

'India?'

'You saw the complexion of those three men,' said Colbeck. 'They have clearly spent time in a hot country. Also, Harry Seymour made his first slip. The custody sergeant told me that he had the gall to ask when tiffin would be brought to his cell.'

'Tiffin?'

'It's an Indian word for a midday meal.'

'The bare-faced cheek of the man!' said Leeming,

angrily. 'What does Harry Seymour expect – a dozen oysters and a pint of beer, with apple pie to follow? He'll be asking for a butler next.'

'My guess is that all three of them were in an infantry regiment. The brothers would certainly have served together and they treat Jukes with that mixture of jocularity and respect that soldiers reserve for a corporal or a sergeant. When people have been in the army for any length of time,' observed Colbeck, 'they can never entirely shake off its effects.'

'You only have to look at Mr Tallis to see that.'

Colbeck smiled. '*Major* Tallis, please.'

'Did *he* have any idea which regiment they might have been in?'

'Not his own, anyway – the 6th Dragoon Guards. None of them would have lasted a week in that, according to the Superintendent. He had a very low opinion of them as soldiers.'

'Someone obviously values their abilities.'

'The most likely person,' said Colbeck, 'is an officer from the same regiment, someone whom they would instinctively obey. When you find where they served in India, make a list of any officers who have retired from their regiment in recent years.'

'Yes, Inspector.'

'After that, I have another assignment for you.'

Leeming grimaced. 'I thought that you might.'

'Visit all of the slaughterhouses within the London area,' suggested Colbeck. 'If Vernon Seymour used to work in one of them, they'll remember him and might even provide an address.'

'Regiments and slaughterhouses.'

'That should keep you busy.'

'This job never lacks for variety.'

'The more we can find out about those three men, the better.'

'What about Jukes? He's the only one who has a wife and family.'

'So?'

'Should we not try to track them down, sir?'

'No need of that, Victor. You saw the fellow earlier on. The one moment he looked vulnerable was when we touched on his marriage.'

'Yes,' recalled Leeming. 'He obviously cares for his wife.'

'Then she will doubtless love him in return,' said Colbeck. 'When he's been missing long enough, she'll become alarmed and turn to us for help. All that we have to do is to wait.'

'I'll make a start with those regimental records.'

'The Superintendent will be able to offer guidance. I daresay that he'll reel some of the names straight off.'

'I was banking on that, sir.' He opened the door. 'This may take me some time – well into tomorrow, probably. What about you, sir?'

'Oh, I'll be here for hours yet. It will be another late night for me.'

'At least we do not have to spend it underneath a locomotive.'

273

Colbeck laughed and Leeming went out. Three nights without sleep were starting to take their toll on both of them but the Inspector drove himself on. There was no time to rest on his laurels. The man he was after was still in a position to make further strikes against railways and Colbeck was determined to get to him before he did so. Sitting behind his desk, he took out his notebook and went through all the details he had gathered during his interviews with the three prisoners. What stood out was the similarity of their denials. It was almost as if they had agreed what they were going to say even though they had deliberately been kept in separate cells. Someone had drilled them well.

An hour later, Colbeck was still bent over his desk, working by the light of the gas lamp that shed a golden circle around one end of the room. When there was a tap on the door, he did not at first hear it. A second and much louder knock made him look up.

'Come in!' he called. A clerk entered. 'Yes?'

'Someone wishes to see you, Inspector.'

Colbeck's hopes rose. 'A young lady, by any chance?'

'No, sir. A man called Gideon Little.'

'Did he say what he wanted?'

'Only that it was a matter of the utmost importance.'

'Show him in.'

The clerk went out and left Colbeck to speculate on the reason for the unexpected visit. He remembered that Little was the suitor whom Madeleine Andrews had chosen to turn down. Colbeck wondered if the man had come to blame him for the fact that he had been rejected, though he could not imagine why. As soon as he saw Gideon Little, however, he realised that his visitor had not come to tax him in any way. The man was hesitant and agitated. Dressed in his work clothes, he stepped into the room and looked nervously around it, patently unused to being in an office. Colbeck introduced himself and offered him a chair but Little refused. Taking a few tentative steps towards the desk, he looked appealingly into Colbeck's eyes.

'Where is she, Inspector?' he bleated.

'Who?'

'Madeleine, of course. She came to see you.'

'When?'

'This morning.'

'You are misinformed, Mr Little,' said Colbeck, pleasantly. 'The last time that I saw Miss Andrews was yesterday when I called at the house. What gave you the idea that she was here?'

'You sent for her, sir.'

'But I had no reason to do so.'

'Then why did the policeman come to the house?'

'He was not there on my account, I can promise you.'

'Caleb swore that he was,' said Little, anxiously. 'Madeleine told him that she had to go out for a while to visit you but that she would not be too long. That was the last her father saw of her.'

Colbeck was disturbed. 'What time would this have been?'

'Shortly after eight.'

'Then she's been gone for the best part of the day.'

'I only discovered that when I finished work, Inspector,' said Little. 'I stopped at the house on my way home and found Caleb in a dreadful state. It's not like Madeleine to leave him alone for so long.'

'You say that a policeman called?' asked Colbeck, on his feet.

'Yes, sir. A tall man with a dark beard.'

'Did you actually *see* him?'

'Only from the corner of the street,' explained Little, suppressing the fact that he had been watching the house for the best part of an hour. 'I was going past on my way to work when I noticed that Madeleine was getting into a cab with a policeman. They went off at quite a gallop as if they were eager to get somewhere, so I was curious.'

'Is that why you went to the house and spoke to her father?'

'Yes, I let myself in. The door was on the latch.'

'And what did Mr Andrews tell you?'

'That you wanted to see her at Scotland Yard and had sent a cab to bring her here.' Gideon Little wiped the sweat off his brow with the back of his hand. 'If he was not a policeman, who could that man be?'

'I wish that I knew,' said Colbeck, sharing his concern.

'Do you think that she could have been kidnapped?'

'I sincerely hope that that is not the case, Mr Little.'

'Why else would she disappear for so long?'

'Could she have visited relatives?'

'I doubt it.'

'Or called on friends, perhaps?'

'Not when her father is stuck in bed all day like that,' said Little. 'Madeleine is very dutiful. She would never desert Caleb.'

'No,' said Colbeck, his brain spinning as he saw the implications of the news. 'The only thing that would keep her away from home is that she is being held against her will.'

'That's our fear, Inspector. Find her for us – please!'

'I'll not rest until I've done so, Mr Little.'

'I know that she'll never be mine,' said the other, quivering with apprehension. 'Madeleine made that obvious. But she'll always be very dear to me. I cannot bear the thought that she is in danger.'

'Neither can I,' admitted Colbeck, worried that he might somehow be responsible for her abduction. 'Thank you for coming, Mr Little. I only wish that you'd been able to raise the alarm sooner.'

'So do I, Inspector. What am I to tell Caleb?'

'That we'll do everything in our power to find his daughter. I will take personal charge of the search.' He thought of the injured driver, stranded in his bedroom. 'Is there anyone to look after him?'

'A servant who comes in three days a week. She's agreed to stay.'

'Good,' said Colbeck. 'You get back to Mr Andrews

and give him what support you can. I, meanwhile, will institute a search.' He shook his head in consternation. 'Taken away in a cab – wherever can she be?'

Madeleine Andrews was stricken with quiet terror. Locked in an attic room at the top of a house, she had no idea where she was or why she was being kept there. It had been a frightening ordeal. When the policeman had called for her, she had looked forward to seeing Robert Colbeck again and was so lost in pleasurable thoughts of him that she was caught off guard. Once inside the cab, she realised that she had been tricked. The man who overpowered her had slipped a bag over her head so that she could not even see where they were going. The last thing she recalled about Camden was the sound of a train steaming over the viaduct.

She cursed herself for being taken in so easily. The policeman's voice had been far too cultured for an ordinary constable, and his manner too courteous. What had misled her was that he had behaved more like Colbeck than a typical policeman. That had appealed to her. His demeanour had changed the moment they were in the cab. He had threatened her with physical violence if she tried to resist or cry out, and Madeleine knew that he was prepared to carry out his threat. All that she could do was to submit and hope that she would somehow get out of her predicament.

The room was small and the ceiling low but the place was well-furnished. Under other circumstances, she might even have found it snug. There were bars across the window to discourage any hope of escape over the roof, and she had been warned that, if she dared to shout for help, she would be bound and gagged. Madeleine spared herself that indignity. A manservant had twice brought her meals in the course of the day and, on the second occasion, had lit the oil lamp for her. Though the food was good, she had little appetite for it.

Fearing for her own safety, she was also distressed on her father's behalf. He would be alarmed by her disappearance and, unable to stir from his bed, would be completely frustrated. Madeleine felt that she was letting him down. The other person about whom she was concerned was Robert Colbeck. During her abduction, she had been ordered to obey if she wished to see the Inspector again. Did that mean *his* life was in danger or merely her own? And how had the counterfeit policeman known that she was fond of Colbeck? It was baffling. As she flung herself down on the couch, she was tormented by one question.

What were they planning to do to her?

Sir Humphrey Gilzean believed in dining in style. When he was staying in London, therefore, he always made sure that his cook travelled with him from Berkshire. Over a delicious repast that evening, washed down with a superior wine, he mused on the ironic coincidence.

'You know how much I detest railways, Thomas,' he said.

'They are an abomination to you.'

'So why do you bring a railwayman's daughter to my house?'

'Madeleine Andrews is the chink in Colbeck's armour.'

'Can this really be so?' asked Gilzean. 'The only way their paths could have crossed is as a result of the train robbery. There has been very little time for an attachment to develop.'

'Nevertheless, Humphrey, I was given to believe that it has. The gallant Inspector was seen to take a fond farewell on her doorstep. And while she may only be a railwayman's daughter,' said Sholto with a well-bred leer, 'she is a fetching young woman. I'd hoped that she'd struggle more so that I could have the pleasure of manhandling her.'

Gilzean was strict. 'She must be treated with respect.'

'Am I not even allowed a little sport?'

'No, Thomas.'

'But she might like some company in the middle of the night.'

'Miss Andrews must be unharmed,' insisted Gilzean, filling his glass from the port decanter. 'I draw the line at molestation.'

'Where women are concerned,' teased Sholto, 'you were always inclined to be too soft.'

'I behave like a gentleman, Thomas. So should you.'

'There are times when courtesy is burdensome.'

'Not to me.'

Sholto laughed. 'You really are the strangest creature,

Humphrey,' he said. 'Who else would send me off to murder a man then insist that I leave a substantial amount of money with his widow?'

'Mrs Ings needed it – we do not.'

'I always need money.'

'Even you must be satisfied with what we have accrued.'

'It only makes me want more.'

'Apart from what we gained in the robbery, there were the profits from blackmail. In total, it amounted to almost three thousand pounds. We are in a position to be generous.'

'Giving money to that woman was unnecessary.'

'It salved my conscience and appealed to my sense of fair play.'

'Fair play?' echoed the other with a derisive laugh. 'Having her husband killed hardly constitutes fair play.'

'He betrayed her for that money, remember,' said Gilzean. 'He abandoned his wife and family to live with a whore in the Devil's Acre. I have no sympathy for him – but I did feel that Mrs Ings deserved help.'

Sholto was disdainful. 'I do not believe in charity.'

'Cultivate a little benevolence, Thomas.'

'Oh, I have plenty of that,' said the other, 'but I put it to different uses. You see a grieving widow and tell me to put money through her letterbox. When I see a female in distress – Madeleine Andrews, for example – I have the urge to comfort her in a more intimate way and offer my full benevolence.'

'Miss Andrews is only a means to an end.'

'My belief, entirely.'

'I am serious,' said Gilzean, forcefully. 'When she is under my roof, she is under my protection. Dismiss any thoughts you may have about her, Thomas. Miss Andrews is here for a purpose.'

'How long will we keep her?'

'As long as we need her.'

'What about the elegant Inspector?'

'He will surely be aware of her disappearance by now,' said Gilzean, sniffing his port before tasting it, 'and, if he is as enamoured as you believe, he will be extremely fretful. That was my intention – to give Inspector Colbeck something to occupy his mind.'

Robert Colbeck slept fitfully that night, troubled by dreams of what terrible fate might have befallen Madeleine Andrews. The news that she had been kidnapped aroused all of his protective instincts and he came to see just how fond he was of her. It was no passing interest. His affection was deep and intensified by her plight. The thought that she was in great danger left him in a fever of recrimination. Colbeck felt responsible for what had happened. She had been taken, he believed, as a way of striking at him. Because he had arrested three men, Madeleine had become a hostage.

He woke up to the realisation that his efforts to find her had, so far, been fruitless. In the wake of the visit from Gideon Little, he had sent police officers to Camden to question all the neighbours in her street in case any of them had witnessed the abduction. One had remembered seeing a policeman outside the door of Madeleine's house, another had watched the cab setting off, but neither could add to what Colbeck already knew. He had nothing to help him. Madeleine could be anywhere.

Rain was scouring the streets when he stepped out of his house, making London seem wet and inhospitable. Colbeck had to walk some distance along John Islip Street before he found a cab, and his umbrella was dripping. He was glad to get to Scotland Yard. Although it was still early, Superintendent Tallis had already arrived to start work. Colbeck met him in the corridor outside his office. Having been informed of the crisis, Tallis was eager to hear of developments.

'Any news, Inspector?' he asked.

'None, sir.'

'That's worrying. Miss Andrews has been missing for the best part of twenty-four hours. I would have expected contact by now.'

'From whom?'

'The people who abducted her,' said Tallis. 'In cases of kidnap, there is usually a ransom demand within a short time. Yet we have heard nothing. That bodes ill.'

'Not necessarily, Superintendent.'

'It could mean that the poor woman is no longer alive.'

'I refuse to believe that,' said Colbeck. 'If the object were to kill Miss Andrews, that could have been done more easily. Nobody would go to the trouble of disguising himself as a policeman so that he could lure her into a cab, when he could dispatch her with one thrust of a dagger.'

'That's true, I suppose.'

'Look what happened to William Ings and Daniel Slender, sir. They were both killed with brutal efficiency – so was Kate Piercey.'

'You are still making the assumption that this abduction is the work of the train robbers.'

'Who else would kidnap Miss Andrews?'

'She lives in Camden, Inspector. It's not the most law-abiding area of the city. Any woman who is young and pretty is potentially at risk.'

'Of what?'

Tallis was sombre. 'Use your imagination,' he said. 'When we get reports of abductions, young women – sometimes mere girls – are always the victims. They are dragged off to Seven Dials or the Devil's Acre and forced into the sort of life that Kate Piercey lived.'

'That is certainly not the case here.'

'It's something that we have to consider.'

'No, Superintendent,' said Colbeck. 'You have obviously not seen the house where Mr Andrews and his daughter live. It's a neat villa in the better part of Camden and the neighbours can be trusted. If that were not so, Miss Andrews would never have gone out and left the door on the latch. And there's something else,' he continued. 'On the two occasions when she visited me here, Miss Andrews walked all the way to Whitehall. If she found Camden a source of peril, she would never have ventured abroad on her own like that.'

'You know the young lady better than I do.'

'Miss Andrews is very practical and level-headed. She knows how to take care of herself. Only a man in police uniform could have won her confidence. That, after all,' Colbeck pointed out, 'was how her father was deceived. One of the robbers who flagged the train down was dressed as a railway policeman.'

'I see what you mean. There is a pattern here.'

'The kidnap was an act of retaliation.'

'Against what?'

'The arrest of Jukes and the Seymour brothers.'

'But why pick on Miss Andrews?' said Tallis, puzzled. 'She is only indirectly connected with this investigation. Why choose her?'

'I wish I knew, Superintendent.'

Colbeck sensed that Madeleine had been abducted in order to get his attention, though he did not mention that to Tallis. It was important to be cool and objective in the Superintendent's presence. To confess that he had feelings for Madeleine Andrews would be to cloud the issue and to incur the other man's criticism. Tallis did not look kindly on members of his division who became involved with women whom they met in the course of their duties. He viewed it as distracting and unprofessional. While he knew nothing of Colbeck's fondness for Madeleine, however, it appeared that someone else did. That unsettled the Inspector.

'What do you think they will do?' asked Tallis.

'Get in touch with us very soon.'

'To demand ransom money?'

'No, sir,' replied Colbeck. 'Caleb Andrews does not have the sort of income that would interest them. Besides, they are not short of funds after the robbery. No, I suspect that they will wish to trade with us.'

'In what way?'

'They will return Miss Andrews if we release the prisoners.'

'Never!'

'They can always be re-arrested, Inspector.'

'What is the point of that?' snapped Tallis. 'We did not go to all the trouble of catching them in order to set them free. Heavens above, man, have you forgotten what they tried to do?'

'No, sir. I was there at the time.'

'The Great Exhibition is the first of its kind, a world fair that enables British industry to show why it has no rivals. A massive amount of money and energy has gone into the venture. Prince Albert has worked valiantly to contribute to its success. Millions of visitors are expected,' he stressed, 'and what they want to see is the Crystal Palace – not a heap of twisted metal and broken glass.'

'I appreciate the seriousness of their crime, Superintendent.'

'They were also involved in the train robbery.'

'That is not the point,' argued Colbeck. 'A young woman's life may hang in the balance here. If you refuse even to listen to their offer, you may be condemning her to death.'

'I will not sanction the release of guilty men.'

'At least, *discuss* it with them.'

'What good will that do?'

'It will earn us time to continue our search,' said Colbeck, 'but its main advantage is that it may keep Miss Andrews alive. Refuse even to listen and you will only anger them. Employ delaying tactics.'

'I make the decisions, Inspector.'

'Of course. I merely offer my advice.'

'If we let these villains go, we will be made to look like idiots.'

'You are thinking solely of your own reputation, sir,' said Colbeck. 'My concern is for the safety of the victim. Miss Andrews has already suffered the shock of abduction and of being locked away. If the one way to ensure her survival is to release Jukes and the Seymour brothers, I'd unlock the doors of their cells myself.'

The journey was a continuing nightmare. Bound, gagged and blindfolded, Madeleine Andrews sat in the coach as it rolled through the suburbs of London and out into the country. The familiar noises of the capital were soon replaced by an almost eerie silence, broken only by the clatter of hooves, the creaking of the vehicle and the drumming of the rain on the roof. The one consolation was that she was alone, not held in the grip of the bearded man who had called at her house with the false message. She could still feel his hot breath against her cheek as he grabbed her.

Hours seemed to pass. Wherever she was, it was a long way from London. The rain stopped and so did the pace of the horses. When the animals slowed to a trot, she realised that they were letting another coach catch them up. Both vehicles soon came to a halt and there was a discussion between the coachmen. She strained her ears to pick up what they were saying but she could only make out a few words. The door opened and someone gave a grunt of satisfaction. She presumed that they were checking to see that she was still trussed up safely. The door shut again. A minute later, they set off.

Madeleine no longer feared for her life. If they had wanted to kill her, they would surely have done so by now. Instead, she had been imprisoned in a house that, judging by those she could see opposite from the attic window, was in a very respectable part of London. To her relief, she had been treated reasonably well and was subjected to no violence. What she missed most was conversation. The manservant who had brought her food had been ordered to say nothing to her, and the bearded man who tied her up that morning had confined himself to a few threats before carrying her downstairs over his shoulder.

During a normal day, Madeleine would talk to her father, her friends, her neighbours and to various shopkeepers. Conversations with Gideon Little were more fraught but at least he represented human contact. She longed for that now. For some reason, she had been isolated in a way that only served to heighten her fears. The person she really wanted to speak to was Robert Colbeck, to report her misadventure to him, to seek his reassurance, to enjoy his companionship and to listen to the voice she had come to love for its bewitching cadences. Colbeck was her one hope of rescue. It gave them a bond that drew them closer. Knowing that he would be trying hard to track her down helped Madeleine to find a reserve of courage that she did not know existed.

For her sake, she had to maintain hope; for Colbeck's sake, she was determined to keep her spirits up. The agony could not go on forever. He would come for her in time.

Adversity taught Caleb Andrews just how many friends he had. When he had first been injured, most of his visitors had been other railwaymen, people with whom he had worked for years and who understood how he felt when he heard of the damage to his locomotive. The kidnap of his daughter brought in a wider circle of friends and well-wishers. Once the word had spread, neighbours to whom he had hardly spoken before came to offer their help and to say that they were praying for the safe return of Madeleine. Andrews was touched by the unexpected show of concern.

Frank Pike could hear the emotion in his voice.

'There were six of them in here earlier this morning,' he said. 'I thought that the floor would give way.'

'It shows how popular you are,' said Pike.

'I'd prefer to be the most hated man in Camden if I could have Maddy back home, safe and sound. I didn't sleep a wink last night.'

'What do the police say?'

'That they're doing everything they can to find her. Gideon spoke to Inspector Colbeck yesterday, who told him that he'd lead the search himself.'

'That's good news.'

'Is it?' said Andrews, doubtfully.

'Yes. Inspector Colbeck caught those three men at the Crystal Palace. They included that ugly bastard who knocked you out. If he hadn't been locked up,' vowed Pike, flexing his muscles, 'I'd have beaten him black and blue.'

'He's the least of my worries now, Frank.'

'I know.'

'All that I can think about is Maddy.'

'Did nobody *see* her being taken away?'

'Only Gideon,' said Andrews. 'He claims that he was just passing the end of the street, but I think he was standing out there and watching the house. He's so lovesick, he'll wait for hours for the chance of a word with Maddy. If she comes out of this, she'll have reason to thank him.'

'What did he see, Caleb?'

'A policeman with a dark beard, talking to Maddy

on the doorstep then helping her into a cab. The driver cracked his whip and off they went. Gideon had no idea that she was being kidnapped. Luckily, he called in here later on. I sent him off to raise the alarm.'

'Is there anything I can do?'

'You've done it just by being here, Frank.'

'I could send Rose over to fetch and carry for you.'

'No,' said Andrews, 'your wife has enough to do as it is.'

'You only have to ask.'

'Rose would have to wait in the queue. I've got dozens of offers.'

Pike grinned. 'All these women, banging on the door of your bedroom – you always did have a way with the ladies, Caleb.'

'Not when my arm was in a sling and my leg in a splint.'

'They want to mother you.'

Andrews became solemn. 'I tell you this, Frank,' he said. 'If they paraded in here naked and danced in front of me, I'd not even look at them. There's only one woman on my mind right now.'

'Maddy.'

'Why the hell can't they *find* her?'

The letter arrived late that morning. Written in capitals on a sheet of exquisite stationery, it was addressed to Inspector Robert Colbeck. The message was blunt.

RELEASE ALL THREE PRISONERS OR MISS ANDREWS WILL SUFFER. WE WILL BE IN TOUCH TO MAKE ARRANGEMENTS.

A shiver ran through Colbeck. It gave him no satisfaction to see that his guess had been right. Madeleine Andrews was being used as a bargaining tool. Colbeck's problem was that the Superintendent was not prepared to strike a bargain or even to pretend to do so. Releasing anyone from custody was like retreating on the battlefield to him. When Colbeck went to his office to show him the letter, Tallis was defiant. He thrust the missive back at the Inspector.

'Nobody tells me what to do,' he asserted.

'Does that mean you are prepared to let Miss Andrews suffer, sir?'

'Not deliberately.'

'Ignore their demands and that is what will happen.'

'It could be bluff on their part,' said Tallis. 'If they harm her in any way, they lose the one lever that they have at their disposal.'

'I prefer to take them at their word, sir.'

'Yes, Inspector. We know you have a fondness for releasing felons from custody. It was by your connivance that Mulryne walked free.'

'Brendan Mulryne is no felon,' retorted Colbeck.

'He is in my eyes.'

'He acted with outstanding bravery at the Crystal Palace.'

'That does not excuse what he did.'

'Mr Mayne felt that it did, Superintendent. I wonder what his reaction to this demand would be?' he said, holding up the letter.

Tallis was hostile. 'Do not go over my head again, Inspector.'

'Madeleine Andrews's life may be at stake.'

'So is your career.'

Colbeck was unperturbed by the threat. Madeleine's safety meant more to him at that moment than anything else. Baulked by his superior, he would have to find another way to secure her release.

'Excuse me, sir,' he said, politely. 'I must continue the search.'

'You can tear that letter up for a start.'

Ignoring the command, Colbeck went straight back to his office and he was delighted to see that Victor Leeming had finally returned. The Sergeant had the weary look of someone who had pushed himself to the limit. Before he allowed him to deliver his news, Colbeck told him about the kidnap and showed him the letter. Leeming's response chimed in with his own. Even if they did not intend to release the prisoners, they should enter the negotiations so that they could purchase some time.

'One other thing you should know,' explained Colbeck. 'Early yesterday morning, a cab driver reported the theft of his vehicle while he was having breakfast. Later the same day, it was returned.'

'You think that it was involved in the kidnap?'

'Yes, Victor. No self-respecting cab driver would have agreed to take part in a crime like that. And the fact that the cab was returned is significant. These people will destroy a steam locomotive but they will not harm a

293

horse. But how did you get on?' said Colbeck, wrinkling his nose. 'You smell as if you've just come from a slaughterhouse.'

'Several of them, sir. And they all stink like old blue buggery. Do you know how many slaughterhouses there *are* in London?'

'I'm only interested in one of them.'

'Needless to say,' complained Leeming, 'it was the last that I visited. However,' he went on, taking out his notebook and referring to a page, 'they did remember Vernon Seymour and they had an address. He lived alone in a tenement near Seven Dials. The landlord there told me that Seymour had come into some money last week and moved out. I saw the room where he lodged – it still had a whiff of the slaughterhouse about it.' He flicked over a page. 'According to the landlord, Seymour received a visit from a tall, well-dressed man with a beard. Shortly after that, he left the place.'

'What about his brother?'

'Harry came there from time to time, apparently. That's all I can tell you.' Leeming turned over another page. 'But I had more success with the regimental records. Mr Tallis gave me a list of possibilities and told me where to find the records. Arthur Jukes, Vernon Seymour and Harry Seymour all served in India in the 10th Queen's Regiment.'

'Infantry?'

'Yes, Inspector. It's the North Lincoln.'

'Any officers listed as retiring?'

'Quite a few,' said Leeming, running his finger down

the page. 'I went back five years and wrote down all the names.' He handed his notebook over. 'It's probably easier if you read them for yourself.'

'Thank you.'

Colbeck ran his eye down the list. While he could never approve of Leeming's scrawl, he had to admire his thoroughness. The names were listed alphabetically with their ranks, length of service and date of retirement noted alongside.

'We can eliminate some of these men immediately,' said Colbeck, reaching for the pen on his desk and dipping it in the inkwell.

'Can we, sir?'

'Yes, I refuse to believe that Colonel Fitzhammond is our man. He's given a lifetime's service to the army and will be steeped in its traditions.'

He scratched through the name then put a line through three more. 'We can count these officers out as well. They'll be too old. All that they will want is a quiet retirement.'

'I know the feeling,' said Leeming.

'Two of these men left the army within the last few months,' said Colbeck, pen poised over their names. 'They would not have had the time to set up such a complicated crime as the train robbery. We can cross them off the list as well.' The pen scratched away. 'That leaves five names. No, it doesn't, Victor,' he added, as he spotted a detail. 'I think that it leaves two whom we should look at more carefully.'

'Why is that, Inspector?'

'Because they retired from the army on the same day.'

'Coincidence?'

'Possibly – or they could be friends who joined at the same time.'

'When did they return to civilian life?'

'Almost five years ago,' said Colbeck. 'Of course, we may be barking up the wrong tree but I have the feeling that we may have found something important here. My belief is that one or both of these men was involved in that train robbery.'

'What are their names?'

'Major Sir Humphrey Gilzean and Captain Thomas Sholto.'

'Mr Tallis will never accept that army officers are responsible for the crimes. In his book, they are above suspicion.'

'Then let's first try these two names on someone else,' decided Colbeck. 'Men who served under them.'

Standing in the hallway of Gilzean's country house, Thomas Sholto stroked his beard and watched two servants bringing another trunk downstairs. He turned to his friend.

'You do not believe in wasting time, Humphrey, do you?'

'Forewarned is forearmed,' said Gilzean.

'What if Inspector Colbeck does not run us to ground?'

'Then we have no need to implement our contingency plans. As you know, I'm a great believer in covering all eventualities. This luggage will be loaded into a carriage in readiness for a swift departure.'

'Will our hostage be travelling with us?' asked Sholto.

'Only if we need to take her, Thomas.'

'Given the opportunity, I'd have taken her already.'

'Keep your hands off Miss Andrews.'

'You should at least have let me share the same coach as her.'

'No,' said Gilzean. 'The woman is frightened enough as it is. I do not wish to add to her distress by having you lusting after her. I prefer to encourage your virtues, not indulge your vices.'

Sholto laughed. 'I didn't know that I had any virtues.'

'One or two.'

'What are you going to do with this resourceful Inspector?'

'Keep him guessing, Thomas.'

'How will you contrive that?'

'By pretending that we really do intend to hand over Madeleine Andrews for the three prisoners. A letter will be delivered by hand to him tomorrow, setting up a time and place for the exchange to be made, two days from hence. Only when they arrive at the designated spot will they realise that they've been hoodwinked. By that time,' said Gilzean, leading his friend into the library, 'I will have emptied my bank accounts and put all my affairs in order.'

'Would you really be prepared to turn your back on this house?'

'Yes. It holds too many unpleasant memories for me now.'

'That was not always the case,' Sholto reminded him.

'No, I agree. When I grew up here, I loved it. After my army days were over, I could think of no finer existence than running the estate and keeping a stable of racehorses.' His face hardened. 'I reckoned without the railway, alas.'

'It does not actually cross your land, Humphrey.'

'Perhaps not but it skirts it for over a mile. It's far too close for comfort. Trains from the Great Western Railway go past all the time. If the wind is in the right direction, I can hear the noise of that damned whistle whenever I am in my garden. Nothing makes my blood boil so much as that sound.'

'I hope that you do not have to sacrifice this place,' said Sholto, gazing fondly around the room. 'It's a splendid house. There are some things that you'll miss a great deal about this estate.' He raised an eyebrow. 'One of them, in particular.'

'All that has been taken into consideration,' said Gilzean, knowing what he meant. 'Whatever happens, I will return somehow from time to time to pay my respects. Nobody will prevent me from doing that. It's a sacred duty. Besides,' he went on, his face brightening, 'I have another good reason to come back.'

'Do you?'

'Yes, Thomas. I simply have to be at Epsom on the first Wednesday in June. I intend to watch my colt win the Derby.'

'What if he loses?'

'That option does not even arise,' said the other, brimming with confidence. 'Starlight is a Gilzean – we never lose.'

'Sir Humphrey Gilzean?' asked Superintendent Tallis, eyes bulging.

'Yes,' replied Colbeck. 'I'm certain of it, sir.'

'Then I am equally certain that you have the wrong man.'

'Why do you say that?'

'Do you know who Sir Humphrey is – and *what* he is?'

'If my guess is right, he's a man with blood on his hands. He not only organised the train robbery, he sanctioned two murders and ordered the kidnap of Miss Andrews.'

'Do you have any other far-fetched claims to offer, Inspector?' said Tallis, incredulously. 'Are you going to tell me, for instance, that Sir Humphrey is about to assassinate the Queen or steal the Crown Jewels?'

'No, Superintendent.'

'Then do not plague me with your ridiculous notions.'

'Sir Humphrey is our man. Take my word for it.'

'Listen, Inspector. I can accept that men from the ranks, like Jukes and the Seymour brothers, may have

299

gone astray but not someone who was once a senior officer. You have no concept of what it takes to become a major in the British Army. I do. It shapes you for life. Sir Humphrey is no more likely to have committed these crimes than I am.'

Superintendent Tallis was peremptory. Colbeck had come into his office to announce what he felt was a critical breakthrough in the investigation, only to have cold water liberally poured over his suggestion by his superior. Remaining calm in the face of the other's intransigence, he tried to reason with him.

'Will you not at least hear what we found out, sir?'

'No, Inspector. The idea is ludicrous.'

'Sergeant Leeming and I do not think so.'

'Then I have to overrule the pair of you. Look elsewhere.'

'We have,' said Colbeck. 'At a man named Thomas Sholto, who was a Captain in the same regiment. Have you heard of him as well?'

'Not until this moment.'

'Then you will not have prior knowledge of *his* innocence.'

'Do not be impertinent.'

'Well, at least do us the courtesy of taking us seriously.'

'Why should I bother to do that?' said Tallis, sourly. 'It is quite obvious to me that neither you nor Sergeant Leeming are aware of who Sir Humphrey is. Did you know, for example, that he is a distinguished Member of Parliament?'

'No,' admitted Colbeck. 'We did not.'

'He has only been in the House for three or four years yet he has already made his mark. Sir Humphrey is already being talked of as a future minister.'

'That does not prevent him from robbing a train.'

'Why should he *need* to do such a thing, Inspector? He's a rich man with a dazzling political career ahead of him. It would be sheer lunacy to jeopardise that.'

'In his mind,' argued Colbeck, 'there was no jeopardy at all. Sir Humphrey did not expect to get caught. That is why the crimes were planned with such precision.'

'Balderdash!'

'If you will not listen to us, I'm sure that Mr Mayne will.'

'The Commissioner will tell you exactly what I do,' said Tallis, jabbing a finger at him. 'Sir Humphrey Gilzean has a position in society. He has neither the time nor inclination to commit crimes.'

'I am persuaded that he had both,' said Colbeck, unmoved by the Superintendent's belligerence. 'Like you, we had our doubts at first so we sought the opinion of someone else – someone who knew him in the army and who has been employed by him since then.'

'And who was that?'

'Harry Seymour.'

'You questioned him again?'

'No,' replied Colbeck, 'we simply confronted him with two names and watched his reaction. You saw for yourself how convinced he was that he would somehow be set free. So I told him that it could not happen because we had both Sir Humphrey and Thomas Sholto in custody.'

'What did he say to that?'

'Nothing, sir, but his face gave him away. He turned white.'

Tallis shook his head. 'That could simply have been shock at hearing a familiar name from his days in the army.'

'We repeated the process with Vernon Seymour. He was even more dismayed than his brother. Ask Sergeant Leeming,' said Colbeck. 'The look on Vernon Seymour's face was as good as a confession.'

The news forced Tallis to think again. Unwilling to accept that anyone in Gilzean's position would ever be drawn into criminal activity, he tried to refute the claim but could not find the arguments to do so. He had an ingrained respect for Members of Parliament that blinded him to the possibility that they might not always be men of high moral probity. On the other hand, Inspector Colbeck and Sergeant Leeming would not have plucked the name of Sir Humphrey Gilzean out of the air. And it did seem to have upset two of the prisoners in custody. Searching for a means of exonerating Gilzean, he finally remembered one.

'No, no,' he insisted, 'Sir Humphrey would never contemplate such crimes – especially at a time like this.'

'What do you mean, Superintendent?'

'The man is still in mourning.'

'For whom?'

'His wife. I remember reading of the tragedy in the newspaper.'

'What happened?'

'Shortly before last Christmas, Lady Gilzean was killed in a riding accident. Sir Humphrey is still grieving for her.'

After placing a large basket of flowers in front of the gravestone, Sir Humphrey Gilzean knelt down on the grass to offer up a silent prayer. When he opened his eyes again, he read the epitaph that had been etched into the marble. He spoke in a loving whisper.

'I will repay, Lucinda,' he said. 'I will repay.'

CHAPTER TWELVE

During the ten years of its construction, Robert Colbeck had been past the House of Commons on an almost daily basis, and he had watched it grow from piles of assorted building materials into its full Gothic glory. However, he had never had an opportunity to enter the place before and looked forward to the experience. As he approached from Whitehall, he saw that work was continuing on the massive clock tower, though completion was not anticipated for some years yet. Until then, Members of Parliament would have to rely on their respective pocket watches, opening up the possibility of endless partisan strife over what was the correct time of day.

When he entered the building, he found the atmosphere rather cold and forbidding, as if a church had been stripped of its mystery and given over to purely temporal functions. Unlike those who filed into the Lower Chamber to take their seats, Colbeck was not there for the purposes of debate. All that interested him were the heated exchanges of an earlier year. Repairing to the library, he introduced himself, made his request then sat down at a table with some bound copies of *Hansard* in front of him. As he leafed through the pages of the first volume, he reflected that Luke Hansard, the printer who had started to publish parliamentary debates way back in 1774, must have felt that he was bequeathing a priceless resource to posterity. What he had not anticipated was that he might, one day in the future, help a Detective Inspector to solve a series of heinous crimes.

Colbeck was concentrating on the year 1847 for two principal reasons. It was shortly after Sir Humphrey Gilzean had become a Member of Parliament and he would therefore have tried to make a good impression by taking part early on in the verbal jousting that enlivened the Commons. In addition, it was the year when investment in the railways was at its height, reaching a peak of over £30 million before declining sharply when the bubble later burst with dramatic effect. Colbeck knew that, in 1847, a substantial amount of time had been devoted to the discussion of Railway Bills and that one of the most insistent voices in the debates would be that of George Hudson, M.P. for Sunderland, the now disgraced Railway King.

It did not take him long to find the name of Sir Humphrey Gilzean, Conservative, representing a constituency in his native Berkshire and sitting on the Opposition benches. His maiden speech, unsurprisingly, had been delivered on the vexed question of railways. Opposing a bill for the extension of a line in Oxfordshire, he had spoken with great passion about the urgent necessity of preserving the English countryside from further encroachments by the Great Western Railway. It was not the only occasion when he had raised his voice in anger. Colbeck found several debates during which Gilzean had risen in defiance against those with vested interests in the railway system.

Gilzean's speeches were not confined to the railways. As he flicked through the rhetorical flourishes, Colbeck learnt that the man had firm opinions on almost every subject, deploring the repeal of the Corn Laws by his own party, reviling the Chartists as dangerous revolutionaries who should be suppressed by force, and showing a special interest in foreign affairs. But his heavy artillery was reserved for repeated attacks on the railways. Since it mentioned his favourite poet, Colbeck was particularly interested in a speech that denounced the Great Western Railway.

William Blake, may I remind you – a poet with whom I will not claim any spiritual affinity – once spoke of building Jerusalem in England's green and pleasant land. He was fortunate to die before the industrial infidels made his dream an impossibility. Green pastures are everywhere darkened by the shadow of the railway system. Pleasant land is everywhere dug up, defaced and destroyed in the name of the steam locomotive. When Blake wrote of chariots of fire, he did not envisage them in such hideous profusion, scarring the countryside, frightening the livestock, filling the air with noise and smoke, imposing misery wherever they go. And who benefits from these engines of devastation? The shareholders of the Great Western Railway – vandals to a man!

Colbeck had read enough. With the words still ringing in his ears, he went off in pursuit of someone whose hatred of the railways amounted to nothing short of a mania. Sir Humphrey Gilzean was clearly a fanatic. Convinced that he had identified the man behind the crimes, Colbeck was ready to bring his parliamentary career to an abrupt halt. There was, he acknowledged, one problem. Abducted from her doorstep, Madeleine Andrews was being held by Gilzean and that gave him a decided advantage. The thought made Colbeck shudder. It also caused him to break into a run when he came out into daylight once more. He had to find her soon.

They kept her in a wine cellar this time. Long, low and with a vaulted ceiling, it seemed to run the full length of the house and contained rack upon rack of expensive wine. Minimal light came in through the small windows that looked out on a trench alongside the wall of the building. Even on such a warm day, the place was cold and damp. It was also infested with spiders and Madeleine Andrews, liberated from her bonds, walked into dozens of invisible webs as she tried to explore her new prison. It was one more source of displeasure for her.

Madeleine was beyond fear now. She felt only disgust and anger at her captors. Though no explanation had been given to her, she had soon worked out that she was a pawn in a game against Scotland Yard as personified by Inspector Robert Colbeck. If they had not been worried by the detective's skills, she believed, they would not have needed to take a hostage. It was firm proof that Colbeck was getting closer all the time. Madeleine just hoped that she would still be unharmed when he finally caught up with her.

Meanwhile, she intended to fight back on her own behalf. Like her father, she had a combative spirit when roused. It was time to issue a challenge, to show her captors that she was no weak and harmless woman. Her first instinct was to smash as many bottles of wine as she could, venting her fury in a bout of destruction. But she saw that a wine bottle was also a formidable weapon. Used in the right way, it might even help her to escape from her dank dungeon. Madeleine picked up a bottle and held it by its neck. She was armed.

It was not long before she had the chance to test her resolve. Heavy feet were heard descending the steps outside then a key turned in the lock. Keeping the bottle behind her, Madeleine backed against a wall, her heart pounding at her own bravado. When the door swung open, the bearded man who had kidnapped her stepped into the cellar. Thomas Sholto was in a playful mood.

'I wondered how you were getting on,' he said, grinning at her.

'Who *are* you?' she demanded.

'A friend, Madeleine. There's no need to be afraid of me. I'm sorry we have to keep you down here in the cellar, though, in one sense, it may be the appropriate place, for I'm sure that you taste as delicious as any of this wine.' He took a step closer. 'A room is being prepared for you even as we speak,' he told her. 'It is merely a question of making the windows secure so that you will not take it into your pretty little head to try to get away from us. That would be a very silly thing to do, Madeleine.'

'How long are you keeping me here?'

'Until your ardent admirer, Inspector Robert Colbeck, is suitably diverted. I can see why he has been ensnared by your charms.' Sholto came even closer. 'In this light, you might even pass for a beauty.'

'Keep away from me!' she warned, eyes aflame.

'A beauty with real spirit – that's even better.'

'Where are we?'

'In a much nicer part of the country than Camden Town,' he said with a condescending smile. 'You should be grateful to me. Since we first met, I've taken you up in the world. There are not many railwayman's daughters who have stayed in such a fine house as this. At the very least, I think that I deserve a kiss from you.'

'Stand off!'

'But I'm not going to hurt you, Madeleine. Surely you

can spare one tiny kiss from those lovely red lips of yours. Come here.'

'No!' she cried.

Ignoring her protest, he reached out for her. Madeleine tried to fend him off with one hand, using the other to swing the bottle out from behind her back. Sholto ducked instinctively but it caught him a glancing blow on the side of the head before continuing on its way to smash into the brickwork. Glass went everywhere and red wine sprayed over the both of them. Having come off far worse than her, Sholto was incensed.

'You little bitch!' he yelled, his forehead cut and his beard glinting with shards of glass. 'I'll make you sorry that you did that.'

Grabbing her by the shoulders, he pushed Madeleine back against the wall and knocked all the breath out of her. Before he could strike her, however, a voice rang out from above.

'Thomas!' shouted Gilzean. 'What are you *doing* down there?'

The cab was driven as fast as the traffic permitted, the driver using both whip and vocal commands whenever a clear space opened up in front of them. Seated inside the cab, Sergeant Leeming asked for details.

'Upper Brook Street?'

'Sir Humphrey Gilzean rents a house there,' explained Colbeck.

'Do you expect him to be at home?'

'That would be too much to ask, Victor.'

'Does the Superintendent know that we're going?'

'Not yet.'

Leeming was worried. 'He'll be angry when he finds out.'

'That depends on what we discover,' said Colbeck. 'For reasons that we both know, Mr Tallis is temperamentally unable to accept that a man like Sir Humprey Gilzean – in mourning for his late wife – would ever stoop to such villainy. Our job is to enlighten him.'

'He does not take kindly to enlightenment.'

'We'll cross that bridge when we come to it.'

'You can go first, sir.'

When the cab arrived at its destination, Colbeck paid the driver and sent him on his way. After sizing the house up, he rang the doorbell and waited. There was no response. He rang the doorbell again and brought the brass knocker into action as well.

'Nobody there,' concluded Leeming.

'We need to get inside somehow.'

'We can't force our way in, sir.'

'That would be quite improper,' agreed Colbeck, slipping a hand into his pocket. 'So we'll try to manage it without resorting to force.'

Making sure that nobody in the street was watching, he inserted a picklock into position and jiggled it about. Leeming was scandalised.

'What on earth are you doing, Inspector?' he asked.

'Making use of a little device that I confiscated from a

burglar we arrested earlier this year. He called it a betty and swore that it could open any lock and . . .' he grinned as he heard a decisive click, 'it seems that he was right.'

Opening the door, he went swiftly inside. Leeming followed with grave misgivings. As the door shut behind them, he was very unhappy.

'We are trespassing on private property,' he said.

'No, Victor,' asserted Colbeck. 'We are taking steps to track down a man who is responsible for a series of crimes that include the kidnap of an innocent young woman. While her life is imperilled, we have no time to discuss the legal niceties of home ownership. Action is required.'

Leeming nodded obediently. 'Tell me what to do, Inspector.'

'Search the downstairs rooms. I'll take those upstairs.'

'What are we looking for?'

'Anything that connects Sir Humphrey to those crimes – letters, plans, notes, information about the railways. Be quick about it.'

'Yes, sir.'

While the Sergeant instituted a rapid search of the ground floor, Colbeck went upstairs and checked room after room in succession. Disappointingly, there was nothing that could be used as evidence against Gilzean. Empty drawers and wardrobes showed that he had quit the premises. In doing so, he had taken great pains to leave nothing incriminating behind him. Colbeck went up to the attic. The bedroom at the rear clearly belonged to a manservant because some of his clothing was still there, but it was the room overlooking Upper Brook Street that really interested him.

The moment that Colbeck went into it, he experienced a strange but compelling sensation. Madeleine Andrews had been there. With no visual confirmation of the fact, he was nevertheless certain that she had been held captive in the room, kept in by the stout lock on the door and the bars on the window. Sitting on the edge of the bed, Colbeck ran his fingers gently over the indentation in the pillow. He doubted if she had had much sleep but he was convinced that Madeleine's head had lain there. That discovery alone, in his mind, justified the illegal mode of entry. Colbeck hurried downstairs.

Sergeant Leeming was in the library, sifting through some items he had taken from the mahogany secretaire. He looked up apologetically as the Inspector came into the room.

'I thought that this would be the most likely place,' he said, 'but all I can find is a collection of bills, a few invitations and some notes for a speech at the House of Commons. What about you, sir?'

'She was here, Victor. Miss Andrews was definitely here.'

'How do you know?'

'There was something in the atmosphere of an attic room that spoke to me,' said Colbeck. 'Also, the key was *outside* the door. How many hosts lock their guests in?'

'I searched the other rooms without success, though I can tell you one thing. Judging by what I found in the kitchen bin, Sir Humphrey dined very well last night. He obviously enjoys fine wine. There are dozens of bottles here. As for this desk,' he went on, dropping the bills on to the desk, 'it's been no help at all.'

'Perhaps you've been looking in the wrong place.'

'I've searched every drawer thoroughly.'

'No, Victor,' said Colbeck, 'you searched everything that you could see in front of you. What about the secret compartment?'

'I didn't know that there was one.'

'My father and grandfather were cabinetmakers. I watched both of them build secretaires just like this and they always included a secret compartment where valuable items could be stored.' Bending over the desk, he began to tap various parts of it, listening carefully for a hollow sound. 'All that we have to do is to locate the spring.'

'If there was anything of real value there,' said Leeming, 'then Sir Humphrey would surely have taken it with him.'

'We shall see.'

Along the back of the desk was a row of pigeonholes with matching doors. Leeming had left them open but Colbeck closed them in order to experiment with the carved knobs on each door. After pressing them all in turn, he started to twist them sharply. When that failed to produce a result, he pressed two of the knobs simultaneously. The Sergeant was astonished when he heard a pinging sound and saw a hidden door suddenly flip open. It fitted so beautifully into the side of the desk that Leeming would never have guessed that it was there. Colbeck reached inside to take out the single envelope that lay inside. He looked at the name on the front.

'What is it, sir?'

'A letter addressed to me.'

Leeming's jaw dropped. 'He was *expecting* you to find it?'

'No,' said Colbeck, slitting the envelope open with a paper knife. 'My guess is that it would have been sent to me in due course.'

'How? The house is closed up.'

'I suspect that a manservant has been left behind. His clothing is still upstairs. He would probably have been deputed to deliver this. Yes,' he added, perusing the letter, 'it has tomorrow's date on it. I was not supposed to read it until then. It gives instructions regarding the exchange of the three prisoners for Miss Andrews in a couple of days' time. In other words,' he declared, 'Sir Humphrey never intended that he would trade his hostage for the men in custody.'

'Then why did he send that first demand?'

'To confuse us and to gain himself some leeway. Here,' he said, giving the letter to his companion. 'If this does not persuade the Superintendent that we are on the right trail, then nothing will.'

'I hope that you are right – or we are in trouble.'

'Have faith.'

'It's all that I can cling onto.'

'We have firm evidence here,' said Colbeck, taking the original ransom note from his pocket and holding it beside the letter. 'Do you see what I see, Victor? Same capital letters, same hand, same ink, same stationery. What do you say to that?'

Leeming chuckled. 'Thank God your father was a cabinetmaker!'

Sir Humphrey Gilzean had no sympathy whatsoever for him. As he looked at his friend's wounds and his wine-stained waistcoat, he was filled with disgust for Thomas Sholto.

'All I can say is that it serves you right,' he snarled. 'What madness drove you to go into the wine cellar in the first place? I told you to leave her alone.'

'I was curious,' whined Sholto, examining his face in the drawing room mirror. 'Look what she did to me. Cuts all over my forehead. But for the beard, my face would have been lacerated to bits. And this waistcoat is *ruined*.'

'That's the price of curiosity, Thomas.'

'I was merely going to take her up to her room.'

'You were there for sport,' said Gilzean, coldly, 'so do not even try to deny it. You could not bear the idea of having a pretty young woman at your mercy without taking advantage of the fact.'

'And what is wrong with that?' asked Sholto.

'To begin with, it was against my express orders. I told you that Miss Andrews was not to be molested. Think how terrified she must already be.'

'She was not terrified when she tried to take my head off with that wine bottle. There was real venom in her eyes. The woman attempted to *kill* me, Humphrey.'

'No, Thomas. She tried to escape and I admire her for that.'

Sholto was aghast. 'You admire her for attacking me in that way?' he said, gesticulating wildly. 'She could have split my head open. If you want my opinion, she should be bound and gagged as long as we have her with us.'

'I'll make any decisions regarding Miss Andrews.'

'She's dangerous, Humphrey.'

'Only when provoked,' replied the other. 'Had you not gone to the wine cellar, none of this would have happened. You've always been too hot-blooded, Thomas. Try to curb your desires.'

'Some of us do not share your monastic inclinations,' said Sholto with disdain. Seeing his friend's angry reaction, he was instantly contrite. 'Look, I take that back unreservedly. I did not mean to sneer at you, Humphrey. I appreciate your situation all too well. I know how difficult life has been for you since Lucinda died.'

Gilzean stared at him with a muted rage and indignation. Sholto had touched him on a sensitive spot and he was in pain. It was some while before he allowed himself to speak. Retaining his composure, he gave the other man a simple warning.

'Do not *ever* mention my wife again, Thomas.'

'No, no, of course not.'

'There are limits even to my tolerance of you.'

'I did apologise.'

'That was not enough.'

'Wait a moment,' said Sholto, wilting under his stern gaze and feeling the need to defend himself. 'Do not forget what I have done on your behalf. Who helped to set up the train robbery? I did. Who committed the two murders? I did. Who ordered Jukes and the Seymour brothers to blow up the Kilsby Tunnel? I did. Who dressed up as a policeman and abducted Miss Andrews from her house? I did. Ask yourself this, Humphrey – where would you be without me?'

'I would not be looking at a man who disobeyed instructions and was nearly brained by a wine bottle as a result.' His voice softened and he tried to make peace. 'Look, I know that you did all those things, Thomas, and I'm eternally grateful, but you've made a handsome profit out of the enterprise.'

'So have you.'

'In my case, there have been losses as well as gains.'

'Only if Inspector Colbeck overhauls us,' said Sholto, 'and what chance is there of that?'

'None whatsoever – for the next few days at least. Meanwhile . . .'

'Yes, yes. I know. Leave Miss Andrews alone.'

'If you don't,' cautioned Gilzean, 'then I'll be the one coming at you with a wine bottle in my hand. And I can assure you that it will not be to offer you a drink.'

* * *

Victor Leeming could think of several places that he would rather be at that particular moment. Travelling by train on the Great Western Railway, seated opposite Superintendent Tallis and Inspector Colbeck, he was in considerable discomfort. The improved stability offered by the broad gauge track failed to dispel the queasiness that he always felt in a railway carriage, nor did it still the turmoil in his mind. Since it would be late evening by the time they reached Berkshire, they would be obliged to stay overnight at an inn. It would be the fourth time in a week that he would be separated from his wife and there would be severe reproaches to face when he returned home again.

His uneasiness was not helped by the hostile glances that Tallis was directing at him from time to time. He felt the Superintendent's silent reproof pressing down on him like a heavy weight. Observing his distress, Robert Colbeck tried to divert attention away from his beleaguered Sergeant.

'At least, you must now admit that Sir Humphrey is the culprit,' he said to Tallis. 'That fact is incontrovertible.'

'I was not entirely persuaded by your evidence, Inspector.'

'But that letter was clear proof of his involvement.'

'I am less interested in the letter than in the means by which you acquired it,' said Tallis, meaningfully. 'However, we will let that pass for the time being. No, what finally brought me round to the unpalatable truth that Sir Humphrey Gilzean might, after all, be implicated,

319

was a visit from the wife of Arthur Jukes. While you and Sergeant Leeming were making your unauthorised visit to Upper Brook Street, she called to report the disappearance of her husband.'

'What state was she in?' asked Colbeck.

'A deplorable one. I could not stop the woman crying. When I told her why her husband was missing, she wailed even more. I've never heard such caterwauling. Marriage,' he pronounced with the air of a man who considered the institution to be a species of virulent disease, 'is truly a bed of nails.'

'Only when you're lucky enough to lie on it,' muttered Leeming.

Tallis glared at him. 'Did you speak, Sergeant?'

'No, sir. I was just clearing my throat.'

'Try to do so less irritatingly.'

'What did Mrs Jukes tell you, sir?' said Colbeck.

'Exactly what I expected,' replied Tallis. 'That her husband was the finest man on God's earth and that he would never even think of committing a crime.'

'She should have seen him at the Crystal Palace,' said Leeming. 'Jukes was ready to blow the place up. Fortunately, we were there.'

'Yes, Sergeant – you, Inspector Colbeck and a certain Irishman. That's another thing I'll pass over for the time being,' he said with asperity. 'What I learnt from Mrs Jukes – in between her outbursts of hysteria – was that her husband had been out of work. Then he got a visit from a bearded man whom Jukes later described to her as a captain from his old regiment.'

'Thomas Sholto,' decided Colbeck.

'So it would appear. Soon after that, she told me, her husband came into some money. Enough to pay off his debts and move house.'

Leeming sat up. 'Did Mrs Jukes never ask where his sudden wealth came from?'

'She was his wife, Sergeant. She believed every lie he told her.'

'My wife wouldn't let me get away with anything like that.'

'You are unlikely to rob a mail train.'

'Given the choice, I avoid trains of all kinds, Superintendent.'

'We know this is an ordeal for you, Victor,' said Colbeck with compassion, 'but at least we have a first class carriage to ourselves. You do not have to suffer in front of strangers.'

'That's no consolation, sir.'

'Forget about yourself, man,' chided Tallis. 'Do you hear me telling you about my headache or complaining of my bad tooth? Of course not. In pursuit of villains such as these, personal discomfort is irrelevant. While you and the Inspector were otherwise engaged today, I had a further insight into how many lives have been damaged by these people.'

'Did you, sir?'

'I had a visit from a gentleman whose identity must remain a secret, and who would not confide in me until

321

I had given that solemn undertaking. Do you know what he came to talk about?'

'Blackmail?' guessed Colbeck.

'Yes, Inspector,' continued Tallis. 'Someone had accosted him with a letter he was incautious enough to write to a young man in Birmingham, offering him money if he would care to visit London. I did nor care to pry into the nature of their relationship,' he went on, inhaling deeply through his nose, 'but it clearly put him in an embarrassing position.'

'Is he married, sir?'

'No, but he has reputation to maintain.'

'What price did the blackmailer put on that reputation?'

'Two hundred pounds.'

'Just for writing a letter?' said Leeming.

'A compromising letter, Sergeant,' noted Tallis. 'I advised him not to pay and promised him that the people behind the attempted blackmail would soon be in custody.'

'He had the sense to report it to you,' said Colbeck. 'Others, I fear, did not. Stealing those mail bags must have paid dividends.'

'It did the opposite to the Post Office. They have been swamped with protests from those whose correspondence went astray. There's talk of legal action. Having spoken to this gentleman today, I can see why.'

Victor Leeming sighed. 'Murder, robbery, assault, blackmail, kidnap, destruction of railway property, conspiracy to blow up the Crystal Palace – is there any crime that these devils have *not* committed?'

'Yes,' said Colbeck, thinking about Madeleine Andrews and fearing for her virtue. 'There is one crime, Victor, and the man who dares to commit it will have to answer directly to me.'

Madeleine Andrews was also concerned for her safety. She had been moved to an upstairs room at the rear of the house and, through the wooden bars that had been fixed across the windows that day, she could, until darkness fell, look out on a large, blossoming, well-kept garden that was ablaze with colour. The room had clearly belonged to a maidservant but Madeleine did not object to that. She had not only been rescued from the gloom of the wine cellar, she had access to the meagre wardrobe of the former occupant. Soaked with red wine, her own dress was too uncomfortable to wear so she changed into a maidservant's clothing, relieved that the woman for whom it had been made was roughly the same shape and size as herself.

Unlike Thomas Sholto, she had sustained only the tiniest injuries to her face when the wine bottle shattered. Dipping a cloth into the bowl of water provided, she soon cleaned away the spots of blood on her face. By the light of an oil lamp, she now sat beside the little table on which a tray of untouched food was standing. There was no hope of escape. In daring to fight back, she had given herself away. From now on, they would take extra precautions to guard her.

Her abiding concern was for the bearded man who had cornered her in the cellar. Had they not been interrupted at a critical moment, Madeleine might have been badly beaten. Patently, her attacker had no qualms about striking a woman. Once he had subdued her by force, she feared, he would satisfy the lust she had seen bubbling in his eyes. Another long and sleepless night lay ahead. She looked around for a weapon with which to defend herself but could find nothing that would keep the bearded man at bay. Madeleine felt more exposed than ever.

Her mind turned once more to her father. Like her, he was trapped in a bedroom from which he could not move. She knew that he would be in a torment of anxiety about her and Madeleine blamed herself yet again for putting him in such a position by being so easily gulled. Instead of representing law and order, the policeman who had enticed her away was a dangerous criminal with designs on her. She was glad that her father could not see what she was being forced to endure.

Hunger began to trouble her so she nibbled at some of the food, keeping her ears open for the sound of approaching feet. But nobody came to disturb her. Down in the hall, she heard a clock strike the hours. It was only when the chimes of midnight finally came that she felt able to relax slightly. If the bearded man were going to force himself upon her, he would surely have done so by now. Determined not to sleep, Madeleine nevertheless lay down on the hard bed. How long she stayed awake, she could not tell, but fatigue eventually got the better of her and she dozed off.

She was awake again at dawn, sitting up guiltily as fingers of light poked in through the windows. Madeleine got up to check the door but it was still locked. She drank some milk to bring herself fully awake before washing her face in the bowl. When she looked at the oil lamp, still giving off a faint glow, she realised that she might have a weapon after all. Its heavy base could knock someone unconscious if she were able to deliver a hard enough blow. But the bearded man would be more wary next time. Madeleine would not be able to catch him unawares again.

Tired, frightened, worried about her father, imprisoned in a strange house and wearing someone else's dress, she tried to stave off despair by praying that she would soon be released. Madeleine even included the name of Robert Colbeck in her prayers, more in desperation than in hope. While she knew that he would be searching hard for her, she was afraid that he would never find her in such a remote spot.

Still thinking about him, drawing comfort from the memory of the brief times they had spent together, missing and needing him more than ever, Madeleine drifted across to a window and looked out. The first rays of sunlight were slowly dispelling the darkness and she was able to make out a few ghostly figures moving furtively towards the house through the garden. She blinked in surprise. When she peered out again, she saw that the men seemed to be carrying firearms. Madeleine felt the first surge of optimism since her kidnap.

'Inspector Colbeck!' she exclaimed.

Superintendent Edward Tallis had insisted on taking charge of the operation. Having had the house surrounded by armed policemen, he and Sergeant Leeming approached in an open carriage that had been hired at the nearest railway station. Inspector Colbeck preferred to ride alongside them on a horse. Even in the hazy light, they could admire the size and splendour of the Gilzean ancestral residence. It was a magnificent pile with classical proportions that gave it a stunning symmetry. Hampered by the presence of his superior, Colbeck had to follow a plan of action with which he did not entirely agree. He would certainly not have done what Tallis now did. When the carriage reached the forecourt, the driver reined in the two horses so that the Superintendent could stand up and bellow in a voice that must have been heard by everyone inside the building.

'Sir Humphrey Gilzean and Thomas Sholto!' he boomed. 'My name is Superintendent Tallis of the Metropolitan Police, and I have warrants for your arrest.' Within seconds, two upstairs windows opened. 'I have deployed men all around the house. Give yourselves up now.'

Taking stock of the awkwardness of his situation, Gilzean closed his window immediately but Sholto left his open while he retreated into his bedroom. Moments later, he reappeared with a pistol in his hand and aimed it at Tallis. There was a loud report and the Superintendent's hat was knocked from his head. Leeming pulled him down into the carriage. Colbeck, meanwhile, ordered the driver to take the vehicle out of range, following him as he did so. Sholto had now vanished from the window.

When the carriage came to a stop, Tallis was livid.

'He shot at me!' he cried, indignantly. 'He tried to kill me.'

'No sir,' said Colbeck. 'That was just a warning shot to make you pull back. I told you that it would be unwise to challenge them like that.'

'The house is ringed with policemen. They have no way out.'

'By throwing away our advantage, we may have given them one. Sir Humphrey will surely have planned for contingencies.'

'So did I, Inspector. That's why I brought so many men. Your idea was that you and Sergeant Leeming would make the arrests on your own. What could two of you have achieved?'

'An element of surprise, sir.'

'I am bound to agree,' said Leeming.

Tallis was acerbic. 'Who invited *your* opinion, Sergeant?'

'Nobody, sir.'

'Then keep it to yourself.'

'Of course, sir.'

'All we have to do is to wait here until Sir Humphrey comes to his senses. He will soon see how heavily outnumbered he is and accept that resistance is pointless.'

'I hope so,' said Leeming, picking up the top hat and putting a finger through the bullet hole. 'I believe that was Captain Sholto who fired at you, sir. Obviously, *he* does not think that resistance is pointless.'

Tallis snatched the hat from him and put it beside him on the seat. Colbeck was keeping an eye on the house, waving back any policemen who appeared and indicating that they should take cover. It was not long before the window of Gilzean's bedroom was opened. Fully dressed and with a defiant smile, he surveyed the scene below.

'Congratulations, Superintendent,' he called out. 'I did not expect to see you for days yet – if at all. The credit, I am sure, must go to Inspector Colbeck so I will address my remarks to him.'

'I am in charge here,' asserted Tallis, rising officiously to his feet as he turned to Colbeck. 'And not the Inspector.'

'But you do not have the same personal interest as your colleague. He is a gentleman who will always put the safety of a lady first. Am I right, Inspector Colbeck?'

'What have you done with Miss Andrews?' asked Colbeck.

'She is right here. Quite unharmed – as yet.'

Madeleine was suddenly pulled into view. Colbeck could see that her wrists were bound together and that she was shaking with fear. Gilzean put a pistol to her temple.

'If anyone tries to stop us,' he warned, 'Miss Andrews dies.'

'He would never dare to kill a woman,' said Tallis.

'Call your men off, Inspector Colbeck.'

'I give the orders here.'

'This is no time to argue, Superintendent,' said Colbeck, his gaze fixed on Madeleine. 'We must obey him or he'll carry out his threat. I'll not trade Miss Andrews's life for anything.' Before Tallis could stop him, he gave a command. 'Stand back, everyone! Let them go!'

'I have not made a decision yet,' protested Tallis.

'Then make it, sir. Do as he says or tell him to blow out her brains. But bear this in mind, Superintendent,' he went on, looking at him with burning conviction, 'if Miss Andrews is killed, or harmed in any way, I will hold you responsible.'

Tallis wrestled with his conscience. Keen to arrest the two men who had sparked the dramatic series of crimes, he did not want a life to be lost in the process, especially that of a defenceless young woman. He was also swayed by Colbeck's intervention. In the end, trying to attest his authority, he barked his own order.

'Stay where you are!' he shouted. 'Lower your weapons and do not try to stop them!' He sat down heavily in his seat. 'I never thought to see the day when I gave in to the threats of a criminal!'

'They will not get far,' Colbeck assured him. 'But next time, I suggest, we should not arrive with such a fanfare. All that we have done is to endanger their hostage.'

Tallis brooded in silence and stared at the house. They were not kept waiting long. The coachman was the first to emerge, running to the stables at the side of the house with a servant in attendance. Against such an emergency, the carriage was already loaded with baggage but the horses had to be harnessed. While that was happening the front door of the house remained shut. When the carriage finally came round the angle of the building, Colbeck dismounted, tethered his horse to a bush and walked briskly up the drive.

'Wherever is he *going*?' demanded Tallis. 'Those men are armed.'

'Inspector Colbeck has taken that into account, sir,' said Leeming.

'I gave him no permission to move.'

'He obviously feels that he does not need it.'

Colbeck strode on until he was no more than twenty yards from the house. When three figures came out, he had a clear view of them. Dressed in a satin cloak with a hood, Madeleine Andrews was being forced along between Gilzean and Sholto. The men stopped when they saw Colbeck standing there, weighing him up with a mixture of cold scorn and grudging admiration.

'Are you bearing up, Miss Andrews?' asked Colbeck.

'Yes, Inspector,' she replied, summoning up a brave smile. 'They have not hurt me.'

'Nor will we if the Inspector has the sense to do as I tell him,' said Gilzean, letting Sholto get into the carriage before pushing Madeleine after him. 'Goodbye, Inspector. I am sorry that our acquaintance has to be so fleeting.'

'Well meet again soon, Sir Humphrey,' said Colbeck.

'I think not, sir.'

Clambering into his seat, Gilzean ordered the coachman to drive off. The policemen could simply watch as the vehicle was allowed to leave the estate unimpeded. Tallis was fuming with impotent rage. When the departing carriage was out of sight, he told his driver to take him to the house. Colbeck was standing at the front door when they arrived.

'Have you taken leave of your senses, Inspector?' said Tallis, getting out of the vehicle to confront him. 'From that distance, they could easily have shot you.'

'I wanted to make sure that Miss Andrews was unhurt.'

'You should not have put your own life in danger, man.'

'I survived,' said Colbeck, removing his top hat and examining it for holes. 'And so did my hat, it seems.'

'This is no time for humour. We have just been compelled to let two of the worst criminals I have ever encountered go free, and all that you can do is to joke about it.'

'Their freedom is only temporary, Superintendent.'

'How can we catch them when we have no idea where they have gone? Their escape was obviously planned.'

'Yes,' agreed Colbeck, 'but they did not expect to put their plan into action for a few days yet. They had to leave in a hurry and that means they will not have had time to cover their tracks. Let us search the house,' he urged. 'We'll soon find out where they are heading.'

Madeleine Andrews did not wish to be seated beside Thomas Sholto but it spared her the agony of having to face him during the journey. Instead, as the carriage rumbled along at speed, she was looking at Sir Humphrey Gilzean, a man who paid such meticulous attention to his clothing that she was reminded of Colbeck. She felt a pang of regret that she had got so close to the Inspector only to be dragged away again. For his part, Gilzean was also reminded of someone. It put sadness into his eyes and the faintest tremor into his voice.

'That cloak belonged to my wife,' he said, pursing his lips as a painful memory intruded. 'Nothing but extremity would have made me loan it to another woman, but it is a convenient disguise.'

'Where are you taking me?' she asked.

'Somewhere you would never have dreamt of going.' He saw her glance over her shoulder. 'Do not bother to look for help, Miss Andrews,' he advised. 'They are not following us. I have kept watch on the road since we left the house.'

Sholto was angry. 'How did they get to us so soon?' he growled.

'Do not worry about that now.'

'I do worry, Humphrey. I thought that you had led them astray.'

'So did I,' admitted Gilzean, 'but we have a formidable adversary in this Inspector Colbeck. I'm sure that Miss Andrews will agree. He is a remarkable man.'

'He is,' she affirmed, 'and he will catch you somehow.'

'Not if he values your life,' said Sholto.

'Besides,' added Gilzean, 'the gallant Inspector will have to find us first and there is no chance of that. His writ does not run as far as the place we are going.'

Madeleine was alarmed. 'And where is that?' she said.

'You will see. But when we get there, I'm afraid that I will have to divest you of that cloak. It suited my wife perfectly,' he went on with a mournful smile, 'but it does not become you at all.'

'No,' said Sholto, harshly. 'You belong in the servant's dress.'

'There is no need for bad manners, Thomas,' scolded Gilzean.

'Miss Andrews will get no courtesy from me – not after she tried to crack my head open with a wine bottle.'

'*Noblesse oblige.*'

'To hell with that, Humphrey! Do you know what I hope?' he said, turning to glare at Madeleine. 'In one way, I hope that Inspector Colbeck *does* turn up again.'

'Do you?' she said, quailing inwardly.

'Yes, I do – because it will give me the perfect excuse to put a bullet through your head.'

Madeleine said nothing for the remainder of the journey.

While the servants were being questioned by Superintendent Tallis, the house was searched by Inspector Colbeck and Sergeant Leeming. The three men met up in the drawing room. Hands behind his back, Tallis was pulling on a cigar and standing in front of the marble fireplace. His expression revealed that he had learnt little from his interrogations.

'It is useless,' he said, exhaling a cloud of smoke. 'The servants were told nothing. Even if they had been, they are so ridiculously loyal to their master that they would not betray him.' He fixed an eye on Leeming. 'What did you find, Sergeant?'

'Only that Sir Humphrey has a lot more money than I do, sir,' replied the other. 'Parts of the house are almost palatial. It made me feel as if I was not supposed to be here.'

'This is where those terrible crimes were hatched.'

'Yes,' said Colbeck, 'and I think that I know why.' He handed Tallis a faded newspaper. 'This was tucked away in a desk drawer in the library. It contains a report of the death of Lady Gilzean.'

'She was thrown from a horse. I told you that.'

'But you did not explain how it happened, Inspector. Read the article and you will see that Sir Humphrey and his wife were out riding when the sound of a train whistle disturbed the animals. Lady Gilzean's horse reared and she was thrown from the saddle.'

'No wonder he detests railways,' commented Leeming.

'Who can blame him?' said Tallis, reading the report. 'It was a real tragedy. Lady Gilzean's neck was broken in the fall. However,' he went on, putting the newspaper on the mantelpiece, 'it is one thing to despise the railway system but quite another to wage war against it.'

'It's time for the steam locomotive to strike back,' said Colbeck.

'What are you talking about, Inspector?'

'This, sir.' Colbeck held up a booklet. 'I found this in the desk. It's a timetable for sailings from the port of Bristol. Sir Humphrey Gilzean and his accomplice are fleeing the country.'

'Going abroad?' gasped Tallis. 'Then we'll never catch them.'

'But we will, sir. They are only travelling by carriage, remember, and they will have to pace the horses carefully. We, on the other hand, will be able to go much faster.' Colbeck smiled at him. 'By train.'

When the carriage reached Bristol, the port was a veritable hive of activity. Though narrow at that point, the estuary was deep enough to accommodate the largest ships and several steamers were moored at their landing stages. Madeleine Andrews viewed it all with utter dismay. Furnished with locks, wharves and quays some 6,000 feet in length, the harbour was a forest of masts through which she could see a vast number of sailors and passengers milling around. Hundreds of seagulls wove patterns in the air and added their cries to the general pandemonium. Madeleine shivered. To someone who had never travelled more than ten miles from London in her entire life, the thought of sailing across the sea induced a positive dread.

Yet she had no option. She had been warned what

would happen if she dared to call for help and could not take the risk. With her hood up, she was taken aboard between Sir Humphrey Gilzean and Thomas Sholto, and – to her astonishment – was described as Lady Gilzean, leaving the country on her husband's passport. Before she knew what was happening, Madeleine was taken below to a cabin, where she was tied up and gagged. Sholto stood over her.

'If we have any trouble from you,' he threatened, cupping her chin in his palm, 'I'll throw you overboard.'

'You'll do nothing of the kind,' said Gilzean, easing him away from her. 'Miss Andrews came to our rescue at the house. Without her, we would now be in custody. Show some appreciation, Thomas.'

'Leave me alone with her – and I will.'

'Come, you need some fresh air.'

'What I need is five minutes with her.'

Gilzean took him by the lapel. 'Did you hear what I said?'

Sholto obeyed with reluctance. After tossing a sullen glance at Madeleine, he left the cabin. Gilzean paused at the open door.

'I am sorry that you got caught up in all this,' he said with a note of genuine apology, 'but there was no help for it. Had your father chosen a different occupation, you would not be here now.' There were yells from above and the sound of movement on the deck. 'We are about to set sail,' he noted with satisfaction. 'Where is Inspector Colbeck now?'

Madeleine could not speak but there was panic in her eyes. Gilzean went out and shut the door behind him, turning a key in the lock. He had been unfailingly polite to her and had shielded her from Sholto, but he was still taking her as a prisoner to a foreign country. As the ship rocked and the wind began to flap its canvas, she knew that they had cast off. Madeleine was out of Inspector Colbeck's reach now. All that she could do was to resort to prayer once more.

A few minutes later, she heard the sound of a key in the lock. Thinking that it would be Thomas Sholto, she closed her eyes and tensed instinctively, fearing that he had slipped back to get his revenge for what had happened in the wine cellar. But the person who stepped into the cabin was Robert Colbeck and the first thing that he did was to remove her gag. When she opened her eyes, Madeleine let out a cry of relief. As Colbeck began to untie the ropes that held her, tears of joy rolled down her cheeks.

'How ever did you find us?' she asked.

'I took the precaution of bringing my *Bradshaw* with me.'

'The railway guide?'

'A steam train will always outrun the best horses, Miss Andrews,' he said, untying her legs and setting her free. 'And I was determined that nobody was going to take you away from me.'

Madeleine flung herself into his arms and he held her tight until her sobbing slowly died down. He then stood back to appraise her.

'Have they harmed you in any way?'

'No, Inspector. But one of them keeps threatening to.'

'His name is Thomas Sholto,' said Colbeck. 'We waited until we saw them come up on deck. There was no point in trying to apprehend them while they had you in their grasp. Stay here, Miss Andrews,' he went on, moving to the door. 'I'll be back in due course.'

'Be careful,' she said. 'They are both armed.'

'They are also off guard. Excuse me.'

Standing at the bulwark, Gilzean and Sholto ignored the people who were waving the ship off from the shore and congratulated themselves on their escape. Gilzean was honest.

'It was a Pyrrhic victory,' he conceded. 'I kept my promise to Lucinda and struck back at the railway, but it means, alas, that I am parted from her for a while. No matter, Thomas. I will be able to slip back from France in time. Meanwhile, we have money enough to live in great comfort and anonymity.'

'What about that little vixen down in the cabin?'

'She will be released as soon as we are safely in France.'

'Released?' said Sholto, mutinously. 'After what she did to me?'

'We have no more need of her, Thomas.'

'You may not have – but I certainly do!'

'No,' decreed Gilzean. 'Miss Andrews has borne enough suffering. As soon as we dock, I'll pay for her

338

return passage and give her money to make her way home from Bristol.'

'But she will be able to tell them where we are.'

'France is a much bigger country than England. Even if they sent someone after us – and that is highly unlikely – he would never find us.'

'According to you, Inspector Colbeck would never find us.'

Gilzean was complacent. 'We have seen the last of him now,' he said. 'Bid farewell to England. We are about to start a new life.'

The detectives crept up until they stood only yards behind the two men. Victor Leeming had a hand on his pistol, but Robert Colbeck favoured a more physical approach. Since it was Thomas Sholto who had spirited Madeleine away, the Inspector tackled him first. Rushing forward, he grabbed Sholto by the legs and tipped him over the side of the ship. There was a despairing cry, followed by a loud splash. Gilzean spared no thought for his friend. He reacted quickly, pulling out a pistol. Before Gilzean could discharge it, Colbeck got a firm hold on his wrist and twisted it so that he turned the barrel of the weapon upwards.

Seeing the pistol, almost everyone else on deck backed away as the two men struggled for mastery. Sergeant Leeming pointed his own gun at Gilzean and ordered him to stop but the command went unheard. And since the combatants were now spinning around so violently, it was impossible for Leeming to get a clear shot at the man. He jumped back as Colbeck tripped his adversary up and fell to the deck on top of him. Gilzean fought with even more ferocity now, trying to wrest his hand free so that he could fire his weapon. Using all his strength, he slowly brought the barrel of the gun around so that it was almost trained on its target. Colbeck refused to be beaten, finding a reserve of energy that enabled him to force the pistol downwards and away from himself.

Gilzean's finger tightened on the trigger and the gun went off. A yell of pain mingled with a gasp of horror that came from the watching crowd. Hearing the sound of the gunshot from below, Madeleine came running up on deck, fearing that Colbeck had been killed. Instead, she found him standing over Gilzean, who, compelled to shoot himself, was clutching a shoulder from which blood was now oozing.

'Why did you not leave him to *me*?' complained Leeming.

'I wanted the privilege myself.'

'But I had a weapon.'

'I am sorry, Victor,' said Colbeck with a weary grin. 'You can arrest Thomas Sholto, but you'll have to haul him out of the water first.' He turned to Madeleine. 'They'll not trouble you again, Miss Andrews,' he promised. 'Horses and ships have their place in the scheme of things but they were not enough to defeat the steam locomotive. That is what brought them down. Sir Humphrey was caught by the railways.'

* * *

Richard Mayne, the senior Police Commissioner, looked down at the newspapers spread out on his desk and savoured the headlines. The arrest of the two men behind the train robbery and its associated crimes was universally acclaimed as a triumph for the Detective Department at Scotland Yard. After sustaining so much press criticism, they had now been vindicated. That gave Mayne a sense of profound satisfaction. While he could bask in the general praise, however, he was the first to accept that the plaudits should go elsewhere.

He was glad, therefore, when Superintendent Tallis entered with Inspector Colbeck and Sergeant Leeming. The Commissioner came from behind his desk to shake hands with all three in turn, starting, significantly, with Robert Colbeck, a fact that did not go unnoticed by Tallis. The Superintendent shifted his feet.

'Gentlemen,' said Mayne, spreading his arms, 'you have achieved a small miracle. Thanks to your efforts, we have secured some welcome approbation. The headlines in today's newspapers send a message to every villain in the country.'

'Except that most of them can't read, sir,' noted Tallis.

'I was speaking figuratively, Superintendent.'

'Ah – of course.'

'No matter how clever they may be,' continued Mayne, 'we catch them in the end. In short, with a combination of tenacity, courage and detection skills, we can solve any crime.'

'That is what we are here for, sir,' said Tallis, importantly.

'Our role is largely administrative, Superintendent. It is officers like Inspector Colbeck and Sergeant Leeming on whom we rely and they have been shining examples to their colleagues.'

'Thank you, sir,' said Leeming.

'On your behalf, I have received warm congratulations from the Post Office, the Royal Mint, Spurling's Bank, the Chubb factory, the commissioners for the Great Exhibition and, naturally, from the London and North Western Railway Company. The last named wishes to offer both of you free travel on their trains at any time of your choice.'

'I will certainly avail myself of that opportunity,' said Colbeck.

Leeming frowned. 'And I most certainly will not,' he said. 'On the other hand,' he added with a chuckle, 'if the Royal Mint is issuing any invitations to us, I'll be very happy to accept them.'

'They merely send you their heartfelt gratitude,' said Mayne.

Tallis sniffed. 'Far be it from me to intrude a sour note into this welter of congratulation, sir,' he said, 'but I have to draw to your attention the fact that some of the evidence was not obtained in a way that I could bring myself to approve.'

'Yes, I know, Superintendent. I've read your report.'

'Then perhaps you should temper your fulsome compliments with a degree of reproach.'

'This is hardly the moment to do so,' said Mayne,

irritably, 'but, since you force my hand, I will. Frankly, I believe that *you* are the person who should be reprimanded. Had you let your men go to Sir Humphrey's house on their own, they might well have made the arrests there. By making your presence known so boldly, Superintendent Tallis, you gave the game away. That was bad policing.'

'We had the house surrounded, sir.'

'Yet somehow they still managed to escape. In all conscience, you must take the blame for that.'

Trying not to grin, Leeming was enjoying the Superintendent's patent unease, but Colbeck came swiftly to his superior's aid.

'It was a shared responsibility, sir,' he told Mayne, 'and we must all take some of the blame. Against anyone but Sir Humphrey Gilzean, the plan that Mr Tallis had devised might well have worked. And the Superintendent did, after all, prove that he is not chained to his desk.'

'That merits approval,' said Mayne, 'it's true. So let us be done with censure and take pleasure from our success. Or, more properly, from the success that you, Inspector Colbeck – along with Sergeant Leeming here – achieved in Bristol. Both of you are heroes.'

Leeming pulled a face. 'That's not what my wife called me when I stayed away for another night, sir,' he confided. 'She was very bitter.'

'Spare us these insights into your sordid domestic life,' said Tallis.

'We made up in the end, of course.'

'I should hope so, Sergeant,' said Mayne with amusement. 'Mrs Leeming deserves to know that she is married to a very brave man. You will have a written commendation to show her.'

'Thank you, sir,' said Leeming, happily, 'but I only followed where Inspector Colbeck led me. He is the real hero here.'

'I'm inclined to agree.'

'The only reason that we finally caught up with them was that the Inspector had the forethought to put a copy of *Bradshaw's Guide* in his valise. It told us what train we could catch to Bristol.'

'I regard it as an indispensable volume,' explained Colbeck, 'and I never go by rail without it. Unlike Sergeant Leeming, I have a particular fondness for travelling by train. I am grateful that this case gave me such opportunities to do so.'

'A train robbery certainly gave you the chance to show your mettle, Inspector,' said Mayne, 'and everyone has admired the way that you conducted the investigation. But success brings its own disadvantage.'

'Disadvantage?' repeated Colbeck.

'You have obviously not read this morning's papers.'

'I have not yet had the time, sir.'

'Make time, Inspector,' suggested Mayne. 'Every single reporter has christened you with the same name. You are now Inspector Robert Colbeck – the Railway Detective.'

After considering his new title, Colbeck gave a slow smile.

'I think I like that,' he said.

Madeleine Andrews could not understand it. While she was being held in captivity, all that she wanted to do was to return home, yet, now that she was actually there, she felt somehow disappointed. She was thrilled to be reunited with her father again, trying to forget her ordeal by nursing him with renewed love, but she remained strangely detached and even jaded. Caleb Andrews soon noticed it.

'What ails you, Maddy?' he asked.

'Nothing.'

'Are you in pain?'

'No, Father,' she replied.

'Did those men do something to you that you haven't told me about? Is that why you've been behaving like this?' She shook her head. 'Well, something is wrong, I know that.'

'I'm still very tired, that's all.'

'Then you should let someone else look after me while you catch up on your sleep.' He offered his free hand and she took it. 'If there *was* a problem, you would tell me?'

'Of course.'

'I'll hold you to that,' he said, squeezing her hand. 'It might just be that you are missing all the excitement now you are back here.'

'There is nothing exciting about being kidnapped,' she

said, detaching her hand. 'It was terrifying. I wish that it had never happened.'

'So do I, Maddy. But the men who held you hostage will be punished. I only wish that I could be there to pull the lever when the hangman puts the noose around their necks.'

'Father!'

'It's what they deserve,' he argued. 'You saw that report in the paper. It was Sir Humphrey Gilzean who set the other man on to commit those two murders. That means a death penalty for both of them. Yes,' he went on, 'and they found a list of all his accomplices when they searched that baggage they took off the ship. The whole gang is being rounded up.'

'I was as pleased as you to hear that.'

'So why are you moping around the house?'

'I'll be fine in a day or two.'

There was a knock at the front door and she went to the bedroom window to see who it was. Recognising the visitor, she brightened at once and smoothed down her skirt before leaving the room.

'Ah,' said Andrews, drily. 'It must be Queen Victoria again.'

After checking her appearance in the hall mirror, Madeleine opened the door and gave her visitor a warm smile.

'Inspector Colbeck,' she said. 'Do please come in.'

'Thank you, Miss Andrews.' Colbeck removed his top hat and stepped into the house. 'How is your father?'

'Much better now that he has me back again.'

'You would gladden the heart of any parent.'

'Did you wish to see him?'

'In time, perhaps,' said Colbeck. 'I really called to speak to you. I am sure that you will be relieved to know that everyone who took part in the train robbery has now been arrested.'

'Were they all men from Sir Humphrey's old regiment?'

'Most of them were. They became involved because they needed the money. Sir Humphrey Gilzean had another motive.'

'Yes, I know,' she said. 'He did all those terrible things because he believed that a train had killed his wife.'

'Even before that happened, he had a deep-seated hatred of the railways. The death of Lady Gilzean only intensified it.'

'But to go to such extremes – it's unnatural.'

'It certainly changed him from the man that he was,' said Colbeck, soulfully. 'Though I'd never condone what he did, I have a faint sympathy for the man.'

Madeleine was surprised. 'Sympathy – for a criminal?'

'Only for the loss that he endured. I know what it is to lose a loved one in tragic circumstances,' he confided. 'If I'm honest, Miss Andrews, it's what made me become a policeman.' He sighed quietly. 'Since I could never bring the lady in question back, I tried to protect others from the same fate.' He looked deep into her eyes. 'That was why it gave me so much pleasure to come to your aid.'

'This lady you mentioned,' she said, probing gently. 'Was she a member of your family, Inspector?'

'She would have been,' he replied, 'but she had the misfortune to surprise a burglar in her house one night, and made the mistake of challenging him. He became violent.' He waved a hand to dismiss the subject. 'But enough of my past, Miss Andrews. I try not to dwell on it and prefer to look to the future. That is the difference between Sir Humphrey and myself, you see. In the wake of his loss, he sought only to destroy. I endeavour to rebuild.'

'That's very wise of you.'

'Then perhaps you will help in the process.'

'Me?'

'I know that it is indecently short notice,' he said, watching her dimples, 'but are you, by any chance, free on May Day?'

'I could be,' she said, tingling with anticipation. 'Why?'

'In recognition of what happened at the Crystal Palace,' he explained, 'His Royal Highness, Prince Albert, has sent me two tickets for the opening ceremony. I would deem it an honour if you agreed to come with me.'

Madeleine was overjoyed. 'To the Great Exhibition!'

'Yes,' said Colbeck over her happy laughter, 'there are one or two locomotives that I'd like to show you.'

ACKNOWLEDGEMENT

*With thanks to Janet Cutler
for her expert advice on
Victorian railway companies.*

THERE'S MORE TROUBLE ON THE LINE FOR THE

RAILWAY DETECTIVE

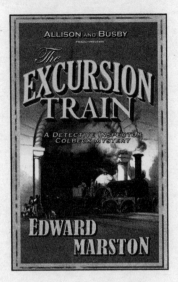

'Historical crime writing of the first order . . .
compulsive reading'
Good Book Guide

'Told with great colour and panache . . . this is how
history mysteries should be'
Sherlock Magazine

To discover more great historical crime and to
place an order visit our website at
www.allisonandbusby.com
or call us on
020 3950 7834